A MOM

'It's not your job t[...]er.
'I know you're only trying to help, but please, [...]sn't mean you can rush in –'

Sarah's eyes widened and she inhaled sharply. 'Rush in?' she demanded. 'Why haven't you spoken to her yet?'

A sharp scream filled the night air.

There was a moment of silence and then a dull, bodily thud.

Vallance was moving before he knew it. He raced back along the drive as lights flicked on in room after room above him. His heart was pounding and he knew with a sickening finality what he would find.

The body was sprawled on a paved area to one side of the building, face down. Blood was beginning to pool like black oil.

CRIME&PASSION

A MOMENT OF MADNESS
A Fairfax and Vallance mystery

DEADLY AFFAIRS
A John Anderson mystery

A MOMENT OF MADNESS

by
Pan Pantziarka
A Fairfax and Vallance mystery

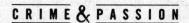
CRIME & PASSION

First published in Great Britain in 1997 by
Crime & Passion
an imprint of Virgin Publishing Ltd
332 Ladbroke Grove
London W10 5AH

Crime & Passion series editor: Pan Pantziarka

ISBN 0 7535 0024 8

Typeset by Avon Dataset Ltd, Bidford on Avon, B50 4JH
Printed and bound in Great Britain by
Mackays of Chatham PLC, Chatham, Kent

To my family, who have walked with me through hell.
To my children Despina and Georgie.
And to the memory of their mother,
Gina Pantziarka (1964–1994).

ONE

Sarah felt the excitement ripple through the room when Tom Ryder stepped back to the lectern. She watched him survey his audience, his pure blue eyes scanning those closest to him as he caught his breath. His technique was excellent. He spoke with the fervour of an evangelist and in the language of science and now he had the audience right where he wanted them. He was good looking too, with short black hair streaked with grey and a face that radiated emotion. She glanced round the room quickly; all eyes were fixed on the charismatic figure standing on the raised platform at the front.

When she turned back he was looking at her with those blue eyes that sparkled with an electric excitement. She held the gaze for a moment and then looked down at her notes. Was she the only person there not totally captivated by the man? He was an imposing figure up on the stage, and with his deep resonant voice he had effectively outlined his views on the world and where it was going. She knew the spiel by heart, but hearing it from him was different from reading it in one of his books. No wonder he was making a fortune on the lecture circuit.

He inhaled sharply and gripped the lectern as though he needed the support. This was going to be it. The sucker punch that was going to set everything up for the next four days of the course. This was what his audience had come to hear.

This was what they were leaning forward on the edge of their seats for.

'And what is the way of the world?' he demanded, his voice booming through the lecture theatre.

He made a show of waiting for an answer but none came from his audience. Tom Ryder didn't want answers. Answers were what he had.

'Wheels within wheels; loops within loops; cycles and systems so deep we can't comprehend what's going on any more,' he continued, gazing into the distance as though he could see the wheels and loops. 'Chaos. Primal chaos, that's the way of the world. When the flutter of a butterfly's wing here causes a tropical storm over the Amazon then we're dealing with chaos. When a bad lunch in New York crashes the stockmarket in London, Paris, Frankfurt, then that's chaos. So how are you – each and every one one of you – supposed to navigate through this crazy, screwed-up, glorious, complicated, mess of a world?

'Coping isn't good enough any more. No sir, to cope means to keep your nose above the water line just long enough to grab some air before you go down again. To survive and prosper – and that's what we all want to do – you need to be able to see through the dense fog of rumour, fear, indecision and confusion. To survive and prosper means getting a handle on the world; it means being brave enough to flourish in the chaos; to embrace that which we instinctively fear.'

Damn but he was good. She could feel the tension rising in the room as he communicated the feeling of fear and dread and excitement. They all knew what he was talking about; their worst fears and brightest hopes were being articulated with a passion that hit home directly.

'Can you think of any system more defined, more logical, more rigorous than the computer? This is the paradigm above all else. We want to run our corporations with the efficiency and the success of a computer program. Don't we? Don't you? Yes! Damn it! This is what we want. The elimination of risk, the destruction of indecision and confusion. We want to destroy the chaos so that order reigns supreme. We want a world we can program. We want a world that gives us the power to predict and to control. Isn't that what you all want? That total certainty that means you can sleep easy at night. The control that means there are no surprises ready to ambush you. The security of knowing that all your carefully worked plans aren't zapped by the unforeseen and the out of control. Hell, you don't want butterflies and tropical storms.

'Well, I've got news for you,' he announced, the American accent suddenly sharper. 'Computers thrive on chaos. The scientists call it fractals. Fractals. These guys are talking about the science of chaos. The science of turbulence. Can you see that? Science. Chaos. Look at that ladies and gentleman. Think of that. Science. Chaos. That's a contradiction, isn't it? Science is about prediction and control. Science is about this force acting on this body and producing this result. That's what we learnt at school, isn't it? Well it's wrong! All of it! Chaos rules here as well. Chaos is the underlying principal of the universe, it drives everything and everywhere. Fractals. Turbulence. Chaos.

'So how are you supposed to live and function in this crazy upside-down universe where nothing makes sense and a broker with heartburn in New York crashes the stockmarket in London? How are you supposed to cope? Because we all know that if you don't cope you're out of the game. I'll tell you how you cope: to navigate through the confusion you need to abandon everything you've ever learnt. The way that scientists have had to ditch the solid laws of physics for the weird ungraspable truths of quantum mechanics and fractal chaos. What you need is inspiration. Inspiration to see through the wheels within wheels, to see feedback loops that loop back on themselves with crazy abandon. You need inspiration to grasp the simplicity that results in the turbulent storms around you.

'My name's Tom Ryder and I'm here to give you that inspiration. Thank you.'

It took a moment to register that he had finished. Ryder stepped back from the lectern and one of his helpers rushed forward to dab at the sweat on his furrowed brow. The stunned silence gave way to applause and Sarah found herself joining in. He was good, there was no way she could deny the man his due. He had spoken with such conviction that even she had been caught up in the feeling of excitement.

'Isn't he gorgeous?' the woman next to Sarah whispered, keeping her eyes fixed on Ryder.

Why lie about it? 'Yes, he is,' she admitted.

'I can't wait to meet him.'

Meeting the man was the real reason people went on the course. If they wanted the message they could buy the book, or the tape, or the CD, or the video. All that was missing was the Tom Ryder T-shirt and Sarah had no doubt that marketing were working on the design. No, people went on the course to meet the medium and not just for the message. That was a good line, she decided. Medium and message. Medium; there was a link there to spiritualism, table-turning and other crackpot stuff. She scribbled the line down quickly, just as Tom Ryder stepped forward once more.

He looked cleaned up, his jacket was back on, the beads of perspiration had been dabbed away. With his transatlantic accent and the sharp blue suit he looked every inch the successful tele-evangelist. He'd done the passion and the fury and now he was back down to earth and ready to speak the language his audience understood best.

'I know you people are probably sick to death of being tested and prodded and questioned. I know I was when I developed this course, and yes, I've been through the whole process so I know just what it feels like. Here's the good news: no more tests. I mean that,' he insisted, as though anyone doubted it. 'Here's the better news, we're ready to start to play. During the next four days we're going to go on a journey together, all of us. This is a journey with a difference. This is a journey to the different dimensions that make up each and every one of us. This is where you discover parts of yourself you never knew existed. Hell, this is where you discover parts of yourself you never even imagined were possible.

'Some people say that you can't teach inspiration. They say Tom Ryder is full of crap!' he shared a smile with his audience, as though none of them could harbour such a thought. 'They say "Tom, why don't you just spill the beans! Why don't you just admit that being inspired is one of those natural born

4

instincts". Well, ladies and gentlemen, I ain't the one who's full of crap! I say that we're all capable of functioning success-fully in the world, and that if we free the faculties and the talents we lock away inside ourselves we'll have the inspiration and the sense to work through anything!

'Now you've been through the mill; now we've pumped you so full of questions you want to scream; now we know enough about you so that we can help and guide you to discover that you – and I mean every single one of you – can work miracles when you want to.

'OK, I guess about now you're sick of me,' he continued, smiling, 'so I'll just hand over to Diane and she'll let you know what we have planned for the next four days. Thank you.'

Sarah's neighbour – her name badge said 'Kate' in big blocky letters – was one of the first to stand up and applaud. Others followed suit until the applause was coming from every side of the room. Sarah joined in reluctantly; he had been good, and no matter how much she wanted to find fault she had to admit that he'd spoken convincingly and had carried his audience with him all the way.

He accepted the applause with a smile, standing at the edge of the stage until it started to die down. One of his assistants, an over-made-up American woman called Diane Bennett, rushed from the wings to stand beside him, applauding as enthusiastically as the people in the audience. She seemed as excited as everyone else, as though she hadn't heard the same speech a million times already. That was what was so slick about the whole thing. Tom Ryder made the same speech at least twice a week and yet it still sounded fresh and exciting, and he still sounded totally sincere about it. The whole thing made Sarah very wary.

Tom Ryder waved at his audience, flashed a smile that was meant for each of them individually and then stepped back into the wings. Diane Bennett, her lips glossed bright red and her hair bleached a shimmering gold, took over the fixed smile that Ryder had left vacant. She looked back towards him as he disappeared, her eyes filled with the same adulation that Sarah could see in Kate and many of the other women around her. With his powerful build, sharp suits and charismatic manner Tom Ryder was an attractive figure, Sarah admitted to herself grudgingly.

'We should get to see a lot more of him now,' Kate whispered, leaning over to Sarah as Diane Bennett began her spiel.

'I hope so.'

Kate smiled. 'So do I,' she said, 'so do I.'

Wherever the high fees for the course had gone it hadn't been on the catering, Sarah decided, casting a jaundiced eye on the buffet lunch. Tired chicken wings, soggy sandwiches, sausage rolls that had seen better days. The same tired spread for the second day running, along with the same cheap plonk and the no-name mineral water. Considering how much it cost to spend a week at the Ryder Forum champagne and caviar should not have been out of the question. No one else seemed bothered though; the tightly clustered little groups were talking about the course, about the tests they'd performed the previous day and above all about Tom Ryder.

She picked gingerly at the food that she had arranged neatly on her plate. Her producer had nearly hit the roof when she'd put in an application to attend the one-week course entitled 'Tom Ryder's Inspirational Management'. She was doing a feature on management fads and fallacies, looking at the different theories and fashions which had taken the previously staid world of corporate management by storm. Downsizing, upsizing, outsourcing, chaos theory, neuro-linguistics – there was an endless list of competing philosophies and techniques, all promising success and power. The only common feature they shared was the ability to part corporate cash from corporate bank accounts.

By all accounts Tom Ryder's course was the sexiest. She had taken the word 'sexy' to be a left-over from eighties yuppie talk. She hadn't realised that it had been meant literally.

'Well, Miss Fairfax, what did you think of Tom's speech?'

Sarah turned to face Diane Bennett. Up close the make-up seemed less manufactured. 'I thought it was very well done,' Sarah said.

6

'Good, I'm glad. I would hate to think that you were going to get nothing from your time with us.'

What did that mean? 'Pardon?'

Diane smiled. 'I said that I hoped you weren't going to go away with a negative image of what we're trying to achieve here.'

There was a sudden flurry of activity towards the door and everybody turned to see Tom Ryder and another of his female assistants enter the room. They were being honoured with a visit from the great man himself.

'If you'll excuse me,' Diane said, eager to get back to her boss.

'Of course,' Sarah said. What had Diane been on about?

Kate came rushing over. 'I told you we'd get to see more of him now that we're going to start the role-playing stuff.'

'I'm surprised,' Sarah admitted.

'Why?'

'Because he's going to have some of this awful buffet,' Sarah said.

Kate smiled. 'It's a bit lame, isn't it?'

'Considering what we've paid to be here.'

'I would have paid double,' Kate whispered. 'It's not my money, this is coming out of the company training budget.'

It was time for a bit more research. 'How did you get approval?' Sarah asked innocently.

'I'm the training manager where I work. It's my budget. Look, he's coming towards us –'

He was too. Kate seemed ready to wet herself, like an adolescent schoolgirl about to meet her favourite pop star. Diane too had gazed at Ryder with unconcealed adoration, the look in her eyes anything but purely professional.

'Kate, Sarah,' he said, 'how are you enjoying the course so far?'

'Fine, just fine, Mr Ryder,' Kate gushed.

'Please,' he said, 'call me Tom, there's no need for this formality. I'm glad you like it so far, Kate. And you, Sarah?'

He was good on the names, but then that was what name badges were for. He was wearing aftershave, not too strong but enough to be noticed. Up close he was even better looking than he had been on stage. 'It's been very interesting, so far,' she said.

He smiled. 'You're the one who doesn't like me, aren't you, Sarah?'

What? 'I – I don't know what you mean, Mr Ryder.'

He looked at her sceptically. 'Let's be straight, Miss Fairfax,' he said. 'I know that you're here because you're investigating me. Isn't that right?'

Sarah suppressed the anger instantly. 'That's not true.'

'Then perhaps my information is incorrect. Perhaps you're not the Sarah Fairfax who works on the television programme called *Insight*. And so you're not here as part of an investigation into the activities of the Ryder Forum.'

Kate looked utterly astounded. She took a step away from Sarah, discreetly disassociating herself.

'I'm researching a programme on management theories,' Sarah said. 'The Ryder Forum is just one of a number that I'm looking at.'

Tom smiled; vindicated. 'And how many other courses have you attended so far in your researches?'

'None.'

'And how many do you plan on attending following ours?'

It was beginning to sound worse than it was. 'None.'

'Then I think that I was right the first time,' he concluded. 'You're here to investigate me.'

Sarah shook her head. 'Firstly this isn't a personal thing. I'm here looking at the Ryder Forum, not at Tom Ryder. Secondly the programme is about a range of management techniques, not just about this one. And lastly I'd like to know just how much else you know about me!'

He looked at her and sipped from his glass of water. 'You'll excuse me for being so direct,' he said. 'I have no objection to your presence here, even if you were attempting to infiltrate this course –'

'That's not what I was doing!'

'– nor do I have anything to hide, Miss Fairfax. Will you answer me one question?'

'Only if you'll tell me how you know so much about what I'm doing here.'

8

'Agreed. I would suggest that you ask your accounts people,' he said. 'When they made the booking for you they negotiated a discount on the price. They explained the purposes of your visit and were keen on lowering the price. In fact we did offer them a discount, and I had fully expected that you would let us know yourself when you arrived why you were attending. It was only after the first day was over, when you had completed numerous questionnaires and tests, that we realised you were going to keep things from us.'

Typical! The bloody accounts people had screwed up again. How the hell was anyone supposed to do any investigative journalism when their cover was blown in the hope of getting a bloody discount!

It was time to backtrack. 'I didn't want to be treated differently to anyone else on the course,' she said, and then attempted a smile.

'Of course,' he agreed calmly. 'Now, I would just like to know one thing.'

'I'm sorry if it appears differently but –'

'One question, remember? I would just like to know if there's anything that you've heard me say today that you think is wrong or dishonest in some way. Do you think that I was wrong when I spoke about chaos theory?'

'No.'

'And the need for inspiration in the modern corporate environment, is that wrong?'

What did Sarah know about the modern corporate environment? Nothing. But everybody needed inspiration. 'No,' she said.

'And do you think that inspiration can be taught?'

A shrug. 'I don't know.'

He smiled again, only this time he seemed more relaxed. 'In that case, Miss Fairfax, I'm sure that you've got things to learn. Thank you for your time, ladies, I'm sure we'll talk again.'

He bowed out graciously, then walked over to join Diane Bennett and a small group by the door. Most of them looked pretty pleased to be meeting Tom Ryder, and his charming manner suggested that he was just as happy to meet them.

'How could you!' Kate snapped angrily.

Sarah sighed and turned to her. 'It's not the way it seems,' she said.

'No? Well I don't believe you even if he does!'

Sarah watched Kate storm off. By the end of lunch every person on the course was going to be primed with the story. What was worse? The fact that Tom Ryder had handled it all so calmly and had made her seem like a sneaky bitch, or the fact that she was now shown up as a non-believer in front of the faithful? Any chance of getting information out of the other people on the course had been effectively scuppered.

Kate lost no time in spreading the news. She was already deep in conversation with a group of similarly-aged females, all of them looking at Sarah with open suspicion if not downright hostility. Most of the people on the course were obviously deeply impressed with Ryder, however it was the women who were his most ardent admirers. The course was split 50-50 men and women, which was a proportion way in excess of the number of women in corporate management, and it said a lot for Ryder's looks and personality that he could attract so many high-flying women to his cause.

'You seem to have caused quite a stir.'

Sarah turned to find that one of the men had wandered over to her. He was tall and gangly, with big round glasses that magnified his wide, grey-green eyes. He didn't seem in the least put out by the fuss. In fact the slight smile on his face suggested a sense of humour that was conspicuously lacking anywhere else in the room. 'Yes, I have I suppose,' she said.

'What was it? Did you fail to fall to your knees at the right time? Or did you have the temerity to suggest that Tom Ryder is not the most desirable man on the planet?'

'No, much worse that that. He exposed me as an undercover journalist.'

'Really?'

'Yes, I'm doing a story on management gurus.'

'Oh? So you're not just working on him then?'

Was he for real? It suddenly occurred to her that she had no idea who she was talking to and what his motives were. She'd seen him in the lecture room earlier, sitting with the rest of them but he could easily have been planted there to keep an eye on them, or perhaps it was just her he was interested in. 'I'm Sarah Fairfax,' she said, the incipient paranoia making her feel nervous.

'Alan Platt,' he responded, offering her a clammy hand to shake.

'And you, Alan, why are you here?'

'To see what it is that this guy's selling.'

'Chaos theory and inspiration.'

'You call that chaos theory?'

She shrugged. 'What do you call it?'

'Stating the obvious in the most banal terms possible. He has as much understanding of chaos theory as he has of quantum mechanics and the history of science. As a scientist I recognise the attempt to co-opt the language of science. He wants to sound cleverer than he is.'

It sounded as though he were telling the truth. 'And I thought I was the only non-believer here,' she said, relieved to find that she was not totally isolated.

'I'm reserving judgement,' Platt told her. 'I think he's trying to blind with science – or perhaps that should be pseudo-science – but I want to see exactly what it is he can teach by way of inspirational management.'

That made sense. Tom Ryder was probably stating the obvious but he did it with panache and that was what his audience were paying for. The true value, if there was any, had to be in what his techniques could deliver.

'Excuse me, Sarah,' Platt said, looking beyond her and right across to the other side of the room.

She followed his gaze and caught a glimpse of a woman leaving through the swing doors. Not one of Ryder's assistants, she guessed, at least not judging by her tight jeans and drab top which clashed with the shiny black handbag she was carrying.

'We must talk again,' Sarah said. Platt nodded and then walked to the door, obviously keen to meet the woman who was probably waiting for him outside.

Sarah watched him go and felt a sudden sense of relief. At least there was one other sane person on the course. Platt had seemed sincere enough, and his analysis was spot on. She made a mental note to find out what sort of scientist he was, and to find out why he was on the course. So far he was the only person she'd met there who didn't work as a manager for a large corporation somewhere. Or perhaps he did. There was probably more money in the management of science than in science itself.

Lunch was drawing to a close and she realised she had hardly touched the cold, tasteless food on her plate. It looked even less appetising than before and she abandoned it on a convenient table top. The afternoon session promised the start of the active part of the course – play therapy for adults was how she thought of it. They were supposed to role-play and in doing so discover the latent creativity that had been knocked out of them by the pressures of adulthood. It sounded like a lot of crap, another ingredient in the strange mixture of new age mysticism, science, management theory and psychology that made up the Ryder technique.

Diane Bennett came over just as Sarah was heading for the ladies' to freshen up.

'Sarah, can I have a moment?'

Sarah looked at her dubiously. 'Yes?'

'I just want to let you know, nothing's changed as far as we're concerned,' Diane explained earnestly, her big blues eyes wide with sincerity. 'You're still on the course. You're still here to learn as well as you can and we're not going to treat you in any way differently to everyone else.'

What was this? Damage limitation. 'Try telling that to everyone else,' Sarah said, aware that they were being watched by some of the others in the group.

'I have. I've spoken to the other helpers and so has Tom. We've also spoken to Kate and the other people who are going to be in the same team as you. Please, just give us a chance to show you what we can all do together.'

'Why's he so paranoid? What makes him think I'm here to do a hatchet job on him?'

Diane's smile wavered. 'Tom's a very direct person, Sarah, he just wanted to cut through to the core. Nothing he said was personal, and we wouldn't want you to think that it was.'

She was on the defensive. 'Then why mention it at all?' Sarah demanded.

'Because we knew why you were here and yet you didn't mention it on any of your forms or answers.'

'Why should I?'

'Because your score was extremely high on personal integrity factors, Sarah. You're basically a very honest person, we know that for a fact. Which was why Tom wanted to talk to you directly about it. You and he are very much alike that way.'

What? Sarah stalled. Were they trying to flatter her? 'What else did my scores say?'

Diane leant closer so that her expensive scent was overpowering. 'High intelligence. Highly motivated. An aptitude for logic and analysis. All-round good use of the left brain. Basically you're a very switched-on person.'

It sounded good and Sarah had to suppress the smile. 'Am I supposed to feel grateful for that?'

'I'm just reporting what comes out of the computer,' Diane said. 'You're a smart person and we like smart people. Just give us a chance, that's all we're saying, Sarah, just give us a chance.'

'But I never said I wouldn't.'

Diane smiled. 'You did, Sarah. Your score also shows a high degree of hostility, emotional imbalance and a basic mistrust of right-brain function. That's why we can help you. Our programme of learning is designed to tackle these areas, to help you open up the dimensions you've deliberately closed down.'

Ouch! 'I haven't ever said I'm not willing to give you a chance,' she insisted. 'You're just reading that into my scores. Not that I'm saying I accept your computer's assessment of my results.'

'You don't accept that you're intelligent and motivated?'

Sarah smiled. 'I don't accept anything without checking it up independently. But then you probably know that too.'

'Yes we do,' Diane agreed, smiling also. 'Tom has made it clear to everyone that you're to be treated like any other client. And we've spoken to Kate and the others, but if you feel that you're being treated differently then please tell me. Will you do that?'

'Yes.'

'Good. Oh, and Tom has asked me to apologise on his behalf if you were offended by his approach. He will of course apologise in person the first chance he gets.'

'I wasn't offended.'

Diane looked relieved. 'Good. I know that we're going to work together just great! I'd better get ready. Enjoy yourself this afternoon.'

Sarah ignored the weird American syntax. 'Thanks,' she said, accepting the peace offering.

All friends together again. Or at least that was what Diane was hoping for. She'd done well, but then as one of Tom Ryder's key assistants Sarah couldn't expect anything less than excellence from her. And using the test results had been a good tactic, Sarah realised. Accepting the good news meant that she then had to accept the bad, there was no arguing with the facts.

She turned to leave once more and, as the double doors swung open for a second, saw that Platt was still deep in conversation with his female friend. She was standing close to him, her face shielded by his body but they were deep in conversation.

'Sarah?'

She turned to Kate. 'Yes?'

'Tom's just had a word with me,' she said. Her face was flushed a little and the excitement was there in her voice.

'Yes?'

'I'm sorry if I seemed a little off-hand earlier. It's just that, well, I got the wrong end of the stick.'

'That's OK,' Sarah said, 'you're forgiven.'

'Good, I wouldn't want an atmosphere, it would spoil the course completely for us.'

'I agree. So, what do you think of him?'

Kate waved her hand in front of her face, getting some air. 'I still think he's a catch,' she said, grinning. 'My husband already thinks I'm obsessed because I've got all the books and articles Tom's ever written. To be honest I'd even be willing to leave my husband for him.'

'I know what you mean and I don't even have a husband,'

Sarah admitted. In spite of everything – her doubts about his work, her doubts about his show-biz style and lack of sincerity – she still felt a sense of attraction to him. If anything his directness made him seem even more appealing. There was something almost sexual about his forceful personality.

Sarah's group, one of a half dozen groups into which the hundred or so people on the course had been organised, had been split into three teams of three. Apart from Kate her other team mate was a slim, quiet man in his late fifties called Peter Shalcott. He sat between Kate and Sarah, his hands together in his lap as he listened intently to one of Ryder's identikit American females outline the plan for the session.

Sarah only half listened as she scribbled notes to herself. A lot had happened and she didn't want to lose any of it. She listed her keywords for Tom Ryder: mesmerising, evangelical, sexy. She also noted the way he had been careful to play on the fears of his audience before offering them the hope of inspiration (INSPIRATION was how she wrote it).

'Are you writing this down?' Peter whispered, looking down at Sarah's pad.

She covered it up quickly. 'No, not this.'

'Do you do shorthand?'

His voice was soft, wavering almost. 'Shorthand?'

'I had a secretary who could do shorthand,' he said.

Was he joking? No. His wistful voice carried no hint of humour, but then nor was he being deliberately patronising. He looked and sounded as though he'd wandered into the room by mistake. 'We'd better pay attention,' she said, putting her pad down for the moment.

'It's all nonsense,' the older man assured her, patting her hand absently.

'Was that a question?' the American woman asked, looking pointedly at Peter and Sarah with a thin-lipped and disapproving expression.

Was she called Mary-Lou, or was it Kelly-Jo? Sarah couldn't remember, besides it didn't much matter. 'Sorry,' she said.

'I'll run that by you all one more time,' the American decided. 'This is a group test and it's designed to get you into

15

the swing of things. We want you to really go at it all the way now. OK? Good, now using the kit of parts in the boxes in front of you, we want you to build a structure to bridge the gap between the two lines drawn on the floor. Think of the two lines like the banks of a river, you understand? Good. You gotta use every piece of kit in the box and the structure must be capable of carrying the weight of a member of your team.

'Y'all got that? Good, because you've got 30 minutes to design and build the structure. Oh, and when you're done we're gonna test what you've built,' she paused to laugh. 'That's rightie folks, you get to walk across your creations. Remember, this is a game, enjoy it. Remember also that it's a competition. The last team to finish makes the tea and coffee for the rest of us. Right! Let's get to it!'

Kate stood up and then turned to Sarah and Peter. 'Sarah you can do the testing when we're finished,' she said instantly.

'Why me?'

'Because you're the lightest,' Kate said seriously. 'Now, Peter, what do you know about bridges?'

'Bridges? I was never one for engineering,' he announced. 'Though obviously one had to study a fair amount of mathematics and a good deal of mechanics as I recall. Compton,' he said, as though testing the word. 'Yes, Michael Compton. He was a bit of a swot when it came to mechanics, easily the best mathematician in the school. Read Physics at Cambridge I believe, did rather well for himself.'

Kate looked at Sarah, who smiled and shrugged back. 'Peter,' she said, 'what exactly are you doing here?'

He looked at her strangely and then seemed to snap out of his wistful state. 'Here? To learn about managing things,' he said tentatively, standing up at last. 'Yes, to learn about how to manage things and people.'

'Were either of you two listening to Sally?' Kate asked, looking at Sarah particularly suspiciously.

Sarah also stood up. 'Yes, of course we were. Now, Peter, our task is to build a bridge using this stuff,' she pulled the wooden tray of plastic building blocks and thin plywood towards her. 'Do you have any ideas?'

Peter looked bemused. 'A bridge? Whatever for?'

'Peter, why don't you let us girls get on with this,' Kate suggested, taking possession of the box of tricks.

'A bridge? The physics is bound to be a bit rusty,' Peter said, 'but let me have paper and pencil and I'll see how much of Newton I can remember.'

The old boy was definitely out of it, Sarah realised. Kate was right, he'd be no use to them. She pulled a few pages from her pad and handed them to him along with her pen. 'You get on with that,' she suggested, 'and Kate and I will see what we can do with these things.'

'Excellent idea,' he agreed, sitting down again, 'you mock up a model and then we can compare with the predictions from the equations. Excellent.'

Kate made a face at Sarah and then they walked over to the front of the room where two parallel lines had been painted on to the polished wooden floor. Already the other two groups were busy making plans, discussing earnestly how to bridge the metre gap between the lines.

'This shouldn't be too hard,' Kate decided.

Sarah looked into the box piled high with interlocking red bricks made of plastic and two pieces of plywood. 'How big are the flat bits?'

'Probably not long enough to go right across when they're end to end,' Kate guessed.

She was wrong but only just; placed end to end the plywood slats sat on the edges of the painted lines. It was a tight fit but at least it meant there'd be no doubt about that part of the bridge.

'Ideas?' Kate said.

'Copy everyone else?'

'Sarah!'

She smiled. 'OK, let's build a sort of thing in the middle where the flat bits go together, and then platforms on either line to hold them up.'

'Can it really be so simple?'

'Why not? We've only got half an hour, anything too complicated and we won't get it done.'

'It looks like everyone has had the same idea.'

The other groups were already busily putting together the building blocks to form different-sized boxes on which to balance the pieces of plywood. Kate knelt down on the floor and emptied the box, spilling the bright red pieces of plastic all over the floor.

'This is what my nephews and nieces do when they play with Lego,' Kate explained, smiling.

'See, you're rediscovering your latent childhood skills,' Sarah said.

'And you. Come on, we've already lost the nutty professor.'

'Don't call him that,' Sarah said, feeling sorry for the old boy.

'I'm sure he's here by mistake,' Kate whispered.

Sarah knelt down beside her and began to snap pieces of plastic together. 'I know, I know.'

For a long while she concentrated on the game, deciding that she may as well go along with it, no matter how ludicrous it felt. When she finally looked up she saw that Peter had walked out of the class completely. She was about to remark on it to Kate when the door to the room opened and she saw him returning. He was smiling and, as he closed the door quietly, she glimpsed a shadow of a figure behind him. Although the glimpse had been brief it was enough for Sarah to catch sight of a the shiny black handbag that had been carried by Alan Platt's mysterious female friend.

'Well, at least it looks like Peter's made a friend,' she said, looking over towards him. Already he was sitting down, returning to the notes he had been making earlier.

Kate looked up sharply, as though annoyed by the interruption. 'What friend?' she asked.

Sarah shrugged. 'He went out to chat to her just now,' she said.

'A woman friend?' Kate asked, smiling broadly. 'At his age too.'

'I didn't mean that at all.'

'I'm sure I saw him with a woman yesterday,' Kate said, looking back down at their bridge, 'perhaps they both work for the same company.'

Sarah hadn't thought of the old man working for a

company. 'You think they're here together?'

'Why not? Anyway, enough about him, he's no bloody use at the moment. So, what's your television programme going to be about?'

That was a damn good question. 'It's not about Tom Ryder,' she said. 'It's not even about the Ryder Forum particularly.'

'So he was wrong then?'

'Yes. Now, about this bridge, do I really have to test it?'

Kate smiled. 'We can always get Peter to test it. That can be his contribution to the team.'

TWO

The sky was a thick, miserable grey that sat heavily over the horizon, merging with the ragged line of trees that marked the edge of Ryder Hall. In the early morning light the landscaped gardens, the expanse of perfectly manicured lawn and the rest of the grounds, merged into a single muddy stain. It hadn't always been called Ryder Hall. It was one of the first things that Sarah had asked on arrival on the Sunday evening, intrigued as she was by the impressive Victorian building which seemed ideally suited for its present purpose.

With the reception area still featuring all the original fixtures, from the solid oak front desk to the maze of connecting corridors, and with dozens of rooms to house guests she had imagined that it had once been a grand hotel. It was only when she had been shown into her room that she appreciated that it had in fact once housed an English public school. The cramped bedrooms and the narrow corridors suddenly made a lot more sense, though it didn't make them any easier to accept. However the lecture theatre, the classrooms and the massive dining room were all well suited to current use.

Sarah yawned once more and glanced forlornly at her alarm clock. It was almost seven, which meant time for a shower before she joined the sleepy line trooping down for breakfast. From her window she could see the brave and the foolhardy jogging across the grounds through the early morning drizzle.

God, at least her room was warm. She'd dressed for exercise again that morning: trainers, jogging bottoms and a sweat shirt. For the third day in a row she'd dressed the part but each time one look at the cold grey weather had persuaded her to do some work instead.

Instead of trekking through the drizzle she'd written up her first experience of 'inspirational' game playing. She and Kate had worked diligently building the struts to support the pieces of plywood which were to act as the span of the bridge they were making. Peter had spent the time deep in his notes and equations and had not even bothered to offer any help. Not that it mattered. Kate was confident that the task would be finished and tested within the allotted thirty minutes.

The first attempt had collapsed under Sarah as soon as she had set foot on it. She had almost taken Kate down with her and the only consolation had been that theirs had not been the only such disaster. The next attempt, after what Kate grandly declared were design improvements, was more successful in that the collapse happened on the second step and not the first. Time was ticking by and the next design was more basic in that there were more supports although they were much smaller as there were only a certain number of bricks to go round.

Sarah had hardly dared breathe as she crossed from one side of the bridge to the next. Kate had almost jumped with joy, and they both stood back to watch one of the other teams putting their last design to a spectacularly unsuccessful test.

'Amateurs,' Kate had called them, with ill-concealed glee.

When Sally blew the whistle to call time both Sarah and Kate were feeling pleased with themselves. It wasn't the best looking bridge in the world, but it could carry Sarah from one painted line to the next and that was all that was needed.

Tom Ryder had chosen that moment to make a reappearance, accompanied as always by a young female assistant with too much make-up on and an American accent.

'I feel inspired already,' Kate had whispered.

The first team proudly showed off their bridge. It had looked needlessly complicated as far as Sarah was concerned, with odd shaped struts and a strange looking arrangement of supports under the plywood. It did the job though, and Tom Ryder seemed to like it.

'We've gone for the simple approach,' Kate had said, as soon as he came over, bringing the jubilant first team with him.

He had agreed easily enough. 'Yep, simple but strong by the look of things,' had been his verdict, delivered in a relaxed, friendly sort of way.

In retrospect Sarah could see that a disaster had been bound to happen. She had known it before she had even stepped on to their simple but strong collapsible bridge. Her heel had caught on the edge and the bridge had fallen to pieces in front of her horrified eyes.

'Sorry,' was all that Sarah could say to Kate's cry of anguish.

Tom Ryder had looked at them both and then begun to laugh. 'This is a game, remember? Don't let it get you down. You learnt from this, didn't you, Kate, Sarah?'

Sarah had looked hopefully at Kate, who nodded vigorously but obviously couldn't trust herself to say anything.

'OK, do you want to see how I'd do this?' Tom Ryder asked, now that it was game over for the two teams who'd had bridges to show off.

Was it possible that he was going to get down on hands and knees and snap building bricks together like an over-grown child? Sarah's first thought was that he'd get his expensive suit dirty. Her second was that it wasn't fair; he'd designed the course, he knew exactly how to build a bridge and make it work. Her doubts seemed not to be shared by the others in the group. Everyone else had been urging him on and Sally was already scooping up the building blocks and pieces of plywood to put into an empty box.

'You don't look convinced, Sarah,' he had said, taking the box of parts from Sally.

Damn but he was perceptive! Even in retrospect she was still astounded that he'd picked up on her doubts. 'I'm sorry,' she had said, 'am I that obvious?'

'Yes,' he said, smiling. 'You're thinking, "Tom Ryder's an expert on bridges, he knows how this game works, that ain't fair!". Am I right?'

She hated to admit it and the memory of it was no easier to take. 'Yes,' she had said simply.

He had turned to the rest of the group. 'Good, that's what I want you all to think. But I'll tell you one thing though, anyone who thinks that is missing the point. Watch.'

He slipped his jacket off and handed it to Sally. His white shirt fitted tightly across his chest and his muscular arms bulged as he moved. They had all stepped back to watch as he had squatted down between the two lines painted on the floor. He had placed the plywood slats on the floor, end to end so that they each touched a line and then he had carefully spread the building blocks on top of them. In a matter of seconds he had formed an even layer of plastic blocks sitting loosely across the plywood. Then he had stood up and walked carefully from one end to the next, stepping on the loose plastic blocks which had easily carried his weight.

He had then turned to face his silent audience. 'Let me say it for you,' he said. 'That ain't fair! Tom Ryder cheated! What kind of bridge do you call that! Isn't that what you're all thinking?'

Sarah wasn't so sure that the others had been thinking that, she was sure they had all been secretly thrilled with the demonstration that they had seen. It wasn't every day they got to see a top management guru scatter Lego on the ground and then walk across it.

'Sally, read back the assignment,' he had instructed.

Right on cue Sally had the story. 'Sure, Tom. This is what I said to everybody: using every piece in the kit build a structure to bridge the gap between the two lines drawn on the floor. Think of the two lines like the banks of a river. Oh, and the structure must be capable of carrying the weight of a member of your team. Those were my instructions.'

'Thank you, Sally. Now, do you see?' he had asked. 'You were not asked to build a bridge, you were asked to build a structure to bridge a gap. Because she used the verb "to bridge" and because she used an analogy of the painted lines as banks of a river you all imagined that you needed to build a bridge. You let the statement of the problem influence your imagination and hence your solutions. You thought you knew what you needed to do and yet you were all wrong.'

'No inspiration,' Kate had said softly.

'That's right, Kate. OK folks, Sally's going to spend some time going through a few quick techniques to help you figure out when you need to drop bricks on the floor and when you need to build the biggest damned bridge in the world!'

That had been inspiration in action. Looking back on it Sarah still felt cheated. The whole problem had been contrived to show Tom Ryder in a good light. It wasn't even a good party trick. And the techniques that all-American Sally spent the better part of the afternoon going through had been so trivial it would have been laughable had the rest of the group not been so earnest in copying it all down.

There was now only one simple question to answer. Where was the meat of the thing? That's all that Sarah wanted: something that could be used to justify the vast expense of the course, something that would elevate Tom Ryder's teachings from a sequence of adolescent word games and riddles into the high-powered, high-performance and high-value set of tools that he promised.

The sharp knock at the door interrupted Sarah's train of thought. She wasn't late, her watch showed that she still had lots of time before the start of the morning's session.

'Sarah? Are you there?'

Kate's voice was unmistakable, even when muffled by the closed door. So, they were still friends, despite the barbed comments and the sarcasm which were Sarah's natural responses to most of what Tom Ryder and his acolytes had to say.

'Something's going on,' Kate reported as soon as the door was open.

'What sort of something?'

'Come on, we can find out,' Kate said.

'But I'm not ready yet,' Sarah said. She was still dressed for the run she had not taken; she needed to change into something else.

'You look ready to me.'

Sarah smiled. Kate always seemed dressed for the office: sensible skirt, safe white blouse and occasionally a jacket that matched the skirt. 'Give me a couple of minutes,' she said.

'No. Come on,' Kate said, taking Sarah by the hand, 'I'm sure something's wrong.'

What could possibly be wrong so early in the morning? There were bound to be hangovers, just as there had been on the other two mornings, but that was no big deal. Part of the fun of a residential course was the chance to get plastered every night and not have to worry about driving home, seeing your partner or having to face work the next morning.

There was a cluster of people at the end of Sarah's corridor, Diane Bennett among them. They were gathered by the door to the last room on that side of the building.

'Alan! Are you in there?' Diane Bennett called through the locked door.

'This isn't like him,' one of the guests was saying. She was dressed in a pair of faded jogging bottoms and a sweatshirt. Her damp hair, red face and running shoes said she'd been out jogging and had just got back.

'I'm sure nothing's wrong, Sue,' Diane told her, rapping on the door again loudly.

'Is anything wrong?' Kate asked, pushing through the small group to speak directly with the anxious looking Sue.

'It's Alan, we normally go running every morning together. I tried this morning and got no answer so I just assumed he was already out there. There was no sign of him and when I got back after my run there was still no answer.'

Alan? Was that the same man she'd spoken to the previous day, Sarah wondered. The scientist who'd shared her doubts about Tom Ryder. 'Are you talking about Alan Platt? He might be in another room,' she suggested, remembering that she had seen him talking with a woman the previous afternoon. She had no idea who the woman was, other than the fact that she was probably attending the course rather than working at Ryder Hall. But the old boy, Peter, he had spoken to her. Or at least it might have been her, it was so hard to be sure.

Sue looked relieved, as though she hadn't considered the possibility. 'What other room?'

Sarah smiled. What was the etiquette in this sort of situation? The other major attraction of residential courses was the chance for some guilt-free casual sex. If that was what you wanted. 'I

26

'can't say,' she said, deciding that discretion was the better part of valour. Sue was obviously close to Alan. Who knew just how close that might be?

'Perhaps he's out cold?' Kate wondered. 'Wasn't he in the bar last night? He might have overdone things a bit.'

'I'm sure that he wouldn't do that,' Sue replied. 'Alan's not a heavy drinker.'

'OK guys,' Diane said, 'I guess it's time for me to get the keys. I'll just go down to reception.'

Sue looked apologetic on his behalf. 'This isn't like him at all.'

'Don't worry,' Diane said. 'I just hope he arrives back before I do.'

Kate took Sarah to one side. 'What do you mean he might be in another room?' she whispered. 'What do you know?'

The woman was fishing for gossip. Kate was just that type. 'I don't know anything,' Sarah said.

'Oh yes? I saw the look on your face when you said he might be in another room. Whose room? Go on, you can tell me.'

Perhaps Kate knew the young woman? If Platt had spent the night with her then everyone was going to find out about it sooner or later. 'Remember that girl you said might work with Peter? The one who was talking to him yesterday afternoon?'

Kate's eyes lit up. 'I didn't see her yesterday. What does she look like?'

It was a question Sarah had already asked herself. 'I don't know, I only caught a glimpse of her,' she admitted.

'That's not very good,' Kate said, her disappointment made clear. 'I didn't really pay attention to her when I saw her with Peter on the first day. She's young, isn't she?'

'I don't know,' Sarah said, 'but I'm sure we can find out from Peter.'

Kate smiled once more. 'You don't suppose that this Alan and her were –'

Sarah shrugged. 'I did see them together yesterday, at lunch in fact. Didn't you see them?'

'No. This Alan's hardly a hunk, is he?'

'Only if you think that lanky scientists with glasses are hunky.'

Kate shook her head. 'He's no Tom Ryder look-alike for sure. Shame.'

'No sign of him, huh?' Diane called, walking back down the corridor and holding a big bunch of keys aloft.

'I do hope I'm just being silly,' Sue said, standing back to let Diane get to the door.

'OK folks, I think I'd better just have a looksie myself,' Diane said, putting the key in the lock. She waited for people to step back before opening the door just enough to slide into the darkened room.

She cried out a few seconds later and then came rushing back to the door. She looked shocked, the cheery grin wiped clean from her face.

'What is it?' they all asked.

For a moment she seemed lost for words. 'Don't go in,' she said finally as Sue went for the door.

Sarah looked at Kate and then she grabbed the door and went into the room. Diane tried to stop her but was too late, and a second later Sue and Kate were there as well. The heavy curtains were still drawn so that even the pale light of the grey morning was cut off. It took a moment to see anything but a fuzz of shape and form.

Alan was lying on the floor, face down and arms spread, his head turned to one side, one leg curled up towards his stomach and the other still touching the bed. The sheets on the bed were still tidy but the pillows were in disarray.

'Alan?' Sarah whispered. 'Are you OK?'

Nothing. She turned to the others but their eyes were fixed on the unmoving body that lay in front of them.

'Is he dead?' Kate asked, whispering as though her voice would wake him.

Sarah knelt down, closed her eyes and touched his hand. Cold. Lifeless. She snatched her hand back and shivered. His eyes were open but there was nothing in them. Up close she could see a trail of vomit on his chin and under his face, and there was dried blood caked around the nose and mouth.

Sue began to sob, turning to Kate who took her in her arms.

The door opened and the light was switched on. There were voices coming from all over the place. Sarah stood up when she felt a hand on her shoulder. She turned to a white-faced Diane Bennett.

'A doctor's on the way,' Diane said.

'It's too late for that. You need to call the police.'

'Tom's on his way.'

Tom Ryder? 'What's he going to do? Make the dead walk?' Sarah demanded angrily. 'Get everybody out of here and call the police. Now.'

Diane looked at her and then began to usher people out of the room. There was a crowd at the door and an excited buzz of conversation. Sue was still crying on Kate's shoulder, her back to the body of her ex-friend.

Tom Ryder was on his way.

Sarah wanted to laugh and cry at the same time.

Diane stopped at the door, closed her eyes and let the weariness wash through her. She felt an ache in her legs and the dull throb of a migraine gathering behind her eyes. It was still so hard to believe what had happened. Alan Platt was dead. How could that be? The previous night he'd been fine in the bar. He'd been drinking a glass of beer and talking in that quietly confident way of his. He had looked fit and healthy then, and pretty sober too; there was no sign that the glass of beer would lead to more. If that was what had done it. Somehow it was hard to figure him as a man who'd drink himself to death.

She gripped the door handle for support as the vision of the dead body flashed through her mind again. Jesus, she just hoped she never had to do something like that again. She couldn't get the picture of the body out of her head: it had been sprawled on the floor as though Alan had just fallen off the bed. She had half expected him to get up, apologise in that mumbling English way of his and then carry on where they'd left off.

The voices on the other side of the door snapped her back to reality. It sounded like Kate was holding court again; boy, could that woman gab when she wanted to. In any case it was better that Kate and the others were out of circulation; that way there would be less chance of the rumours taking root. All the people who'd seen the body – even those who had only caught the briefest glimpse from outside the room – were potential witnesses at the inquest. One of the young policemen had explained to her that there was always an inquest in cases of sudden deaths like this one.

Diane inhaled sharply and went into the room. They were all waiting for her to let them know what was going on, as if she knew any more than they did. For everyone else classes had started late but they had started nevertheless. Tom was insistent that things carry on as best they could – companies paid good money to send people to him and he wanted to make sure that they were happy with what they got.

It took a moment to get silence but the eight or nine people in the room were soon quiet. 'I'm sorry we've had to keep y'all from class this morning,' she began, putting on the gee whiz accent that Tom liked her to use. 'We've just got to wait and see what the folks from your police department want to do before we can let you get on with things.'

It was Sarah Fairfax who spoke first. 'Has the forensic medical examiner arrived yet?'

'The what? A little old guy arrived a while back, the police officer called him a doctor. Is that the same thing?'

The doctor had arrived a long while after the squad car. Did they call them squad cars over here? Diane could never remember what crossed over and what didn't. The doctor was a tired little man in a shabby grey suit and who seemed upset that his daily routine had been disturbed. He wasn't even a forensics guy (or was it pathologists who did the messy stuff?), and not part of the police department either. From what she could work out he was just a local MD who did stuff for the police when needed.

'Yes, it's the same thing,' Sarah confirmed. 'What does he have to say?'

Nothing yet, as far as Diane knew. Tom had wanted to talk to him as soon as he had arrived but the police officers had taken him straight to Platt's room. What did they think? Did they think the doc was a miracle worker about to bring Platt back to life? In any case Tom was keen to get the dead body to the mortuary and out of Ryder Hall as soon as possible. With the body still around it meant that the guy's death would be a permanent topic of conversation. How could people concentrate on the course if all they were talking about was the stiff in room 23?

'The doctor's still in the room,' she said. 'I know it's way past lunch time and we'll be getting some food to you as soon as we can, but I'm sure you can see we've got good reason.'

'Why can't we just go to our classes?' one of the other witnesses asked. One of only three men in the room, he looked mighty angry being stuck in the little room with nothing to do but listen to Kate.

'We're just waiting on your police officers for instruction,' she said. It wasn't true, all they wanted was a list of names and a promise that no one would leave the premises. It was Tom's idea to keep everybody together.

'I don't see why that should be the case,' the man said.

Was his name Harold, Harry? His name badge was obscured. 'I'm sorry,' she said, 'but as soon as Tom's sorted things out I'm sure we'll be getting back to normal.'

That wasn't good enough for him. 'But we've already lost a whole morning.'

'Have some sympathy,' Kate snapped. 'Somebody has just died.'

Harry rounded on her. 'I'm very sorry and all that,' he said, 'but nothing we do is going to change that. Do you realise how much this course costs?'

'Why don't you sue the dead man's company?' Sarah suggested. 'After all if their employee had been considerate enough to die elsewhere then you wouldn't have missed anything.'

The headache buzzed harder and Diane felt the exhaustion tugging at her reserves of energy. 'Please folks, there's no need for any of this. I'm sure that after lunch you can all get back to work, and if any of you feel you've missed out then I'm sure Tom's going to be happy enough to talk refund.'

'How's Sue?' Kate asked, turning her back on Harry.

'Somebody's with her,' Diane said. 'She's taken it badly.

They were obviously friends as well as colleagues and it's come as a real bad shock to her.'

'Was he married?' one of the other women asked.

'The police have informed his wife.'

There were more questions, but the door opened and Sally called her out. 'Get these people something to eat,' Diane told her, 'and for Christ's sake stay with them so they don't get at each other.'

'The food's on its way. Tom wants to see you.'

'Has the doctor finished?'

Sally shrugged. 'I can't say, Tom didn't tell me.'

Tom had his own office on the ground floor, away from the admin section of Ryder Hall. It was his personal territory and he liked to make a clear separation between the organisation of Ryder Hall and all his other work. Laura, his private secretary, was at her desk when Diane arrived.

'Go right on in,' Laura said, buzzing through to Tom immediately.

His office was cool and spacious, the most modern room in the building. After the spartan rooms and the refurbished Victoriana stepping into his office was like stepping into the twentieth century. Plush carpet, a fully stocked bar, monochrome prints on the wall all combined with the sheer acreage of the room to create an atmosphere of peace and serenity. Even the air smelt fresher.

Tom was sitting behind his massive black desk waiting for her. She tried to smile but decided it wasn't worth the effort. He looked pensive, brooding silently as she walked over to him. He didn't look like a man about to deliver good news.

Her legs ached even more and she guessed that it was going to be a long while before she had a chance to get some rest. 'What is it?' she asked, grabbing the chair nearest his desk.

He looked at her for a second before speaking. 'It doesn't look good,' he said. 'It doesn't look good at all.'

Tom was the man who could handle any situation and weather any storm; she couldn't ever remember him looking so tired. 'What do you mean?'

'It looks like Platt's heart gave out. Coronary arrest according to the doctor.'

'Why's that bad?'

'Because he also said that there was a chance it had been brought on by a drug overdose.'

'Hold on,' she said. 'Back up a minute, Tom. Are you saying that Alan was on something? That he OD'ed last night?'

He nodded gravely. 'That's what the doctor said.'

She leant back in her chair trying to let the news sink in. 'That can't be right, Tom, it just can't.'

'The doctor seemed pretty certain, Diane. So, you see why this looks bad?'

'Tom! How can you even think like that? That poor man –'

He shook his head sadly. 'That poor man's dead and it looks like it was self-inflicted. Come on, Diane, how much sympathy can you have for a man in his position?'

She hated it when people were so cold. Maybe – and it had to be a real big maybe – maybe Alan had been taking something, but that was no reason not to feel sorry for him. And what about his wife? How would she react to the news that her husband had been an addict and that he'd overdosed?

'What was it? Cocaine, heroin, what?'

'That's what they're trying to find out,' he said. 'If the press get this then there's going to be dirt flying all over,' he continued, returning to his original point. 'We don't want none of it sticking here, and believe me there's enough people looking for an excuse to get at Tom Ryder. Hell, something like this is even bound to make it back home.'

He was right but something else occurred to her. 'Do the police know who he is?'

He hesitated. 'No, not yet. The doctor's calling in some kind of more senior officers. Police forensics are on their way, photographers, detectives. Diane, this place is going to be crawling with cops for the next couple of days. We've got to keep the press out of this –'

She closed her eyes to let the weariness pass. 'You're forgetting something,' she said.

'What?'

'Sarah Fairfax is with us. She was one of the first on the scene this morning.'

'Hell! Where is she?'

Was he angry with her? It wasn't her fault. She looked at him for a second and then the anger seemed to fade from his eyes. 'She's in with the other witnesses,' she said. 'Don't worry, she's not been able to get to a phone yet.'

'Are you sure?'

'Yes – No. No, I'm not sure, Tom. But she's not acting like she's just walked into a story. I guess she doesn't know who Alan Platt is yet. And don't worry, Sue Beamish isn't with them, she's being looked after by Lucy.'

Tom stood up. 'This is a mess,' he sighed. He walked round the desk and put his hand on her shoulder. 'We've got to handle this carefully, Diane. We've worked too hard to let something like this –'

She turned slightly towards him. His touch seemed to draw away the weariness as he squeezed her shoulder softly. He reached round with his other hand and stroked her face tenderly. She kissed his fingers softly, touching her lips to his powerful but sensitive hands. He looked down at her and smiled, letting her know that he understood her feelings and her concerns. He was always so good to her.

She closed her eyes and savoured the feel of his fingers on her face, stroking her cheek softly, lovingly. He moved behind and massaged both her shoulders, his fingers finding the knots of tension and dissolving them away. He had never lost the healing touch and where the tension faded she felt an electric glow that warmed her body.

He leant over and kissed her softly, his lips cool against her cheek. She turned to him and they kissed quickly, his lips touching hers and lingering for a moment. She took his hands and moved them lower, down from her shoulders towards her breasts. He was down at her level and they kissed again just as his fingers slid under her breasts. His deep blue eyes had never been clearer, filled with the same excitement and want that she felt deep inside her. His fingers closed around her nipples, making her heart beat faster as the excitement grew stronger.

'We haven't got enough time,' he whispered, answering the question before she could voice it.

She wanted him, she felt the desire deep in her sex and in the hardening of her nipples as he teased them with his fingers. They had made love in the office before, why not this time? She put her arms around his neck and pulled him closer for a long, passionate kiss. His tongue parted her lips, opening her mouth to his exploration as he sucked on her breath.

She parted her thighs as soon as she felt his hand on her knee. Her skirt was too tight but she felt a frisson of pleasure as he slid his hand under it, stroking the smooth bare flesh of her inner thigh.

'Please –' she whimpered, half standing and half turning so that she was sitting on the very of the edge of the desk.

He wound his hand in her hair and gently pulled her head back, exposing her throat, opening her mouth. He pushed her thighs apart with his knees as she pulled her skirt up around her waist. She was wet, her pussy aching for his hardness. His mouth joined hers, ground down over her lips violently, passionately and then he moved to her throat, biting, sucking, kissing.

She could feel his hardness against her inner thigh, pressing through his expensive tailored suit. Her cry of pleasure as he touched his fingers to her panties was muffled by another hard kiss. He teased her pussy, rubbing his fingers slowly back and forth over her panties. The wetness of her excitement soiled her panties as he stroked and eased the material between her pussy lips.

She wanted to forget about the horrors of the day. She wanted to wipe out the picture of the dead body. She wanted to forget everything in the pure animal pleasure of sex. 'We do have time,' she sighed. 'Please –'

He let his hands stray higher again, moulding her breasts, pinching her nipples. 'Here?' he whispered, his cool lips and hot breath caressing her throat.

'Here. Now. We can.'

The intercom buzzed suddenly, its harsh electric sound filling the room. He left it unanswered for a moment, giving her hope, and then, cursing angrily, he released her.

35

'Yes?' he demanded, walking round to the other side of the desk. He sounded calm and controlled, despite the excitement in his eyes and the hardness of his cock.

Laura's voice came through as though she were in the room with them. 'More police have arrived,' she said.

'I'll be with them in a second.'

'Tonight?' Diane asked, trying to regain her composure. Her heart was pounding and the excitement was still stronger than anything else she felt.

'I'll do my best,' he said softly. 'Fix yourself up in a minute and then join me, I may need you.'

'OK.'

She smoothed her skirt down quickly and watched him go. He had been reluctant to stop, she was certain of it. His fingers could mould her as he liked; every touch of his was electric and there was nothing she could do to resist. Not that she wanted to resist, she wanted him more than anything. If he had wanted to fuck here there on the desk, or on the floor, or anywhere then she would have done it.

She still felt sorry for Alan Platt but Tom was right. It was hard to figure Alan as a drug taker. He had seemed so straight, definitely not the type. But then who was the type? Alan was dead and if it was true that it was drugs it was his own stupid fault; why should Ryder Hall get caught up in the inevitable scandal?

That Alan was one of the government's top advisors on the drugs industry only made it worse. Not only would he be damned as a drug addict, he'd be damned as a hypocrite as well. The newspapers would have a field day with the story, and through no fault of its own Ryder Hall was going to be associated with it.

Tom was right, they just had to make sure the story didn't get out. Or if it did they needed to keep the damage to a minimum. Having Sarah Fairfax around was going to make that just a whole lot harder.

THREE

Cooper dropped the cigarette on the floor and ground it under heel as soon as he saw DCI Vallance and Diane Bennett approaching. She was doing all the talking by the look of it; Vallance looked like he was only half listening to her monologue as they walked the corridor towards the victim's room. As usual Vallance was dressed all in black, his hands embedded deep in the pockets of his leather jacket as he walked beside the smartly dressed woman.

'Is there any news, sergeant?' she asked when they arrived. She and her boss, another slick Yank, were waiting to find out when the body was going to be moved. Having a corpse in one of the rooms was distracting, they claimed. More like they wanted it off the premises so that they could hire out the room to someone else, he guessed.

'Now that Mr Vallance is here I'm sure everything'll get moving,' he assured her.

'Yes,' Vallance agreed. 'I'll let you know if there's anything I need,' he added, cutting off her next question before she had a chance to start.

She nodded gravely. 'And as I've mentioned already, Tom Ryder would like to see you as soon as possible. I'm sure you understand just how serious this situation is.'

'All dead bodies are serious,' Vallance told her. 'That's just the way dead bodies are.'

Cooper smiled but Diane hesitated for a moment. English humour, Cooper wanted to point out; she had no idea what Vallance was on about. 'Well,' she said, 'you know where to find me or Tom.'

They watched her walk down the corridor, her stiletto heels snapping hard on the polished floor. Good legs, Cooper decided, and the tight skirt did wonders for her backside.

Vallance was watching appreciatively too. 'Who's the Barbie doll?' he asked when she had disappeared.

'Which one? Her or one of the others? This whole place is crawling with dolled-up Barbies like her.'

'Her.'

'I think she sort of runs this place for her boss, Tom Ryder.'

'You've met him?'

'A pain in the arse, sir. He's used to getting his own way, and he seemed a bit put out to have to talk to a mere sergeant,' Cooper smiled at the thought. It had given him great pleasure to tell Ryder to keep out of the way.

Vallance accepted the news without comment. 'So, what's the story?'

'The victim is one Alan Platt. Thirty-seven, married, previously in good health and here for one of the courses. No known history of drug abuse, no previous, nothing remotely dodgy about him.'

'What's he do?'

'This is the problem,' Cooper said. 'He's one of ours, sort of. He's something at the Home Office, part of some committee on the drugs industry. From what I've been told he's made a bit of a name for himself. Can't say I've heard of him but there you go.'

'Sounds like he's been a bit naughty then,' Vallance said calmly. 'What's the quack say?'

'Hard to say really. Cause of death is a coronary, probably brought on by drink and drugs. We've found some nose powder in the room, no toxicology yet but it's coke for sure. There was a half-empty bottle of scotch by the bed too. Looks like he went on a bender and never recovered. No signs of violence, but he'd keeled over and smashed his face on the floor a bit.'

'What's the story then? It all sounds pretty clear-cut to me, sergeant.'

'It's the doctor. First off he'd heard of the victim and seemed to think this is going to be big news. Secondly he kept going on about how unusual it was to have a cocaine overdose. Especially in someone so young and fit, he said it didn't square. He talked to the victim's doctor and that just made him more insistent that things didn't look right.'

Vallance, scratching the dark stubble on his chin absently, considered the facts for a moment. He didn't look like the average DCI, thought Cooper. With his shabby leather jacket, black jeans and well scuffed boots Vallance looked more like a suspect than a policeman. But he was good, so they said. His reputation had preceded his recent arrival in Area. He'd done good at New Scotland Yard according to the canteen gossip but he hadn't been around long enough to live up to it yet.

'We've got no evidence that this is anything but another accidental overdose,' he said. 'The only thing we've got is the suspicions of an overworked GP who makes his pocket money working for the police as a forensic medical examiner. Tell me, sergeant, just how many drug deaths do you think he would have seen in the last year?'

Cooper smiled. Vallance was right. The drug-related deaths at this end of Area you could finger count. Ryder Hall was right on the edge of the Metropolitan Police area, set in rolling countryside a million miles from the city. 'I'd be surprised if he'd seen more than a couple in the last two years, sir.'

Vallance nodded. 'The only thing we know for sure is that this Platt's been a bit naughty and that the papers are going to love him for it. Are the papers on to it yet?'

'Not yet, or at least I ain't seen anybody yet. Except that there's a reporter on one of the courses. Ryder kept going on about her, seemed to think that it was only a matter of time before she twigged who Platt was.'

Vallance laughed. 'She sounds shit hot if she hasn't already sussed that there's a story waiting to happen. All right. I want you to get on to Control and fill them in on the details of who he was. They'll probably have to get someone down from

39

the Home Office to handle it when it breaks. Where's the reporter now?'

'Her name's Sarah Fairfax, she's doing one of the courses somewhere in the building. Her name's on the list of eye witnesses, she was there when they found the body this morning.'

'Right. I'll just have a peek at the scene and then I'll go and see what this Ryder bloke wants.'

'A kick in the arse is what he wants, sir.'

Vallance smiled. 'You're volunteering are you, sergeant?'

At least he had a sense of humour. The last DCI that Cooper had worked with had had his surgically removed. He opened the door and made way for Vallance to enter room 23.

The PC inside the room, a rookie called Paul Hill, jumped to attention, dropping his paperback on the floor. Vallance looked at him and shook his head. Hill, looking embarrassed, bent down to pick the book up. 'I found it in the room, sir,' he explained, as though anybody were interested.

'Reading the evidence lad?' Cooper asked, shaking his head sadly.

The body had been pushed back on to the bed off the floor but the blood and the vomit hadn't been cleaned up. The position of the body had been photographed first, and samples had been taken from the floor. Routine, that's all it was.

Vallance peered at the body for a while, and then he looked around the room. 'How much has been moved?'

'Nothing, sir. We've made sure that nothing's been removed. The door's been locked and PC Hill is already on his second chapter.'

'Is it good?' Vallance asked Hill.

'Not really, sir. It's a book about organisation theory, sir.'

'That's what I like,' Vallance told Cooper, 'a copper not afraid of an intellectual challenge. So, the victim hasn't been tidied up? He was dressed like this when he was found?'

Cooper looked at the corpse. Dressed in a white shirt, black trousers, sensible leather shoes, dressed in fact for a day at the office. 'Yes, sir.'

'Hill, if you were going to do a line of coke and a bottle of scotch don't you think you'd relax a little bit? Undo your tie perhaps, kick off your shoes even?'

'Er, yes, sir.'

'Cooper?'

He hadn't really noticed it before, but Platt still had his trousers belted tight. Far from looking like a man ready to get out of his head he looked as though he were ready to get down to some serious work. 'You're right, sir. He looks ready for a business meeting.'

'Get the scene of crime boys down here pronto,' Vallance decided. 'It looks like the quack's hunch might be right after all.'

Cooper's pulse quickened. Perhaps this one wasn't going to be so routine after all. It made a change, better than the usual boring stuff he had to deal with. 'Yes, sir. Anything else?'

'Yes, find that reporter and get her out of the way for a while. I don't want the papers getting wind of this until somebody from Queen Anne's Gate is here to handle it all. Hill?'

The young PC was almost rigidly to attention. 'Yes, sir?'

'Don't touch anything else! If I find your dabs on any of the evidence I'll give you an example of the tough end of organisation theory in practice. Understood?'

Hill swallowed hard and his face turned an ugly shade of bright red. Cooper realised that he was going to enjoy working with DCI Vallance.

Cooper was right about the Barbie dolls. The place really was crawling with American blondes with big hair, blue eyes and teeth so white they dazzled. Vallance retraced the route he'd taken with Diane Bennett back to the reception area. The woman at the counter flashed him a smile that could not hide the nervousness in the soft blue of her eyes. So, even American Barbies were nervous in the company of the Met.

'Tom's expecting you,' she told him before he had even got to the desk.

'So I understand,' he said, smiling back. She looked pretty cute, with those big blue eyes and full expressive lips.

She picked up a phone and dialled through. 'Detective Vallance is ready to see Tom,' she said, speaking loud enough so that he could hear. Her name tag said 'Josephine'.

'Thanks, Josephine,' he said, leaning against the counter. 'So, what exactly goes on here?'

Fluttering eyelashes while she worked out an answer. 'This is Tom's base in Europe,' she said. 'We run the courses and all –'

'Mr Vallance?' The voice belonged to another one of the female staff. No name badge on her, he noted. 'I'll just take you through to meet Tom,' she said.

Josephine smiled at him nervously. She'd been rescued from having to make small talk with a policeman. The woman he followed had long dark brown hair that cascaded over her shoulders and contrasted with the pure white of her blouse. She was tall, with long legs clad in black stockings and amply displayed by her short skirt with a slit at the back. If this was Ryder's personal secretary than he had better taste in women than the bevy of identikit blondes suggested.

They walked through a door marked STAFF and then into an open plan area at the back. There were seats along one wall, a coffee table with a carefully arranged assortment of magazines laid out on it. The aroma of fresh coffee was hard to ignore; the filter machine was tucked away in a corner. Vallance wandered over hoping that he'd have time for a cup; he'd been up since dawn and he was sorely in need of some caffeine.

He turned when he heard the door to the inner office open. Tom Ryder looked like the boss. Powerfully built, sleek black hair that had started to grey, smart blue suit and an air of authority, he was every inch the successful American business tycoon.

Vallance walked across towards him. 'Detective Chief Inspector Anthony Vallance,' he said, offering his hand.

Ryder gripped his hand for a moment. 'Tom Ryder. I'm glad that you can make time for me, Mr Vallance. You'd like some coffee?'

So, Ryder had noticed him looking at the filter machine. 'White please, one sugar.'

'Laura, two coffees please,' he called to his secretary, who had already taken her place behind her desk.

They walked into the air-conditioned office, Ryder making

42

way for Vallance to go in first. There was a seat in front of the desk and a heavy black leather chair on the other side of it. The polished surface of the desk was bare apart from a blotter and a phone. Ryder waited for Vallance to sit down before sinking down comfortably into his seat.

'I hope your colleague has explained the potential seriousness of the situation to you, Mr Vallance,' Ryder began, looking at him directly.

'I understand your concerns, Mr Ryder, and we'll do our best to minimise any disruption to your operations here.'

'My main concern is not to do with any disruption in the short term. My concern is with the reputation of my establishment; a reputation carefully nurtured and built on solid work these last few years. We both know the sort of thing the tabloid press is capable of in this country.'

He hadn't even expressed an interest in the dead man, but then Ryder was a businessman not a social worker. His concern was with his business, though Vallance had only the vaguest idea what it was that Ryder's organisation did. He knew that Ryder was assuming that everyone knew what his business was. How would he react to the question? 'What exactly do you do here?'

Ryder looked surprised. He really had been under the impression that the police knew what his organisation did. 'I am an expert in management techniques,' he said, leaning back in his seat. 'In the simplest terms I help people to improve the way they manage their companies. I show them how to look at problems in ways which help them towards finding the optimum solutions. I help them to prepare for the challenges presented by the changes in technology and in corporate culture.'

PC Hill's little bit of reading came to mind. 'You mean organisation theory, stuff like that?'

Ryder paused. 'We've had people from Scotland Yard here recently. A Chief Superintendent from the Inspectorate if I remember correctly, and somebody from the Deputy Commissioner's Executive. Perhaps you've heard of what we do?'

Vallance shook his head. 'Can't say that I have, sir. So, you run residential courses in management training. Is that it?'

Ryder shifted uneasily in his seat. 'No, there's a whole lot more to it than that, Mr Vallance. At Ryder Hall we teach a whole new philosophy of management. It's a way of looking at the world rather than just a series of isolated techniques. In addition, this is my European headquarters. From here I organise lecture tours, speaking engagements, television appearances, books, tapes and so on.'

'Do you have a similar headquarters in the States?'

He smiled. 'Yes, Fort Lauderdale, Florida. I spend about half my time in Europe and the rest in North America.'

'It sounds like a very profitable business,' Vallance said, just as the coffee arrived.

Ryder waited until Vallance had taken a sip of his drink before continuing. 'It's hard work but very rewarding, financially and intellectually. Which explains why I am so keen to minimise any negative publicity that might arise.'

'Tell me why you think that's going to happen.'

'Alan Platt was a senior scientist at the Home Office, Mr Vallance. He was a member of the working party looking at the activities of the pharmaceuticals industry. More pertinently he was a consultant to the Advisory Council on the Misuse of Drugs. He was one of the people who report directly to the government on the control of narcotics. If it is true that he was himself a user of narcotics then it will prove highly embarrassing to the government and that in turn will provoke more interest in the media. So you see, Mr Vallance, I have good reason to be wary. I may seem like a callous son of a bitch to some people, but what would you do in my situation?'

Vallance put his cup down. 'I've asked that someone from the Home Office be informed,' he said. 'I want them to handle the press and any kind of political fall-out. That's not a police concern even if we sympathise with your predicament. We're also doing our best to speed things up as regards the investigation. As soon as the coroner makes the decision the body will be transported to a mortuary.'

'How long will that be?'

Vallance had no idea. 'That depends on what the scene of

crime manager decides, and no doubt he'll be talking to the coroner and possibly to a forensic pathologist –'

'Hey!' Ryder demanded furiously. 'What do you mean scene of crime manager? What's going on here. This is an overdose, right? Right?'

Vallance took another sip of coffee. Tom Ryder could get agitated after all. 'Given the circumstances we're not taking any chances, Mr Ryder. This is undoubtedly an accidental overdose, but given the implications we have to be cautious.'

Ryder looked at him warily. 'That sounds mighty like political talk to me,' he murmured. 'If the victim was Joe Average from the bank would you be acting this cautious?'

'No, but then neither would you be so worried. Now, we'll do our best to be unobtrusive. I want to interview the people who found the body this morning, starting with the member of staff who opened the room.'

'Diane Bennett, whom I believe you've already met.'

'Yes, I've met her. Is there a room we can use for interviews?'

Ryder seemed even more agitated. 'Yes of course there is. What do you propose doing about Sarah Fairfax?'

Vallance canned the snide remark. Ryder didn't look the type to appreciate humour. 'She'll be interviewed shortly. Do you know who she works for?'

'Yes, she works for a TV company, they make a programme called *Insight*. She's here to do a piece on me and my work.'

'You don't sound too happy about it.'

Ryder leant forward. 'Let us say, Mr Vallance, that the downside to success is that it makes some folks very jealous. Let us just say that she is less than sympathetic to my work. In fact –'

The sharp knock on the door put a stop to what Vallance was sure was going to be another long speech. For a business-man Ryder seemed very good with words.

Laura put her head around the door; even without a smile she looked good. 'Mrs Platt has arrived.'

'Does she know?' Ryder asked.

'She's here to formally identify the body of her husband,' Vallance said. 'I don't suppose one of your management techniques covers this, does it?'

As a joke it left a bitter taste in the mouth, but not as bitter as showing a dead man to his wife.

If rank had privileges then handling the recently bereaved wasn't one of them, Cooper thought. Vanessa Platt had been inconsolable; her wails of pain must have echoed throughout the entire building. Vallance had taken her into the room and had stayed with her for a long while. When he came out his face was ashen and he looked drained by the experience. Her parents were with her, luckily. Although her mother was crying at least her father was able to take command of the situation.

Vallance had made sure that Mrs Platt was OK before letting her father drive her back home. In the meantime Cooper had been busy. A succession of crime scene specialists had been combing through the room for any evidence of unfair play. The small bag of white powder that had been found on the bedside cabinet was carefully bagged and then taken off for analysis. None of them had any doubt that it was cocaine but until the results came back positive there was always the chance that it might be something else. One of the toxicologists had obligingly listed a dozen or so different compounds that might have killed a man if snorted in the mistaken belief that it was coke.

Platt's bosses at the Home Office had reacted to the news with stunned silence. They retreated behind a civil service silence of the first order. Cooper wasn't surprised. He knew what it was like to pull together against outsiders. Later they'd had a call that someone was going to come down to liaise between the police and the press, as though the Yard's own Directorate of Public Affairs was cack-handed or something.

And now he and Vallance were sitting on stiff wooden chairs ready to interview the first lot of witnesses. As incident rooms went it wasn't ideal, but Cooper knew that Tom Ryder wanted them out and there was no way he was going to make things easy for them. It was late too, and apart from tea and coffee there'd been no offer of food, even though the smell of it pervaded the corridor. There was a canteen somewhere in the building and Cooper longed to find it.

'Do you want me to do the talking?' Cooper asked, sensing

that Vallance was still recovering from his meeting with Vanessa Platt. The poor cow, fancy getting news like that. It was bad enough telling her that her husband was dead, telling her that he'd probably done himself in with a coke overdose was heartbreaking.

'Yes, you start,' Vallance agreed wearily. 'If I've got anything to say I'll say it. Who have we got first?'

'Diane Bennett. She runs the courses mostly, Ryder himself keeps out of the way a lot of the time.'

'Is it my imagination, but do they talk a lot of crap in this place?'

Cooper smiled. 'No, sir. It sounds like crap to me too, but I thought that was because I'm just a dumb cop not clever enough to understand it.'

'Perhaps we ought to get PC Hill to tell us all about it later,' Vallance said. 'OK, let's make a start.'

Diane Bennett had changed out of her work clothes into something more relaxed. But even with a baggy jumper, faded jeans and a pair of trainers she looked immaculate. She came in and sat opposite Vallance, hardly daring to glance at him. Beside her he looked even more down at heel, his unshaven face, scruffy jacket and miserable expression in contrast to her neat clothes, long blonde hair and fresh complexion.

'We won't be long, Miss Bennett,' Cooper began, 'at this stage we're just interested in establishing the sequence of events that led to the discovery of Mr Platt's body this morning.'

'I understand,' she said, looking down at her hands. Cooper wondered what part of the States she was from. She sounded vaguely Southern but it was hard to be sure.

'At what time were you first called to the room?'

She inhaled deeply and began to tell her story.

'It was before eight this morning, I know that for sure. I was down for breakfast so it was probably around seven thirty, no more than that. I always go down around then, Tom likes us to eat with the guests, it makes things friendlier, more personal. Anyways, I was down getting something when I saw Sue Beamish wander over. She'd been out for a run, the way she had every other morning that I'd seen her.'

Cooper checked the name on the list of witnesses. 'Who's

Sue Beamish?' he asked. Sue Beamish was listed but there was nothing to say who she was.

'Oh, she works with Alan. Sorry, she worked with him I should say. Every morning they'd go running together before breakfast. Anyways, she came over and asked me if I'd seen Alan, you know, had he been for breakfast yet? I said not and then she looked really concerned. She said that she'd tried his room before her run and there'd been no answer. She hadn't seen him out on the field and he wasn't there when she got back. I told her that he'd probably gone for a walk someplace but it was raining outside and she said it wasn't like him to miss a run.'

'She'd been out in the rain presumably?' Cooper said.

'That's right, she was soaked and her face was all red. You know, her running shoes were soaked right through. No, she'd been out for a run all right. Well, I could see she was worried so I said I'd go over to try his room again. She kept saying that he was a creature of habit, that he never missed a morning run, you know, talking like that. Well, there was just no answer at his room and she was getting real worried by now. I was hollering through the door at him but nothing. By now there was a crowd out there in the corridor and Sue was apologising almost as much as she was worrying.'

Vallance decided to kick in with a question. 'The crowd around the door,' he said, 'did you notice anyone who shouldn't be there?'

'What do you mean?'

'Someone from another part of the building? A member of staff or a guest from another floor?'

Diane thought for a while before shaking her head. 'No, sir, they were all people from the neighbouring rooms.'

'Are you sure?' Vallance reached for the list of witnesses. 'Kate Thurston? Sarah Fairfax?'

'No, they arrived together as I recall, but their rooms are just down the way. I figure they heard my hollering and banging on the door and came over to investigate.'

'Then what happened?' Cooper said.

'There was still no answer so I headed down to Josie in reception to get a key. When I got back there'd been no response so I went in,' she stopped for a second and then continued. 'The light was out and the curtain was drawn but I knew something was wrong. I saw the outline of something on the floor and at first I thought it was a suitcase or something tipped over. When I got close I saw that it was a body. I ain't never seen a body before, and I tell you something, I don't ever want to see one again. It was horrible.'

'And then?'

'Then I screamed and people rushed in. Things get a bit confused, I was sort of shocked for a minute. I know that Sue came in and that Kate was there to hold her back. Sarah Fairfax was pretty calm, she's the one told me to call the police department.'

'Think carefully now,' Cooper told her. 'Did anyone touch anything in the room? Can you remember anyone acting suspiciously?'

'No, sir, I can't remember anything like that.'

'Do you know when he was last seen alive?' Vallance asked.

'No, sir. I mean I saw him down in the main bar last night. He looked fine then.'

'What time was that?'

'I can't say for sure. Between nine and ten at a guess, but I can't put my hand on heart and swear to that.'

'Was he alone?'

Vallance noticed the momentary hesitation too. 'I spoke to him briefly,' she said. 'That was the last time I saw him.'

She was either lying or skipping something. Cooper was ready to go in harder but Vallance got in first. 'How well did you know Mr Platt?' he asked.

It wasn't the question Cooper would have asked, and from the expression on Diane's face not the one she feared. 'I sort of knew him a bit,' she said. 'I met him and Sue before they came here. But that was it, I mean we weren't friends exactly.'

'Yes?'

She shrugged. 'We do a lot of presentations to corporate clients. Sales stuff, showing them what we do and how we do it. Most people have heard of Tom but there's a lot don't know about the courses. A while back we were working with people in some of the big pharmaceutical companies, that's where we made contact with the Home Office people.'

Vallance again. 'I see. And when you saw him last night what sort of mood was he in?'

Another shrug from Diane. 'Normal I guess. I mean Alan was never the most outgoing person in the world. You know, he was the kind that's always got something on his mind, always thinking things over.'

'Is there anything else you can think of that might help us?'

Cooper looked at Vallance. Was that it? He felt cheated. Diane was holding back, it was obvious.

'I'm sorry,' she said, shaking her head slightly. 'If I think of anything I'll let you know.'

'Thank you, Miss Bennett,' Vallance was saying, 'you've been most helpful.'

She looked relieved on the way out. Cooper waited for her to shut the door before turning to Vallance. 'She was lying, sir!'

'I know.'

'So why –'

Vallance smiled. 'Because I want to find out what she's lying about before I use it against her. Forewarned and all that sort of stuff. If she thinks she's got one over on us then that's good. Next time she won't be ready for us.'

Cooper smiled. 'Bit of a sneaky bugger on the quiet, aren't you, sir.'

Vallance laughed. 'A sneaky bugger? Sneaky bastard I think is the phrase you're looking for.'

'Yes, sir, I'll remember that.'

'Good. I want you to play the same tack when you interview the rest of them. Get PC Hill or one of the others in here with you.'

'You getting back, sir?'

He stood up wearily. 'No, I want to talk to this Fairfax woman. Have you seen her?'

Had he seen her? She'd almost bitten his head off when he'd asked her to go to the library. 'Yes, sir, I've met her.'

'Yes?' Vallance looked interested, his dark eyes lighting up at the prospect.

'She was bloody angry, sir. She was spitting blood and that was three hours ago. Do you want me to deal with her?'

'No, I think Miss Fairfax might be even more pissed off if she doesn't get to chat with me directly,' Vallance replied, obviously relishing the impending confrontation. 'One more thing, what's she look like?'

Cooper smiled. 'A bit of a looker, sir.'

Sarah stood against the door and listened, certain that of the two men she had spotted from the window one was Detective Chief Inspector Vallance. One had been dressed in traditional detective garb of sober blue suit and tie, the other looked as though he'd been dragged out of bed and forced into clothes rescued from the wash. Vallance was certain to be the one in the black leather jacket; only rank gave him the privilege of dressing down like that.

The heavy oak door muffled sound but the murmur of voices was all she needed. After three long and tedious hours she was about to be set free. Being locked in the library would not have been so bad had there been anything interesting to read, but the shelves were stacked with countless Victorian tomes on livestock, arable farming and turgid volumes of second rate poetry. It seemed obvious that the library had come with the house, and with typical American reverence for all things English and Antique the Ryder Forum hadn't bothered to change a thing.

It was a point worth making – American psycho-babble contrasted with English stately home. She wasn't sure how significant it was. Perhaps it meant nothing, but then again perhaps she could look back to Victorian quack cures, snake oil salesman and patent medicines. Not for the first time that day she suddenly felt naked; without paper to write on or her cassette recorder to tape her thoughts she was defenceless.

She crossed the room quickly, realising that DCI Vallance was about to honour her with a visit at long last. Why hadn't she been allowed to stay in her room? Why was Alan's death such a big deal that the local constabulary had forced her out of her class into the library? A coronary wasn't such a big deal, even in a man of Alan's relatively young age –

which meant that it was a suicide or murder.

She sat back on the edge of the desk as the door opened and she suppressed a smile – she was right about Vallance being the man in black. It was not only his clothes that looked dishevelled, he was sorely in need of a shave and the rings under his dark eyes suggested that he needed sleep as well. He strode into the room, a half smile already playing on his lips and a hint of amusement in the dark eyes that fixed on her.

'I'm Detective Chief Inspector Vallance,' he began to say.

She cut him off instantly. 'You've taken your time!' she snapped angrily, finally able to voice the frustration that had been building up over the hours.

'I was about to apologise for the slight delay,' he replied calmly.

She suppressed the urge to scream. 'Slight delay? You call three hours a slight delay?'

'I do apologise, Miss Fairfax, for not attending to you before checking out the scene of death.'

'Please, Detective Inspector,' she said, echoing his sarcastic tone, 'don't let me detain you any longer.'

His eyes widened a fraction and for a moment she thought he was about to laugh. 'That's a good trick,' he said, walking to the window. 'Does it ever work?'

The snappy answer she had ready and loaded was instantly redundant. She realised suddenly that he was much sharper than the shabby clothes and insolent manner suggested. 'Does what work?'

'Deliberately forgetting rank,' he said, turning from the dull view at the window to face her. 'I suppose there are some people who'd get offended by that. I'm not one of them. Just like there are some people who genuinely forget details like an officer's rank, but you're not one of them, are you?'

Full marks for observation. He was right, verbal demotion was always a good way of cutting through people's defences. It was a trick she'd learnt by accident but a good one nevertheless.

'You're here now,' she said, 'so perhaps you can start by explaining why I've been kept prisoner.'

'No, Miss Fairfax,' he told her, walking back to slump into one of the heavy old armchairs nearer the door, 'I think you ought to explain what it is you're doing here.'

Didn't he know? She was surprised that the Ryder Forum people hadn't informed the police yet. Or else they had and Vallance wanted to hear what she had to say for herself. Certainly he was waiting for an answer. His dark eyes were scanning her intently.

It was time to play for some answers; that was the least that was owed to her. 'Mr Vallance, am I under any obligation to answer your questions? I would remind you that I have been locked in this room for the last three hours, much against my will. Your colleague's answer to my questions was to tell me to wait for the arrival of the fount of all knowledge – namely you. In the event don't I have the right to know what's going on?'

'No.'

Her anger rose suddenly; it wasn't enough that she'd been held prisoner all evening now she had a bloody-minded cop to deal with as well. 'I demand to know what's going on! If I don't get any answers I'll –'

'Miss Fairfax,' Vallance interrupted calmly, 'please don't even think about threatening me. I appreciate the fact that you work in the media and so you feel that gives you rights above the rest of us, but in this case making threats is going to be counter-productive to say the least.'

It was a good speech, far better than she had expected of him, but he had it wrong of course. 'Mr Vallance, while I appreciate the fact that you are a serving police officer and so imagine that that gives *you* rights above the rest of society, I would remind you that I am not obliged to make any statement whatsoever.'

She glared at him, hoping that the insolence in his eyes would finally give way to anger.

Instead he looked at her and laughed. 'That's a good come-back,' he said, 'I like that.'

He wanted to make friends now. His dark eyes shone with a playful humour that invited complicity. The dark stubble on his chin looked etched permanently into his skin. She was

53

looking a mess by accident but his looked deliberate. It was time to put him in his place once and for all, and there was still mileage in playing up her outrage.

'I'm glad that I amuse you, Detective Chief Inspector. Unfortunately the feeling is not mutual, I'm less than impressed with your conduct so far.' For a second she felt like threatening him again but then she relented. 'Now, please, can we get on with things?'

He sighed heavily. 'I'm dying for a coffee,' he said, glancing quickly at his watch. 'Have you had anything to eat?'

Food. She was starving. 'Nothing,' she admitted.

'That makes two of us then. If you'd just answer some simple questions I'll see about getting some food sent up.'

It was her turn to want to laugh. Couldn't he see how transparent his ploys were? The tatty leather jacket matched his tatty little tricks. 'Is that a bribe?' she sneered. 'I always imagined that it took two officers to play good cop bad cop.'

'Cuts in spending,' he replied. 'It's hell when I have to hold a prisoner down and beat him up at the same time.'

She allowed herself a smile at last. There seemed to be no way to dent his good humour. 'That is in extremely poor taste, Mr Vallance,' she said.

He returned her smile with one of his own. 'I'll see about some food,' he said, getting up.

Were his defences down now? She had to take the chance that he'd cooperate at last. He turned and their eyes met unexpectedly; deep, dark brown, fringed with long lashes. For a second she couldn't turn away, and when she finally averted her eyes her heart was beating faster. Damn! She hadn't expected this.

She walked to the door with him, hoping that he hadn't noticed her momentary lapse. In any case she couldn't let it get in the way. 'Will you trade?' she asked.

He stopped dead in his tracks. 'What do you mean?'

'I'll swap you question for question.'

'That's not the way it works,' he said. His smile had faded suddenly and his eyes were blood red with exhaustion.

'OK, I'll answer all your questions if you answer just one of mine.'

He hesitated for a moment, looking at her as though for the first time. 'The answer to your question is I don't know,' he said wearily.

There was no way he was answering the right question – no way on earth. 'What was my question?' she demanded.

'Is it suicide or murder?'

Damn! How the hell had she given herself away?

'That's very good, Mr Vallance,' she admitted, her smile less certain than it had been.

FOUR

Vallance was disappointed that the canteen – Sarah had rather grandly called it the refectory – was closed. He was starving no matter what it was called. On the other hand she seemed more interested in fishing for information than in finding food. Not that there was much to fish for; probably the only thing worth knowing was that Alan Platt worked for the Home Office and was considered an expert on illegal substances. Just how much of an expert was only now becoming apparent.

'We could try the bar,' Sarah suggested.

'You know the way,' he said. She avoided looking at him even though she was trying out a smile for size. Cooper had been right, Miss Sarah Fairfax was definitely a looker: dark brown hair, blue eyes, slender build but curvaceous in just the right places. Yes, definitely a looker, Vallance decided, walking with her along the corridors of Ryder Hall towards the bar.

She was quiet, probably working out her next line of attack. Not that he was in the mood for any more verbals, at least not with her. Like a lot of reporters she obviously felt that she had a God-given right to be arrogant, demanding, intrusive and difficult. In her case she was a natural; he could see that she was the type who excelled at her job.

'Do the police always devote so much energy to investigating sudden deaths?' she asked, holding open the door to the bar.

'Let's get something to eat first and then we can talk,' he

said, taking the door and waiting for her to go in first.

The atmosphere in the bar was only a few degrees above funereal. A few of the tables were occupied and a couple of the stools at the bar were playing host to bored-looking customers. Not a happy atmosphere – the conversation was so muted it might have been switched off completely. The bloke behind the bar looked up from his newspaper as Vallance and Sarah walked over.

'Do you serve food?' Vallance asked, peering over the bar in search of a micro-wave.

The barman shook his head apologetically. 'There's the refectory for food,' he said.

'But that's shut.'

'You're a bit late,' the barman pointed out.

'Couldn't you rustle up some sandwiches?' Sarah suggested hopefully.

'But the kitchen staff will have gone home.'

Vallance smiled. 'Why don't you nip down and make some then?'

'But I'm looking after the bar.'

'You're not being very helpful,' Sarah told him. 'I've paid a lot of money to attend this course, the least I can expect is a bit of service.'

The barman looked adamant. 'I'm sorry, but the kitchen's closed and there's nothing I can do about it.'

Sarah looked even more determined than the barman. 'Is this how Tom Ryder's principles get applied?' she asked loudly.

'Look, I just work behind the bar,' came the reply, delivered at the same volume as her question. 'If you want principles you have to go somewhere else.'

'It wasn't principles I was after,' Vallance said quietly. 'A hot pie and some chips would do me fine.'

'I'm sorry, mate, but the bar's for drinking not for food. I don't make the rules, I just work here.'

'Leave it,' Vallance said quietly, taking Sarah by the arm. 'What do you want to drink?'

'A gin and tonic, slimline.'

'And a whisky for me,' he added.

Sarah glared at the barman but he ignored her as he got

the drinks. One of the other customers looked at Sarah and half-smiled but she ignored him completely. Vallance paid for the drinks and then they moved to a table by the door.

'Is it always this quiet in here?' he asked, grabbing an empty chair and putting his feet up.

'No, it's usually a lot livelier. People go a bit mad when they're away from home like this.'

Not her though, she wasn't the type to go wild. He ditched the comment because he knew she'd start to argue and he didn't have the energy for it. 'Was it livelier last night?'

'Yes, or at least it was when I popped in here briefly.'

'What time was that, do you think?'

She sipped some G&T. 'Is this an interrogation?'

'No, it's a gin and tonic.'

'Do you make these up as you go along or do you have a book?'

'You twigged it,' he sighed. 'There's a chapter in the Police Training Manual which covers crap jokes in bars. It's required reading.'

She smiled but not with any real feeling. 'Will you tell me now why there's all this fuss? I mean what is it about a man having a heart attack that necessitates the presence of a squad of police and a Detective Chief Inspector?'

She didn't know about the coke. She didn't know about Platt's job at the Home Office. She didn't know that the doctor was unhappy about it being an accidental overdose. It was time to give her some ground, he decided. 'Alan Platt's coronary was probably brought on by an overdose of cocaine.'

Her eyes widened a fraction. Deep blue eyes that contrasted with her dark brown hair. Nice eyes which looked into his and then darted away quickly. 'That's so hard to believe,' she said.

'Why?'

She seemed shocked by the question. 'Because he didn't look like a cocaine user to me.'

'And what does a coke user look like?'

'Have you forgotten I work in the media? I've seen no end of people snorting charlie, it's the done thing in this industry.'

'But not you,' he said.

'No, not me.'

He believed her. Doing coke was for other people. The sort of people who went on residential courses and got plastered, or went to bed with complete strangers, or had a puff of grass or did a line of coke. Vallance knew that Sarah did none of those things. What she did was work and argue, or perhaps her work was arguing. 'What about Platt, was he the type?'

'No, I don't think so.'

'You met him then?'

'Just the once. I wanted to talk to him again after it; he seemed a very interesting man.'

'Why's that?'

She took another sip of her drink. Even with that she was being careful, taking tiny sips as though testing it all the time. 'Because he was the only other person on the course not completely mesmerised by Tom Ryder.'

'Tell me about that. I'm just a dumb cop, I don't know anything about organisation theory or management techniques. What's it all about?'

There was no flicker of reaction when he called himself a dumb cop. He would have liked her to disagree, or perhaps it would have been funnier if she'd agreed, but there was nothing. He was a dumb cop and she was the clever reporter.

'Mr Vallance,' she began, 'are you familiar with the phrase "money for old rope"? Tom Ryder's an excellent speaker, very glitzy, very American, very show biz. There's even an element of truth and insight in what he says, I'll grant him that. However from what I've seen he milks that grain of truth – if you'll pardon the mixed metaphor – and makes a fortune doing so.'

Vallance nodded. It was time to play up the dumb cop if that's what she wanted. 'So it's all crap then?'

'Yes and no. He has a particular outlook on things. He likes to call it a philosophy but it's nothing so grand. Along with that he claims to have a set of techniques which help people apply his outlook to their problems. He calls it inspirational management, and that's what we're here to learn.'

'Has it inspired you?'

'No.'

'But it's inspired everyone else apart from the late Mr Platt?'

'Is that significant?'

'No, it was just an observation. This Ryder bloke, he seems to have a lot of women working for him. Young, attractive women. And there's a lot of women on the course too, isn't there?'

Sarah looked at him and nodded. 'Yes, he's very popular with the women on the course. If you'd seen him in action you'd understand why. He's a very charismatic speaker, very forceful, very sincere.'

'You like him too?'

'No,' she said, but her eyes said differently. 'Did they find cocaine in Alan's room?'

There was no point denying it, she'd find out soon enough. 'It's being analysed but we'll be very surprised if it's anything but nose powder.'

'Mr Vallance, why are you here?'

He finished the last of his drink. Food would have been good, but if there was nothing to eat he couldn't think of anything he'd rather drink than neat Scotch. 'I'm here to investigate Mr Platt's death.'

'There's nothing else?'

Should he say more or cut the conversation dead? She was a reporter, anything he said could be taken as evidence and used in print. The rules dictated he keep his mouth firmly shut. But she did have blue eyes that told their own story.

'Will you promise me one thing?'

'That depends, doesn't it, Mr Vallance.'

'Just promise that you won't drop me in it.'

She smiled. 'Are you asking me to keep a confidence?'

'I'm asking you to use your judgement, Miss Fairfax. So far I've not heard anything from you to say that your judgement is skewed. I'm going to trust you to keep things quiet until we have more idea of what's going on.'

She looked at him again. For a moment she was unguarded, vulnerable almost. She was gorgeous and he hadn't even noticed till now. Her eyes lingered on his for a split second and then the look was gone. Him and her? For a second the idea didn't sound too crazy but then the second had passed and she had turned away. The two of them? No; too complicated, even though he was sure she had felt something too.

'I'm here,' he said quietly, 'because Alan Platt worked for the Home Office and was a government advisor on street drugs.'

She blinked. 'But that's just so –'

'I hope that you're not going to rush to print with this story.'

'What? I'm a television journalist, I don't rush to print for anything.'

'You know what I mean.'

She did know. She was playing for time while that cool calculating brain of hers worked out all the possibilities. After all, he was the ignorant copper and she was the sophisticated media person with all the savvy. 'Has there been a press statement yet?'

He glanced at his watch. 'No, but someone from Queen Anne's Gate should be here soon. You can get the scoop now, if you want it.'

She was savvy enough to understand a trade was in order. 'Or?'

'Or you hang on and get the deeper story.'

'I see no reason for rushing things.'

He smiled. Yep, she wasn't the type to rush into anything.

Cooper was just washing down a bacon sarnie with a mouthful of coffee when DCI Vallance returned from his skirmish with Sarah Fairfax. Or at least it should have been a skirmish; Vallance looked pretty relaxed.

'Where'd you get that?' Vallance asked, pointing to the discarded polythene wrapper on the table in front of Cooper. A dollop of ketchup still marked the wrapper.

'One of the SOCO guys brought some over with him.'

'And where's mine?'

Vallance didn't look as if he was joking. 'Well, er, I didn't think you'd – er –'

'I get the picture,' Vallance murmured. 'Did you get anything out of the other witnesses?

The boss was not in a good mood. Cooper hoped it was down to the Fairfax woman giving him a hard time and not down to forgetting to grab him something to eat. Besides, the boss knew the score; the scene of crime officers were always well stocked up with goodies to eat. That's why they had portable fridges and ice-boxes. Using them for bio samples was just a handy bonus.

It was easy to condense the long series of interviews that had stretched through the afternoon and into the evening. 'Most of them gave the same story,' he reported. 'It all ties in with what Diane Bennett told us. The only one who remembers seeing him last night is a Kate Thurston. She says she saw him with Diane Bennett. She can't be sure but she thinks they were having an argument of some kind. Nothing violent, but enough to stick in her mind.'

The news did nothing to change Vallance's scowl. 'Anything else?'

'Yes, she said that she'd heard a rumour that Platt was at it with some woman.'

'Yes?'

'That's it. She didn't know the woman in question, but she did let on where she'd heard the rumour.'

'Who was it?'

'Sarah Fairfax.'

The boss suddenly looked interested. 'She doesn't strike me as the gossippy type. She was sure she'd heard it from Fairfax?'

'Kate Thurston is definitely your gossippy type. I couldn't get her to stop once she'd started. But she was sure about Diane Bennett arguing with Platt on the night he died, and she was sure that Fairfax had told her Platt was having it off with another one of the guests.'

Vallance looked at his watch again. 'I think we're going to have to talk to Diane again,' he said. 'We know now what she was covering up earlier. Do that tomorrow. Did anyone else have anything to say?'

'No. What about Fairfax? If Platt was having it off then we need to find out who the lucky woman was and see what she's got to say for herself.'

'I know. We'll have a chat with Sarah Fairfax tomorrow as well. We'll make it a nice formal little interview. Right, what have SOCO got to show apart from supplying you with sandwiches?'

Cooper flicked through his notebook. 'No signs of violence. Lots of dabs, a few fibres. No change in the cause of death but they've not had anything back from the blood samples they've taken. The coroner's given the all clear to get the body out of here.'

'Make sure that there's a guard on the room tonight,' Vallance said. 'If anyone complains then tell them to talk to me. Also, get on to Tom Ryder and tell him that we're going to carry on with the interviews tomorrow, so we want a room to use. If he complains then tell him I'd be happy to let SOCO loose on the rest of the building.'

'Yes, sir. Anything else?'

Vallance looked at his watch and inhaled sharply. It was late. Outside it was already dark and the strain of the long day was suddenly etched on his face. 'Yes, I need a place to kip tonight,' he said. 'Is there anywhere local that's OK but cheap?'

Cooper looked at Vallance. He wasn't joking. There'd been nothing in the canteen about him having trouble at home. It probably wasn't a good time to ask. 'There's a pub not too far from here. The Fox and Frog. There's rooms upstairs and the landlord pulls a nice pint.'

'Good. Get someone to sort that out for me.'

'Yes, sir.'

'No,' he decided on second thoughts. 'You sort it for me, and if word of this gets back to the nick then you can think about going back into uniform. Understood?'

Cooper nodded. 'Don't worry, sir, I'll have the room sorted and no one'll know anything.'

Vallance smiled. 'Good. Now, all that's left is to brief the bloke from the Home Office.'

'It's a she, sir. Arrived about half hour ago. Her name's Philippa Brady, she's waiting for you downstairs.'

'One more thing, when you ring the Fox make sure there's something to eat when I get there.'

★

Philippa Brady was waiting near the main entrance to Ryder Hall, mobile phone in hand as she paced up and down the gravel drive beside her car. Vallance was guessing that it was her car; sleek, metallic, powerful, it was just the sort of car that a woman like Philippa Brady sported. She was wearing a dark-coloured business suit of grey jacket, short skirt, white top and shiny patent high heels.

It looked like rain, he thought, glancing up at the night sky that rippled with thick black cloud. Where was the Fox and Frog? If one of the uniforms drove him there then his sudden stay away from home might as well be broadcast on the radio. He knew what canteen gossip was like. Within days there'd be a book on the state of his marriage, with odds on that it'd end in tears. He trusted Cooper to keep quiet. He was a keen copper and clever enough to know that you stayed on the boss's good side if you didn't want the police equivalent of latrine duty.

He jogged down the granite steps of Ryder Hall and towards Philippa Brady. She continued jabbering into the mobile until the last minute and then she turned to him. Her glance swept over him quickly; sharp appraising eyes that seemed to take him in completely before meeting his own.

She covered the mouth-piece of the phone with her hand. 'Yes?

'Philippa Brady? I'm Detective Chief Inspector Vallance.'

The look of surprise was only momentary, if he'd blinked he would have missed it. 'I'll call you back,' she told the phone and then snapped it closed. 'That was the drug section of the forensic science labs. They're not happy about it, but you'll get a provisional result from them by tomorrow.'

The turnaround at forensics was normally measured in weeks. If she were telling the truth then it meant that the Platt case was in a different league to most of the cases Area dealt with. 'What about the other labs?' he asked, leaning back against her car casually.

'They're working overtime on this one,' she said, smiling slightly.

The first drops of rain started to fall. They both looked up at the sky and then at each other. 'We can talk in my car,' she suggested quickly.

She walked round to the driver's side and he slipped into the passenger seat before she had opened her door. The car smelt new, all leather trim and the slight scent of her perfume. He tried to guess how much the car cost but gave up. It was expensive, that was all he could say. He eyed her long legs, clad in black stockings, as she swung into her seat. Her skirt was short enough for him to glimpse the dark band at the top of her stockings before she smoothed it down again. When he looked up she was smiling at him.

'Now, Mr Vallance, what do you have to tell me?'

He smiled darkly. There was a lot he wanted to tell her but he had to can it. For the moment at least. 'Drugs are going to confirm that the powder was cocaine, there's no doubt on that score. The only thing I'm interested in is the quality of it. If it's low-grade street stuff then that opens a new line of investigation. If it's good quality and uncut then that changes things completely.'

'How so?'

The rain was falling more heavily, pattering on the windscreen and smearing their view of the entrance to Ryder Hall. 'If it's street stuff then we have to investigate the possibility that the victim may have been leading a double life. He wouldn't be the first who's been whiter than white on the outside but a bit of a sleaze on the inside. You've worked these things before,' he said, taking a guess, 'you know how it is.'

She nodded. 'And if it's not from the street?'

'You do know that cocaine is still used in certain medical procedures? It could mean that we'd be looking at that supply route. I don't know if he's medically qualified or not, but I'm presuming that in this case he would have had access to laboratory samples or something.'

'From our perspective the medical route is the lesser of two evils,' she said, staring at the rivulets of water that cascaded down the windscreen. 'Anything low rent – like drug pushers and everything else that it entails – means there's a greater chance of people running to the tabloids. If it's a case of being liberal with medical supplies we can always pin it down to individual aberration. You know the story: the poor man was under immense pressure, unable to cope, out of his depth, that kind of thing.'

She spoke calmly and without obvious emotion as she outlined her preferred scenario. It meant rubbishing the dead man's life but that seemed incidental to her. There was another possibility that he had not mentioned yet, and now that he had heard her talk he decided not to mention it at all until he was more certain of the facts.

'What are you going to say to the papers?' he asked, glancing at his watch.

'I'll issue a press statement tomorrow morning. It'll be a straight coronary to start with. It won't be noticed except by some of the broadsheets. They'll get the obits out of the way before the full details become known.'

'In a couple of days most of the people who were on the course with him will be back home. They'll be spread all over the country, which makes it a pain in the arse for us but it's easier for you – there's no focus of any rumours then.'

She laughed softly. 'If only that were true. Alan Platt was very highly regarded by his colleagues, and that includes a number of Ministers of State as well as the Home Secretary himself. Unfortunately there are a number of photographs of the Home Secretary and Alan Platt together at different social occasions, as well as at various official meetings. Once it gets out that Alan Platt was a junkie then the tabloids will splash those pictures all over the front pages. So you see, we have to keep this thing quiet for as long as possible.'

Vallance glanced at his watch again. It was getting late and he was shattered. 'In that case I'm sure we've got a lot to discuss in the morning.'

'Yes, I dare say we have. I'd like us to talk about Tom Ryder as well, first thing if possible. I'd like to know what you think of him before I go in to meet him.'

Vallance smiled. Philippa was young and attractive – just Tom Ryder's type. 'OK, we can meet first thing tomorrow. Are you staying here or driving back up to London?'

'I had planned on driving back, but now I'm not so sure,' she said, peering into the dark, pouring rain. 'Is there a good hotel around here that you'd recommend?'

'There's a quaint old place not far from here,' he said. 'It's called the Fox and Frog. It's not the Dorchester but the food's good and the landlord pulls a terrific pint.'

'Is it comfortable?'

Vallance smiled sincerely. 'Very.'

'In that case where can I find it?'

'It's OK, I'll navigate.'

She looked at him dubiously. 'Is it on your way?'

'Sort of.'

It was past midnight when they finally pulled into the car park of the Fox and Frog. It had taken nearly an hour to find the place instead of the ten minutes that Vallance had promised. Philippa eased the car to a stop as she mentally listed the lies he'd told her so far: he knew where he was going; he was a good navigator; it was on his way. She was tempted to ask for proof of identity; he'd probably lied about who he was as well.

'I told you we'd find it,' he declared, grinning.

She looked at him and laughed. He looked exhausted but there was no sign of flagging in his good humour. It had taken an hour to find the place but it had been an entertaining hour. 'Do you think they're still up?' she asked, looking at the building in front of them shrouded in darkness.

He'd probably lied about that too; far from being comfortable it gave every impression of being one of those olde worlde places with poky little rooms designed for midgets or tourists with more money than sense.

'I'm sure they're still about.'

'And do you think they're going to have a room for me?'

'Bound to,' he promised. 'I mean this is the middle of nowhere, how much business can they be getting off season?'

She grabbed her case from the boot and passed him his tatty sports bag. It was only after they'd been driving around for half an hour that he let slip that he was going to be staying at the Fox as well. And then, in case it hadn't occurred to her, he assured her that he hadn't suggested the place merely so that he could get a convenient lift there.

They walked round to the front but it was firmly locked,

as were the doors to the other bars at the side. It was a big place with a main bar that was crossed with oak beams and which flickered with the shadows thrown by the dying flames from the original fire place. The walls were lined with sporting posters, trophies and country bric-à-brac. Just the sort of place that tourists like to think of as quintessentially English.

Vallance found an open door round the back, near to the pub garden that was full of sodden wooden benches drying out now that the rain had stopped. They walked in slowly, peering round in the hope that they'd find someone waiting.

'This must be for you,' Philippa said, finding an envelope pinned to the door leading to the kitchen.

He read the note quickly. 'Can you believe this?' he asked, showing her a door key. 'They've left the key here for me. I could be anyone, what's wrong with these people?'

'Obviously they're a lot more trusting than you are,' she said, pushing the door open and walking into the kitchen. She found the light switch and the fluorescent strips flickered for a while before casting a dull white light over the stainless steel work tops and tiled floor.

'I'll get one of the crime prevention boys to have a word,' he said, following her into the kitchen. 'Now, there should be some food here.'

She turned to face him, her arms crossed over her chest. 'Aren't you forgetting something?'

He raised his eye brows questioningly. 'Like what?'

'Like where am I going to sleep tonight?'

'I thought they'd be awake when we arrived,' he explained, hunting around for food. 'I didn't think they'd all be tucked up in bed.'

'If we'd got here in time they would have been up waiting for us, but then we hadn't counted on your navigational skills.'

He was methodically working down a row of fridges and freezers, peering into each one hopefully before moving on to the next. 'I'm sorry about that – Here it is!'

She shook her head sadly. He'd found a plate of food in one of the ovens and was grinning triumphantly. 'Where are you going to sleep?' she asked him.

He looked at her for a moment then down at the food

again. 'On the couch?' he suggested hopefully.

'These places don't have couches in the rooms.'

'All right,' he said, throwing his arms in the air to admit defeat. 'I'll kip on the floor if I have to.'

Philippa smiled. 'Yes, you'll have to.'

'You want some?' he asked, pointing to the dried-up potatoes, solid peas and the crust of a steak and kidney pie.

She looked at it and felt a little queasy. 'No, you go ahead. What room are we in?'

He threw her the envelope with the key in. 'Room 12. You go up, I'll just finish this and then I'll stake my claim to the floor.'

She turned to go and then stopped. 'I just want you to know,' she said, 'that I don't normally share a room with a man I've only just met.'

'Don't worry about it. I'm pretty used to kipping on the floor these days.'

Was he joking? Probably not she decided. He obviously wasn't staying at the Fox because of the convenience.

The narrow flight of stairs curved tightly before opening up on to a first floor landing. Room numbers were signposted with arrows and she followed the narrow corridor round until she found number twelve. The key was stiff and for a minute she struggled with it before it finally gave and she almost tumbled into the room. As expected the room was a tiny cupboard with barely room to move. A big double bed was the only luxury but it meant that floor space was minimal. No couch.

Vallance was cute, in a shabbily sexy sort of way. Not her usual type, but he made her laugh and there was something very honest about him, despite all the little lies and excuses. She liked his eyes too. Dark, sensual, piercing eyes. But liking him was one thing, letting him into bed was something else altogether.

She carefully eased her case on top of the bedside cabinet and flicked open the catches. Normally she would have slipped out of her clothes and straight into bed. How would Vallance cope with that? She could easily imagine him slipping between the sheets too, giving her a leery smile and making a joke of

70

her outrage. He'd know that her protests were of the coy, come-on type.

'Snap out of it!' she told herself. A man was dead and all hell was threatening to break loose. Her mind should be focused on that, she scolded herself mentally. Not on wondering what Anthony Vallance was like in bed.

She unclasped her skirt and eased it down slowly. In the car every time she'd looked round his eyes had been on her legs. At least there had been no pretence from him, none of that furtive glancing or sneaky excuses when she'd caught him. And what had she done about it? Smiled sweetly and carried on, enjoying the attention.

She took her jacket off next and placed it neatly on the back of a chair. And then her blouse so that she was wearing nothing but Janet Reger's finest lace bra, panties and silk stockings and a pair of black high heels. There was no mirror around, but she didn't need one to know how sexy she looked; if she felt sexy then she looked it whether she was dressed in rags or pure silk.

'Hold on!' she cried when there was a gentle knock at the door. He was back already? She grabbed a bath towel from her case and held it up in front of her. 'OK.'

Vallance started to come in and then stopped. His eyes lingered on her for a moment and then he looked around the room quickly. When their eyes met she felt drawn to him. His smile was gone and his eyes were fixed on her, making her look away as she felt a familiar feeling of excitement ignite deep inside her.

'I don't normally do this sort of thing,' she said, holding the towel in place as he closed the door behind him.

'But you'll do it now,' he stated softly.

She held the towel in place as he walked over to her. They faced each other for a moment and then he put his lips to hers. They barely kissed, lips touching softly, the feel of each other's breath so close. He leant closer and put his hands on her shoulders, drawing her toward him. They kissed again, his mouth harder against hers, his tongue moving in between her lips.

She let go of the towel and put her arms around him,

71

pressing her body against his as he took her completely in his arms. They kissed passionately, voraciously, his tongue exploring her mouth, his teeth forced on to her lips. She felt dizzy suddenly and tried to push away.

'Give me a chance,' she said, shakily. Her face was flushed with excitement and her heart was racing.

'If I gave you a chance you'd get away,' he told her, smiling darkly. He held her face in his hands and kissed her again, pulling her towards him, tilting her face, taking possession of her mouth. She shivered as he pulled her bra straps down over her shoulders, first one and then the other. His fingers massaged her breasts and then closed over her nipples until she uttered a cry of pain which he sucked away.

She stood still while he tugged her bra down without undoing it. She watched his eyes devour her. He stroked her naked breasts, his strong masculine fingers toying with her hardening nipples. She felt the excitement in her sex like a liquid fire as he began to kiss her throat again, his teeth biting into her flesh while he explored her body with his hands.

She cradled his head in her arms, easing him towards her breasts. She wanted his mouth on her nipples, she wanted to feel the frenzy of his desire on the most sensitive points of her breasts. Her gasp was one of pain and pleasure as he began to bite and suck and kiss her flesh. With his hands he began to stroke her thighs, sliding up and down her silky stockings towards the heat of her pussy.

They fell back on the bed together, side by side but he moved round quickly and pushed her beneath him. Each time his fingers touched her sex she shivered with pleasure. She parted her thighs, opening herself to his fluid touch but he seemed to back away. She reached round to him and stroked the hard cock she had felt pushed into her thigh.

He pushed her back down and then stood up quickly to remove his clothes. She watched him, aware of the intensity of his gaze and the controlled way he moved. In moments he was naked and beside her again. His chest was patterned with curls of black hair and the muscles flexed with every movement of his powerful arms. She stroked his hard cock with her fingertips and watched for the pleasure in his eyes.

She closed her eyes and sighed when he stroked his fingers over her panties once more, pressing the lacy material between the moist lips of her sex. She moved for him, parting her thighs, opening herself further. She touched him softly, tracing her fingers over the ridged muscles of his stomach and then through the dark hair of his chest.

He pulled her panties aside suddenly, exposing her sex obscenely and rubbing her pussy bud with the clenched fabric that he gripped tightly. He played rough and it was exciting. She felt the desire swell inside her, turning her sex to honey. His fingers teased her pussy lips apart and she gasped with pleasure. She wanted him. She wanted him to fuck her. Fuck her.

She raked her long nails across his back as his fingers penetrated deeper into her sex. He knew how to excite and to give pleasure, every caress seemed to electrify her body. She sighed and moaned softly as he pushed his fingers hard into her pussy. Her lace briefs were soaked with her pussy juices, stretched tight into her backside and used to tease her pleasure bud.

He moved between her thighs and she opened herself to him. His thick erection touched her inner thigh and then pushed against the open petals of her pussy. He looked into her eyes and she saw the power and the fear and the desperation and the pleasure all there. She closed her eyes and felt him go deep into her body. It felt so good, so good, so good –

'Fuck me hard,' she murmured, digging her nails into his arms.

He kissed her mouth and throat and sucked hard on the flesh of her throat. He began to fuck her with powerful, rapid strokes, his hardness pushing deep into her sex. Each wave of pleasure made her gasp as she clung to him. Her panties rubbed hard against his cock and she could feel the disarray of her stockings and the tightness of her bra constricted under her breasts.

She took his hand and kissed his fingers, perfumed with her body and with his animal scent. He looked at her and smiled that dangerous smile of his that she found so exciting. She took his hand and put it in her hair, winding her long blonde locks in his fist. He tugged sharply and the pain merged with the pleasure in her cunt. She kissed him greedily just as her climax tore through her body.

He lay aside for a moment, kissing her shoulder and running his fingers across her back. 'I want to fuck you every way there is,' he whispered, his breath hot on her body.

She sighed and lay down flat. Already his hands were stroking her pussy from behind.

FIVE

Philippa was still asleep when Vallance opened his eyes. She lay beside him, warm and naked, sleeping on her side with both arms tucked under her head. Her body rose and fell with the soft flow of her breath and he was afraid to move in case he disturbed her. She was covered well by the heavy quilt and her bare shoulder was all that he could see of her body, though he could feel the enticing warmth of her nakedness against his skin.

Should he wake her up gently with kisses on the back of the neck and with glancing, tantalising touches down her back and along her thigh? He didn't know how she'd react. In the cold light of morning things were always different and what might have been greeted with a purr of pleasure the night before might easily elicit nothing but a whisper of embarrassment or even a disdainful look of boredom. He was tempted to try; she looked so sweetly innocent, curled up tight and warm beside him. He kissed her softly on the shoulder, putting his cool lips to her soft, satiny skin but there was no reaction from her.

He turned away, closed his eyes and inhaled deeply before opening them again to glance around the cramped confines of the room. Sleeping away from home had not been his idea, but with Mags back there he'd had no choice. There was probably a law of nature that said impulsive and chaotic marriages turned into vindictive and extremely painful divorces. Mags had probably seen it written down somewhere and had taken it to heart.

Her unexpected return to the flat had screwed things up in a big way. She was claiming it as her territory. Their room had become her room and his things had become garbage to be dumped around the house as she saw fit. Staying away from home was the easiest option until the lawyers had swapped stories and banked their fees.

If only Mags could see Philippa beside him. The malicious grin with which she had seen him out of the flat would have turned into a scream of jealous rage. The idea of it brought a smile to his face. He lazily rubbed a hand through the thick stubble on his chin as he considered what to do next. It should never have happened with Philippa. He wasn't her type, though being young, female and attractive she was definitely his type. She was probably telling the truth when she said that she didn't sleep around. If she'd asked him the same question he would have lied that neither did he, but she would have known it was a lie and smiled.

So what was it that had worked between them? It was a question he always asked himself. He could never figure it out, but whatever it was that he had, or whatever it was that he did, when it worked it worked brilliantly. When the chemistry reacted things just happened and for the life of him he could never suss out how to make it happen every time. It had worked with Philippa, against all the odds. When had he known? When he'd first set eyes on her? When he'd eyed her long legs in the car? When he'd made her laugh? When he'd got them lost in the car?

It was all so complicated. He couldn't see it working with Sarah Fairfax. He wasn't her type either. But he'd made her laugh. And he'd surprised her by second guessing what she was thinking. But there had to be a whole lot more to it than that. He closed his eyes again. Yes, Sarah Fairfax. It was a nice idea though.

Cooper glanced at his watch impatiently: the boss was running late and he had news to deliver. For a second he considered making a call to the Fox and Frog but then decided against. In spite of his good humour and easy, laid-back manner Vallance was the sort of man to be wary of. He was definitely not the sort of bloke you wanted to cross. Cooper could see that there was an understated toughness in him and a temper that could flare unexpectedly.

The sun was shielded by unsettled swathes of grey cloud and the cool air was ready for the rain to come. He walked down the granite steps and on to the gravel drive in front of Ryder Hall. Behind him the building squatted uneasily, the blood red brick and row upon row of sash windows waiting for the sun to bring heat and light. Something modern was what Cooper would have expected the Yanks to go for: steel, shaded glass and chrome fittings. It probably went better with all the modern junk that Tom Ryder was teaching.

He walked along the drive, sucking back hard on a smoke as he figured out where things stood. The results had come back from the drug boys early that morning: an almost pure sample of cocaine, completely uncut and therefore unlikely to have been scored from a street dealer. It wasn't impossible, of course, there were enough dead bodies around to show that occasionally you'd get uncut heroin or coke hitting the streets. A pure dose where you'd been expecting the usual shit was almost a guaranteed overdose. That might explain what happened to Platt but Vallance seemed to doubt it and Cooper was willing to bet that his boss was right.

The autopsy was due later in the morning. Things were moving fast, which meant that the woman from the Home Office was pulling strings, or else Tom Ryder was calling in favours. That was a real possibility too. Ryder seemed like the sort of bloke who'd do anything to keep his name out of the papers, and if he knew people in power then he'd have no problem in putting on the pressure. It wouldn't be such a big deal if the story did make it to the front pages; Cooper didn't like Ryder on instinct and didn't see why they should have to knock themselves out protecting the man's reputation.

The metallic green BMW seemed to speed across the drive on a cushion of air, floating like a missile just above the surface of the ground. It pulled to a halt in front of Cooper, throwing up a spray of gravel as the brakes pulled in hard. The light fell across the windscreen but Cooper recognised the car instantly. It belonged to Philippa Brady. He walked towards it and stopped. The passenger door opened and a shabby black sports bag was unceremoniously dumped on the drive. The boss climbed out a second later, followed by Philippa Brady emerging like a vision from the driver's side.

Philippa looked at him and then at Vallance and then she slammed her door. She was in uniform: short skirt, black stockings, high heels, a jacket with hard lines that gave out warning signals.

'Have the labs been in touch yet?' she demanded, her heels crunching hard on the gravel as she walked around her car.

'Yes, first thing,' Cooper replied, pulling the crumpled fax from his pocket. 'The powder we found yesterday is high grade cocaine, an almost pure sample in fact.'

She turned to Vallance. 'Good. That makes life easier,' she said.

'Not for Platt it doesn't,' Vallance replied. 'Which sample was that? The one in the bag or the stuff they found on the body.'

'It's the same. The stuff in the bag is the same as the stuff he'd been snorting.'

'I need to see Tom Ryder,' she said. 'As soon as I'm finished I'd like us to have a debriefing then we can formulate the steps we take next.'

She was speaking as though she were in charge, the tone of command came effortlessly to her glossy red lips. Cooper looked at Vallance who half smiled in return.

'Good idea,' Vallance said, 'we can have a debriefing after you've spoken to Ryder and that'll give us a chance to interview a few more witnesses.'

'Good. I'll see you later then.'

She turned on her expensive heels and strode off. Vallance was watching her, his eyes fixed on her backside and long legs. 'Right, who've we got lined up first?' he asked, turning to Cooper.

'Sarah Fairfax and then Diane Bennett. We've got the same room as yesterday. Sir, you're not being serious about having a debriefing with Brady are you?'

'Don't worry,' Vallance said, picking up his bag. 'This is still a police operation, but you've seen how she's got things moving and I don't want that messed up. Understand?'

So, it was down to politics. 'Yes, sir,' Cooper agreed. 'I'll get one of the uniforms to fetch Sarah Fairfax.'

They began to walk towards Ryder Hall which reflected the pale light in a thousand panes of glass. The grey sky seemed to hover above it, like a cold, dark aura.

What had the boss being doing with Philippa Brady first thing that morning? The question buzzed in the brain but Cooper couldn't ask it. On the other hand a quick call to the landlord of the Fox wouldn't hurt anybody.

Sarah looked at the brown slurry that had settled in the bottom of her mug and wondered uneasily at how much of it had also settled in the bottom of her stomach. What had happened to the American love of good coffee? Had the Ryder Forum really settled for second rate because they imagined that the British knew no better, or was it another example of their miserliness when it came to spending the high fees that people paid to attend their courses?

With only another two days to go, the course was more than half over and she still felt that there was no meat to it. She had been looking hard for examples of 'inspired' management but there had been none worth reporting. Had she learnt anything of value? Was there anything in the course that she could not have got from buying half a dozen paperbacks in an airport bookshop?

There was only one thing that she could think of: meeting Tom Ryder. Meeting him had been the high point of the course for most people. People like Kate Thurston and Sue Beamish were converts, for whom the chance to meet the guru in the flesh was worth any amount of money. The chance to bask in the great man's presence, to talk to him, to gaze into his piercing, all-knowing eyes – these were ample rewards in themselves and justified going on the courses even if they learnt nothing from them. For the privilege of meeting him they were willing to be bored rigid in silly lectures and to play adolescent games in the pretence that they were discovering hidden talents. A talent for gullibility perhaps, but nothing more as far as Sarah was concerned.

And now this. She had been called from her class by a spotty young policeman who looked barely old enough to be in uniform. She had been escorted to the cramped little room that had been set aside for interviews, provided with a mug of Ryder Hall coffee and then left alone to await the arrival of DCI Vallance. Had there been developments in that story? Not that it interested her very much. She was more concerned with what the Ryder people were doing than with the personal tragedy that had befallen Platt and his family.

The door opened and Vallance ambled in, following by one of his more traditionally dressed associates. Vallance had had a shave, but already she could see the stubble gathering under his skin ready to break out again. His dark brown eyes met her own and she looked at him warily. There was something about those eyes that made her feel unnerved, as though he could see things in her that she did not want him to see.

'I'm sorry for the delay, Miss Fairfax,' he said, taking a seat opposite. 'This is Detective Sergeant Cooper, he'll be joining us for this little chat.'

She glanced up at the thin-faced policeman who moved to take his place beside Vallance. His eyes were full of suspicion and he had none of Vallance's shabby charm. 'You do realise that I'm missing yet another chunk of my course?' she said coldly. She'd been glad to be out of the class, but there was no point in giving that away.

'We do appreciate the time you're giving us, Miss Fairfax,' Vallance told her calmly.

Why was he being so relaxed? 'Is this a formal interview? Am I going to be cautioned?' she asked.

'No, we're not taking a statement, we just want another chat.'

Vallance looked tired, as though making up for a sleepless night, one of many by the look of it. Detective Sergeant Cooper, on the other hand, seemed wide awake. 'Haven't we been through everything already?' she asked with exaggerated weariness.

'Probably,' Vallance conceded, 'but we'd just like to go back over a few things with you.'

'OK, just be quick,' she said, slightly disappointed that Vallance was refusing to rise to the bait. He'd been a better sparring partner the first time around.

'Tell us about Alan Platt.'

Again? What more was there to say about him? 'We met very briefly, I can't have exchanged more than a few sentences with him.'

'How did you meet?' Cooper asked.

'It was after Tom Ryder's big speech, which makes it the day that Alan Platt died. After the speech we were treated to another second-hand buffet during which Tom Ryder came over to talk to me. No,' she paused, thinking back to the vivid memory of her confrontation, 'it was more like he came over to put me in my place. He had found out that I was an investigative journalist and came over to accuse me of being out to get him.'

'And are you?' Vallance asked.

'No, of course not. I've already explained that I'm looking into the whole area of fashionable management theories. Tom Ryder's just one of a number of people I'll be looking at. In any case he managed to cause a bit of a scene and then he casually walked away, leaving me completely isolated. You should have seen the looks I was getting from some of his fans.'

'What about Platt?'

'He came over a little bit after that and we spoke for a moment about Tom Ryder and then he walked off to talk to his friend.'

Cooper shifted uneasily in his seat but there was no reaction from Vallance. 'Which friend would that be?' Cooper asked.

She realised that she hadn't mentioned the mysterious woman to the police before. Was it significant? Was it possible that she was a drug dealer and had passed cocaine to Platt? 'I don't know her name and I don't know what she looks like,' she said. 'I didn't get a proper look at her at all in fact. I just saw them together for a moment.'

'Was she young, old, black, white?' Cooper demanded.

There was little point in pretending that she knew more than she did. 'I only caught a glimpse of her,' she said. 'I didn't see her face at all, Alan was standing very close to her. She was wearing jeans and a top and carrying a shiny black bag, that's all I can say for sure. I sort of assumed from the way Alan was looking at her that they knew each other fairly well, that's all.'

It was Vallance's turn to speak. 'Well enough to be sleeping together?'

'You've been talking to Kate Thurston,' she realised. 'It was a possibility that occurred to me, that's all. People do that sort of thing,' she added. There was a hint of amusement in Vallance's dark eyes and it annoyed her but she decided to bite her tongue.

'This woman, was she in the same group as you?' Cooper asked. 'Can you help identify her for us in any way?'

'Why do you need to talk to her?' she demanded, deliberately directing the question at Vallance and not at his subordinate.

'Because we need to understand the circumstances leading to Mr Platt's death.'

'Do you think she's involved in that?'

'We need to talk to her to discover precisely what, if any, the relationship was between them.'

Was there more to it than that? 'Do you think she sold him the drugs?'

Vallance ignored the question. 'Can you help us to identify her?'

She shrugged. 'Try talking to Peter Shalcott,' she said. 'I think he might know her.'

'Does he work here or is he on the course as well?'

'God only knows what the old boy's doing here,' she sighed. 'He's a rather muddled old man but he's here on the course. Not that he seems to be paying much attention. The only thing I can think is that his company must be sending him on the course to keep him out of the way.'

'And his connection to the woman?'

'I saw him duck out of one of the classses and when he came back I thought I saw her behind him. I could be wrong, I only caught a glimpse of her both times. And before you ask,' she added, pre-empting Vallance's obvious next question, 'I don't think she and Peter are sleeping together as well.'

Vallance smiled. 'Thank you. Now tell me about Diane Bennett.'

She looked at him suspiciously. 'What about her?'

'Did she know Mr Platt?'

She hadn't given the question any thought previously. She had assumed that Diane knew him because he was attending the course. Looking back though she seemed to know both Platt and Sue Beamish fairly well. 'I think so, but I can't be sure.'

'Did you ever see them together?'

'I can't remember.'

'Were you in the bar on the night he died?'

'No.'

Vallance smiled again. 'Busy working?'

She glared at him icily. 'Yes, is there anything wrong with that?'

'Not at all,' he said, still smiling. The more he smiled the more she could feel the anger rising within. Did he think that because he was a slob with a casual attitude to work that everyone else had to be the same? 'About Diane Bennett,' he continued, 'how did she react when she discovered that you weren't in love with Tom Ryder?'

'Who told you I'm not in love with him?' she demanded. His eyes widened a fraction; the first hint of a feeling other than that blasted good humour of his. 'All right,' she agreed, calming down again, 'I'm obviously not in love with him. Let me think. After Tom Ryder had publicly confronted me with what he thought were the facts he had walked away smiling. As though it were a big game he were playing. A little bit later Diane came over to try to smooth things over again.'

'Did you speak with Platt before or after Diane came over?'

'Before. Tom had walked off leaving me effectively ostracised. Kate was livid and there were lots of dirty looks from around the room. Alan obviously picked up on it all but he didn't seem that concerned. His attitude was that Tom Ryder had some mildly interesting things to say, not that much of it would stand up to scientific scrutiny in his opinion. Anyway he came over, we chatted and then he left. Diane Bennett approached me after that.'

'What did she say?'

'She apologised for Tom Ryder's direct approach. She fed me a lot of junk about my test results and then promised that I'd still be treated like everyone else on the course.'

'How likely is it that Diane Bennett saw you and Alan Platt together?'

'Pretty likely I think. I mean she didn't mention it but she was in the room at the time. Look, Mr Vallance, is this significant?'

He stifled a yawn and shrugged. 'Did you hear any rumours of Diane and Platt arguing?'

Rumours? Being in the same group as Kate meant that she was privy to no end of rumour and scandal. The woman was a tabloid newspaper on legs, and she automatically assumed that everyone else would be interested in who was sleeping around, who was a secret alcoholic and who was making a mess of things on the course.

'Yes, I'd heard a rumour,' she said.

'And?' Cooper prompted impatiently.

'That's it. I'd heard a rumour that Alan Platt and Diane Bennett had had a row one evening in the bar. To be honest, Mr Vallance, I don't pay much attention to rumour and silly bits of gossip.'

'No, I don't suppose you do,' he said. Was there a hidden barb there? She couldn't tell.

'Talk to Kate Thurston,' she suggested.

'Thank you, Miss Fairfax,' he said, leaning back in his seat casually.

She looked at him angrily. Was that it? She felt cheated in some way. She had expected a quid pro quo of sorts, some snippet of information that would let her know how things were going. She stood up to leave but Vallance was already flicking through a set of notes given to him by DS Cooper.

Was he deliberately ignoring her? She checked the anger instantly. Why should she care what he thought? But she did, and that angered her still more.

★

The call from the pathologist came in just as Diane Bennett arrived. Cooper would have been able to handle the interview alone but Vallance decided against. Diane Bennett could wait. He despatched Cooper to get the car and then walked with Diane Bennett down to reception. He didn't tell her anything but he took his time about it, keeping her guessing until the last moment.

'There is one thing, Diane,' he said. 'We need to talk to everybody who's had contact with Platt in the last few days. Obviously we want to keep the story under wraps so we're not taking any chances.'

Diane looked relieved, as though she'd been expecting worse. Keeping the story under wraps was probably what she had wanted to hear but feared she wouldn't. 'How can I help?' she offered.

Her eyes were nervous but Vallance pretended not to notice. 'A few people have said that Alan had struck up a friendship with one of the other people attending the course. We don't have a name for her, but as I understand it she may have been in a class with Peter Shalcott. Do you know who I mean?'

'I can't say that I do,' she said, 'but I can try and find out.'

He smiled. 'What about a list of people in the different groups?'

'We don't work that way,' she explained nervously. 'It's Tom's policy to improvise. The classes and groups are always temporary; they come together for one session and then that's it.'

It sounded like a lot of crap, which meant that it was probably true. It was also true that she knew exactly who the woman was. 'I'm sure you can find out for me,' he said. 'Tom's going to want me to have a word with her, isn't he?'

'Sure,' she agreed readily. 'I'll do my best.'

Doing her best meant asking Tom Ryder first, Vallance realised. Whatever else inspirational management was about it wasn't about taking the initiative or being independent. Diane Bennett was frightened to death of disappointing Tom Ryder.

The car pulled up at the steps just as Vallance reached the bottom. The clouds were still threatening rain and casting a dull gloom over the rolling green lawns and landscaped gardens.

He could see the unsettled sky reflected in the gleaming roof of the dark blue car.

'What about the Brady woman?' Cooper asked as Vallance got into the passenger seat.

'She can wait for news like the rest of them.'

Cooper smiled grimly. 'You're going to have her on your back as well as Fairfax,' he said.

'Philippa Brady is still being seduced by Ryder. We don't matter for the moment.'

The car jerked forward in a spray of gravel, Cooper turning a tight circle and then heading towards the wrought iron gates that guarded the entrance to Ryder Hall. 'And Fairfax?'

Vallance shrugged. 'Don't underestimate the woman,' he warned. 'She's smart enough to be suspicious of Ryder's bull. We might need that.'

'You think there's something dodgy going on?'

Vallance instinctively knew that the answer was yes. 'We'll know when we hear what the pathologist has got to say. Now, just drive and let me get some kip.'

It wasn't much of a nap. With traffic low and Cooper's driving it took them less than fifteen minutes to pull into the car park of the local hospital. The different departments were signposted in a confusing array of colours but Cooper knew exactly where to go. The hospital was a typical and confusing mixture of decaying Victorian municipal architecture, prefabricated huts that had been standing for a decade and a smart new building that stood incongruously beside its older and shabbier neighbours.

The mortuary was in the basement of the oldest part of the hospital, down in the darkness and the silence. Dr Raymond, the pathologist, was a tall, greyish man in his late fifties, with tired eyes and flat feet. His eyes were probably tired from spending too long down in the pit that served as his domain.

Vallance was assaulted by the sharp chemical smells that attacked the senses as soon as the double doors swung open silently and he and Cooper walked into the cool darkness.

'DCI Vallance?' Dr Raymond asked, emerging from the shabby den that served as an office.

'That's right, and this is DS Cooper. Well, doctor, what can you tell us about our late Mr Platt.'

Dr Raymond stepped back into the office, jabbed at a phone and called for one of his assistants to wheel the body into the lab. 'This is my first cocaine overdose in ten years,' he remarked conversationally, leading the way to the operating room at the far end of the mortuary.

The sharp electric light cast stark shadows in the tiled room that stank of formaldehyde and the sharp antiseptic smell of laboratory death. They waited in silence for a moment, listening to the approach of the trolley carrying the dead man.

'It's definitely the cocaine then?' Cooper asked.

The double doors swung open on silent hinges and the tubular steel trolley was pushed into the centre of the room by a dark-skinned orderly. The body was covered by a dull blue sheet but the impression of head and arms and feet were clearly visible.

'Thank you, Hamid. We won't be long,' Dr Raymond said.

The orderly stepped forward and quickly pulled the sheet down as far as the shoulders. The head of Alan Platt stared with empty eyes at the strip of fluorescent light above him. The blood and vomit had been cleaned away and already his face had lost the impression of pain or distress.

'Oh, yes,' the pathologist said, finally getting round to answer Cooper's impatient question, 'it was definitely cocaine. I've seen the results from your labs and they're spot on. There were samples in both nostrils which I managed to salvage before it was absorbed into the mucous membranes. Pure cocaine.'

It still didn't ring true. Vallance felt vaguely disappointed. 'You're sure it was an overdose?'

'Oh, yes. His blood samples contained a cocaine level of about 0.3 mg. Deaths have been recorded with levels as low as 0.1 mg. I would definitely say that it was that which caused the coronary.'

'That's it then,' Cooper sighed, 'an accidental overdose. End of story.'

'Try not to sound so disappointed by it,' Vallance snapped.

Dr Raymond looked mildly surprised. 'On the contrary,

I don't think it was an accidental overdose.'

Vallance waited for more, but the pathologist was busy examining the body. He had bent over and was gazing intensely at Platt's left shoulder. 'Here,' he said. He pointed to a tiny blemish that marked the skin just below the neck.

Vallance could see nothing unusual. The waxy skin was slowly leaching colour and detail. 'What is it?'

'A small puncture in the skin. Not very deep. Probably caused by a standard 0.8 needle,' the pathologist reported.

It didn't make sense. 'Is that the entry site for the cocaine?' Vallance asked.

'Possibly but not probably. I would imagine that it was used to inject the procaine first.'

The pathologist was beginning to get on Vallance's nerves. Why didn't he just come out and tell them the whole story instead of feeding them piece by piece? 'What the hell's procaine?'

'A sedative. Funnily enough it's related to cocaine. It's a synthetic drug, similar to the coca bush alkaloids. Very fast acting, even with small doses such as this one.'

'What would be the effect of injection?'

'In a high enough dose it would cause dizziness, muscular tremors, convulsions, irregular breathing, and cardiac arrest eventually. In this case I would suspect that it acted very quickly to weaken the victim, perhaps causing a temporary loss of consciousness during which time the cocaine was applied.'

'Applied?'

Dr Raymond nodded and then bent over the corpse again. 'I've examined both nostrils, and both feature an unfamiliar dispersal pattern. If he had snorted the powder it would have been sucked high into the nasal passages and been absorbed almost immediately by the mucous membranes. In his case there were traces of powder much lower down.'

'Couldn't he have snorted it like that?'

The doctor considered the possibility for a moment, pushing his tongue around his mouth as though chewing on the idea. 'Unlikely in my opinion. The fact that both nostrils show the same pattern suggests that this was not an accident. I believe that a very high dose of cocaine was sprayed into his nose once he had been incapacitated by the procaine. Along with the effects of the sedative the cocaine was almost guaranteed to kill him.'

Vallance felt a surge of excitement that was tinged with sadness and relief. Sadness because it was murder and he now had the task of tracking down the killer. He also felt a strange sense of relief in that at least it showed that Alan Platt had not been a hypocritical drug user. It was small consolation to his wife and family but it spared them the further pain of seeing his name dragged through the mud.

'You were right all along, sir,' Cooper muttered.

'Thank you, Hamid, that will be all,' the doctor said, covering up the body once more.

Vallance waited for the body to be wheeled out before speaking once more. 'There didn't seem to be any evidence of violence.'

'Yes, that's right. The puncture in his shoulder was very clean, which suggests that the victim was relaxed. There was a level of alcohol in the bloodstream, though it was below legal intoxication level. His shirt shows the same puncture, and there's a tiny spot of blood there.'

'So he was with someone he knew,' Vallance concluded. 'He was probably having a drink with someone who injected him from behind and then squirted the coke into his nose. Any ideas what they would have used?'

'None, though I suspect that we're looking for someone with a degree of medical knowledge. The dose of procaine was of the right level to weaken him without causing a suspicious death, and of course the dosage of cocaine was high enough to guarantee it.'

There was also the skill with which the procaine had been injected. The needle mark was so clean it could have been easily missed. 'What about the time of death?'

'It's difficult to say precisely. The procaine would have caused a number of physiological changes which complicate things. I would say between two and four a.m., I can't be more accurate than that. The procaine would have been administered at the beginning of that time, the cocaine soon after.'

'Do you think there's any more you can tell us?'

'Not for the moment, Detective Chief Inspector,' the pathologist reported apologetically. 'But I think you've sufficient information to begin the murder investigation.'

SIX

Cooper said nothing during the short drive back to Ryder Hall, but Vallance could sense his colleague's grim satisfaction. The news wasn't that much of a surprise, it merely confirmed Vallance's initial hunch. However that simple process of confirmation changed everything.

'I want all the statements gone over again,' Vallance told Cooper as the car turned off the road, slowed to a crawl as it passed the empty guardhouse by the wrought iron gates of Ryder Hall and then speeded up on to the drive.

'Yes, sir. Will we be talking to Diane Bennett first?'

The squat red brick building sat uneasily under the same murky grey sky as when they had left. Although surrounded by tended gardens and rolling lawn it seemed closed and claustrophobic, turned in on itself as though jealous of its secrets.

'No, I need to talk to Philippa Brady first, and possibly Tom Ryder.'

'And are we going to interview him as well?'

'Later, maybe. We'll need to get statements from witnesses who saw Platt in the bar on the night he was killed. I want to know exactly what he was doing and where. If he was drugged at two in the morning then we need to find out what went on between the time he left the bar and the time he died.'

★

That it was now a murder investigation meant that the case had taken a big step up in importance. A senior government official had been killed in a manner guaranteed to cause a maximum amount of political embarrassment. Did that mean there was a political motive? Vallance felt that the answer was no, but he knew that such considerations would be uppermost in the minds of his superiors.

Philippa Brady had been assigned a small office near to the reception area and she was there waiting for Vallance when he arrived.

She was sitting behind a cramped little desk, her attention fixed on the screen of her lap-top computer. A phone sat on the far corner of the desk, and in front of it she had carefully positioned her mobile phone as well.

She looked up at him sharply as soon as he came in, her eyes meeting his for a moment, and then she looked away. Was she embarrassed by what they had done the night before? In any case he knew that it was over and there was no way he was going to let it get in the way of what they had to do.

'How did your meeting with Tom Ryder go?' he asked. There was only one other chair in the office and he dragged it over to the side of her desk so that he could sit down.

'It went very well, I think,' she said, taking her cue from him and keeping things formal. 'We're in agreement on the main thing; we both want to keep the fall-out to a minimum.'

Vallance couldn't help the smile. 'That's just got a lot harder to do,' he said.

She didn't return the smile. 'What did the post-mortem show?'

'It showed that Alan Platt was murdered.'

The colour drained from her face and it took a second for her to speak. 'How?'

'The cocaine overdose was deliberately administered after he'd been drugged with something else.'

Again there was a pause while she accepted the facts. 'Is the pathologist certain?'

'Yes, there's no doubt.'

'But I've been working on the press release,' she said.

He wanted to laugh. 'That doesn't change the fact that he

was murdered. When the press get hold of this now then it's going to be dynamite. Your pictures of the Home Secretary and Alan Platt are going to be plastered on every front page in the country.'

She looked appalled at the prospect. It was her worst nightmare coming true. 'Do you have any leads?'

It was time to make his pitch, probably the best chance he'd get. 'I've had my suspicions from the moment I saw the body. Given the right circumstances I'm certain that my team and I will be able to solve the case very quickly. I'm sure that a quick resolution to the case is in all our best interests.'

'Is that really in your best interest?'

Behind her, through the sash window set high in the wall, he could see the rain falling in the distance. The news was shocking, but already she was beginning to work things out. Like Sarah Fairfax, she had a job to do no matter what. 'My best interest is to remain on this case,' he said. 'I know that my superiors are going to be keen to assign a much bigger team to this case, and that team may or may not include me. One thing's certain and that's a different team will have a different commander.'

She closed the lid of her lap-top computer and leant forward. Her perfumed skin was so close, her scent familiar and intoxicating. 'What exactly is the deal?' she asked softly, looking into his eyes for the first time.

He wanted to reach out and touch her, to stroke the smoothness of her soft skin and to put his lips to hers. He looked away, tearing his eyes away from hers in an effort to resist. 'I want to keep this investigation. Someone's killed Alan Platt and I want to find out who and why and to put them behind bars. It's that simple.'

'Tom Ryder's keen to call in someone more senior. He's not sure that you're the right man for the job.'

That figured. Tom Ryder was certain that if he pulled enough strings he'd eventually get a puppet leading the case. 'This is a murder case now. If Tom Ryder thinks he can run that then he's dreaming. This isn't one of the stupid little games they play here. We're talking about the life and death of a real person.'

'If this is political then it's not your job,' she pointed out, leaning back in her seat.

'It's not political.'

'How do you know?'

'I just know,' he said. 'How do you think Sarah Fairfax is going to react to this news?'

'If she's got any sense then she'll be on to her boss immediately.'

'If someone else takes on the case then I can guarantee that that's exactly what she'll do.'

Philippa looked at him sharply. 'What does that mean?'

'It means you ought to get on to your boss, or to the Home Secretary himself if you have to, and tell them that the best man's on the case already.'

He could see that she looked slightly shocked by his demand. There was nothing like the direct approach at times, and he was sure that she'd appreciate it in the long run.

'Let me see what I can do,' she said.

Good. The case was his. All that he needed to do was deliver one murderer as quickly as possible.

Vallance had his feet up on the table when Cooper backed into the interview room with a tray full of sandwiches and two mugs of coffee. The boss was looking pleased with himself and even the dark rings under his eyes seemed to have cleared up a bit.

'Good man,' Vallance said as Cooper set the tray down on the table.

'I figured that if I turned up with no grub I'd end up doing crossing duty at a local primary school, sir.'

Vallance picked through the sandwiches wrapped in cellophane until he found one he liked. 'There's no chance of that for a while,' he said. 'I've just had a meeting with Ms Brady.'

The dark smile on Vallance's face meant that it had been a good meeting. 'What did she say when you broke the news?'

'Not a lot, really. She was a bit pissed off because she'd drafted a press release. That's the thing with these murderers, no bloody consideration for other people's work.'

The boss was definitely in a good mood. 'So what happens next?'

'She's going to get on to the Home Office and make sure that we're not shifted sideways by someone from the Yard. So it looks like the case is ours for a while at least.'

Cooper hadn't considered the possibility that the case could be taken away from them. On reflection he could see that Vallance was right to have acted. A big-wig from the Home Office being murdered meant that the case had stepped up a league and that would have meant either a team from the Regional Crime Squad or direct from Scotland Yard. Vallance knew how these things worked and had acted accordingly. There was a lot to learn from watching him manoeuvre.

They ate in silence for a while, the sandwiches washed down with mouthfuls of cheap but strong coffee. While Vallance had been sorting things out with Philippa Brady, Cooper had been working out the last movements of the dead man. There were gaps of course, both in time and in the statements of various witnesses.

'Before we call in Diane Bennett,' Vallance said, finishing the last of his coffee, 'go through her story for me.'

There was no need to refer to his notebook. Cooper had been going over it in his mind all morning. 'The classes finished at about five-thirty and we believe that Platt returned to his room directly. He came down to eat at around six-fifteen.'

'Did he eat alone?'

'Yes, sir. He was reading at dinner apparently. Definitely on his own. We don't have an exact time when he finished but we know that he arrived in the bar at about eight. He kept himself to himself pretty much, though he was seen with an unidentified young female on previous occasions in the bar. Kate Thurston saw him with Diane Bennett at around eleven. The barman remembers him leaving at around eleven-fifteen. He was dead the next time he was seen.'

'This mysterious woman who might or might not have been Platt's away date, do we have any more on her?'

'No, sir. Fairfax pointed us in the direction of Peter Shalcott, but we've not talked to him yet. Shall I reel him in?'

'Not yet, I want to see how helpful Diane Bennett can be.'

'Shall I call her in now?'

Vallance glanced at his watch. It was way past lunch time. 'Yes, it's time we had another chat with her.'

She arrived a few minutes after being called. Her hair had been ruthlessly coiffured and her face disguised behind a gloss of red lipstick, thick mascara and layer of foundation. There was a nervous flicker of a smile on her face as she came in and sat down opposite the two detectives.

'I just can't believe it's true,' she said, shaking her head sadly.

'You think that Platt killed himself?' Vallance asked.

'No, that's just as hard to believe. But I mean murder? It's just so awful.'

Vallance looked bored by her expressions of disbelief. 'We'd just like to go back over the events of the night of Mr Platt's death,' he said.

'I already told you everything I know. The last time I saw him was in the bar. I was bushed, to be honest, and I just didn't have the energy for too much socialising.'

'At what time did you say you saw him?'

'I can't say for sure.'

'Roughly.'

She shifted uncomfortably in her seat. 'Hand on heart I can't say for sure, but I'd guess it was about 9.00, maybe 9.30 at most.'

Vallance paused before speaking calmly. 'We have a witness who saw you talking with him at around 11.00.'

She swallowed hard and averted her clear blue eyes. 'That late, huh? I guess I was just too tired to notice the time.'

'What did you talk about?'

'Just general chit-chat, nothing specific.'

'Can you be more precise?'

'I think we talked about the course.'

Vallance laughed. 'What about the course? Was he happy with it, excited, angry, tired? What exactly did you talk about?'

Cooper could see her struggling for answers. 'I think we talked about how much he was learning from Tom.'

'You think?' Vallance demanded. 'Do you think or do you remember?'

'Please don't shout,' she said softly. 'I'm doing my best here.

You've got to understand that I'm just not used to dealing with the police department. This has been a terrible shock to me, that's all.'

'So, you remember Alan Platt telling you how much he'd learnt from Tom Ryder. Is that right?'

She must have realised that it sounded like bullshit. 'No, I guess I must've been a bit confused. Alan was talking about the classes, saying how's he'd never done anything like it before.'

Cooper noticed the half smile that Vallance suppressed. 'How did he say it?' Vallance asked.

'What do you mean?'

'Did he say "I've never done anything so wonderful before", or was it more along the lines of "I've never done anything so stupid in my life"?'

She looked miserable as she answered. 'He wasn't happy, that's true. I guess you can't please all the folks all of the time.'

'And how did you react to this news?'

'I guess I was none too happy about it,' she admitted softly. 'Tom puts a whole lot of effort into these courses. I mean he don't need to. Most folks are just happy to hear him speak, more than happy even. But Tom's got a real message, and he makes sure that these courses spread that message the best way they can.'

'So Alan Platt was unhappy with the course,' Vallance continued. 'You were none to happy with him. What happened?'

'Nothing happened.'

'Nothing? You just accepted what he had to say and left it at that?'

'Yes.'

'Did you argue?'

'No, sir. We disagreed but we didn't argue. There's no point in arguments, it don't get you nowhere but it gets you there real fast.'

Cooper smiled to himself as he jotted down her remark. He had no doubt that she was quoting Tom Ryder again.

'Was it a violent disagreement?' Vallance asked.

'Ain't that another way of saying argument? I told you, we disagreed but we didn't fight. There's just no point to that. No point.'

'We have witnesses who say they saw the two of you arguing at eleven o'clock.'

'What are you saying, mister?' she demanded, suddenly rising from her seat. 'Are you saying that I argued with Alan Platt and then killed him later that night?'

Vallance inhaled slowly, looking at her calmly. 'I just want to understand what happened. In your original statement you mentioned seeing him in the bar between nine and ten; nothing about an argument and you were way out on the time. All I want to do, Miss Bennett, is establish the facts.'

She hesitated, uncertain whether to sit down again or carry on out of the door. The anger had drained instantly, as though the mere fact of raising her voice had been enough to bring her round.

'I honestly can't remember the time,' she said. 'If people say it was eleven then that's what it was. We didn't fight, we disagreed, that's all. A difference of opinion, that's all it was, no big deal. That's it, that's all there is to know.'

'And after you left the bar?'

'I checked in with Tom to see if there was anything I should know about and then I went to my room.'

'What time?'

'I was with Tom for about five minutes, maybe less but no way more than that. If people say I was in the bar at eleven then I was in bed by eleven thirty. And before you ask, I was alone and there ain't any witnesses.'

Vallance accepted that without comment. 'Do you know of anyone who'd want to murder Alan Platt?' he asked instead.

'No one,' she replied automatically.

'Thank you, Miss Bennett. We may have to speak to you again,' Vallance warned.

She walked to the door, shoulders drooping a little, as though the confrontation had deflated her. 'Am I a suspect?' she asked, turning back to Vallance.

He looked at her coldly. 'Miss Bennett until the murderer is apprehended everyone at Ryder Hall is a suspect.'

Far from being inspired, Sarah felt increasingly dispirited by the course as it drew nearer to a close. It had started with a long, dull series of tests, questionnaires and interviews, had brightened for a moment when Tom Ryder had delivered his keynote speech and then it had been downhill all the way. What could she report on? A series of stunningly banal group sessions; a number of adolescent word games; endless exhortations to think positive; and the words 'chaos', 'inspiration' and 'success' repeated in countless permutations as a kind of management mantra.

She felt disappointed but not surprised. Tom Ryder had the kind of charismatic personality which could turn the commonplace into the miraculous so long as you looked at him and not at what he was saying. He worked his audience with the expertise of a skilled con-man and the sincerity of an evangelical preacher. He instilled fear and uncertainty on the one hand and then promised deliverance on the other. Unfortunately, judging by the course, he had singularly failed to deliver on his grand promises to inspire.

The afternoon session, which had just broken for coffee, had been grandly billed as offering a 'Guide To Perception'. The lecturer, with typical Ryder Hall enthusiasm, had spoken of 'representational systems', 'the keys to submodalities' and other high-sounding jargon. As she sipped her coffee Sarah flicked through her notebook. The grand phraseology boiled down to common sense. The 'representational systems' translated into the fact that some people are more visual than others, some more auditory and others more tactile. Armed with these grand insights the students were supposed to acquire skills of persuasion and powers of influence beyond all imagination.

Sarah's comments were scribbled in a margin: obvious, transparent and laughable. Even people like Kate Thurston and Sue Beamish were beginning to tire of the false enthusiasm of the Americans and the endless round of meaningless role-play. Where was Tom Ryder?

'Still writing all the nonsense down?'

She turned round to find Peter Shalcott peering over her shoulder at her notes. He was still wearing the amiable, slightly absent, smile that she remembered.

'Yes, you're right,' she said, making space for him to sit beside her, 'it is nonsense.'

'Quite so, quite so. The lecture on representational systems was most unsatisfactory,' he said, his voice taking on an uncharacteristic firmness.

'You didn't believe any of it then?'

For a second it seemed as if he had not understood, or perhaps he had not heard her, and then he leant forward conspiratorially to deliver his answer. 'It was very sloppy, very sloppy indeed. I would have been ashamed to deliver that lecture to a first-year class in cognitive psychology. Completely unscientific. All nonsense.'

He was making perfect sense. Sarah canned the surprise for the moment. She was too intrigued to waste the opportunity. 'You've lectured on this subject?' she asked.

'Good heavens no,' he exclaimed, sitting up again. 'Of course we've all done a bit of cognitive psychology but it's not really my area. Jack Divis. He's your man; excellent teacher and a first-class researcher. He's dead now of course, but he'd have put you to rights on cognition.'

He was losing it again. 'So what exactly is your subject?'

He looked at her slyly. 'Management. That's why I'm here.'

'And what exactly do you manage?'

'People. Yes, I manage people.'

As a liar he was probably the worst Sarah had ever met. 'Really? And which firm do you work for?'

His eyes seemed to lose focus for a moment, as though he were looking into the distance and then he stopped. Whatever he had been looking for was out of reach. 'I'm here to learn about management. Yes, that's why I'm here.'

Although he was obviously lying there seemed to be nothing malicious about him. Perhaps it was the fact that he was so transparent, but Sarah felt no urge to probe too deeply. There was probably a better source of information. 'How's your friend?'

'Which friend?'

It was time to play a hunch. 'Alan Platt.'

He paused only for a moment before replying. 'I'm sorry, I don't know anyone by that name.'

He was lying again. 'He's dead.'

'I'm sorry, what was the name again?'

'Alan Platt.'

He shook his head sadly. 'No, the name doesn't ring any bells.'

'He was a scientist, like you.'

He smiled happily. 'I'm in management,' he said, 'I'm here to pick up on some inspirational techniques.'

She exhaled slowly. The game was beginning to annoy. 'It's all nonsense, you said so yourself.'

'I agree with you, all nonsense.'

'What about your woman friend, does she agree?'

He nodded sagely. 'Yes, she agrees. Anita says she's never heard so much rubbish in all her life.'

'Anita?'

The sly smile returned, as though he understood that he had nearly been caught out. 'Yes, she's on the course as well. Do you know her?'

'I saw her with you during one of our classes. Remember?'

'Bridges.'

'Yes, that's right. You were looking at the physics for us. Is she a physicist?'

'Goodness no. Pharmacology, that's her subject.'

Sarah suppressed the triumphant grin. 'Do the two of you work together?'

'Oh no, we've only just met on the course.'

He sounded as though he were reading from a prepared script. 'You know, Peter, for the life of me I can't remember her surname.'

'Walsh. Anita Walsh.'

It was time for one last gamble. 'Was Alan Platt a pharmacologist too?'

Peter shrugged. 'I'm sorry, the name doesn't ring any bells.'

Julie Perkins, an icy blonde goddess in human form, looked up sharply as Vallance strode confidently to her desk. Her blue eyes were fringed with long lashes that did nothing to detract from her habitual look of disdain.

'The old man's expecting me,' he said, flashing her a smile.

The look in her eyes hardened still more. The Chief Super was not 'the old man' as far as she was concerned, and as guardian of his office she took every slight, real or imagined, as a personal insult.

'If you'll just wait a moment please, sir,' she told him, reaching down for the phone. Her tone sounded anything but subordinate. Vallance was a DCI, she was secretary to a Chief Superintendent, and clearly in her eyes she held rank by default.

'Mr Vallance to see you, sir,' she said, speaking into the phone with an altogether more deferential voice.

Vallance wondered if she and the old man ever got it together. Despite her stern features and the icy demeanour, or perhaps because of them, most men seemed to lust after her.

'You can go in now,' she said, putting the phone down firmly.

He smiled at her again, knowing that no matter what he did nothing would crack the ice. Or else nothing to date had managed to crack her.

The call had come in soon after Diane Bennett's interview; Vallance had been expecting it, he knew that Philippa Brady worked fast. There were still too many things to do to drag Cooper away, so reluctantly Vallance had decided to drive himself down to Area to answer the peremptory summons from the old man.

The office was cool and spacious and occupied by a pensive-looking Chief Superintendent Larkhall accompanied by an equally worried looking Superintendent Riley. As a welcoming committee it was pretty impressive. But was it good news or bad that they had gathered together to deliver?

The old man, ensconced in the black leather chair behind his desk, didn't go much on the formalities. 'Well, Vallance?' he demanded. 'What in the hell's going on at Ryder Hall?'

'Murder, sir.'

'We can do without the humour, Vallance,' Riley warned, his thin, sharp face suggesting that he had done without humour for most of his life.

'Yes, sir. The victim is an advisor to the Home Office on street drugs, among other things. His death was rigged up to look like an overdose of cocaine. The pathologist has confirmed that another drug was used to incapacitate the victim first before the cocaine was used on him.'

102

'Was it political?' the old man asked. 'Is that the motive?'

'I don't think so, sir. There's got to be some other motive.'

'How can you be so sure?' Riley asked sceptically.

'Because the story's not made the papers yet, sir. Besides, there are better ways to embarrass politicians, as most of the Sunday newspapers know.' There were ways to elucidate still further but Riley and the old man didn't look as if they'd appreciate anything too graphic.

'So what's your theory?'

Theory? There wasn't any. 'The murderer has some degree of medical training, that's our first line of attack. I've got DS Cooper and DC Manning going through the class lists at Ryder Hall at the moment.'

'Who else have you got working with you on this one?'

Riley chose to answer for Vallance. 'I'm assigning DS Reed and a couple of my lads from CID, sir. If need be I can pull Jack Burn from his armed robbery investigation.'

Philippa Brady had done a very good job. If Riley was willing to get his golden boy off armed robberies then it meant that someone stratospheric at the Yard had been on the phone.

'Do you think you'll need the extra manpower?' the Old Man asked.

'DS Reed and the CID boys would be most helpful, sir.'

'I don't think I need to emphasise this point, Vallance,' the old man said, leaning forward sombrely, 'but this case is extremely high profile. Eyes are on us to do a good job here. As you know, I run a tight ship and I expect you to abide by my rules. I don't want to hear that you've been rocking the boat or steering your own course. Understood?'

Vallance glanced up at the framed photograph on the wall of the Chief Super aboard his yacht. 'No, sir,' he said, 'I'll keep everything on an even keel.'

The old man nodded sagely. 'This is a good case for an ambitious young officer,' he stated.

'Yes, sir.'

'This woman from the Home Office –'

'Philippa Brady.'

'– how closely are you liaising with her.'

Vallance kept a straight face. 'Very closely, sir.'

The old man was suddenly looking serious. 'Good. I don't have to tell you that this case is extremely sensitive. That means that people are expecting results quickly. Quite frankly, Vallance, I don't like that kind of pressure. It causes mistakes. A calm hand weathers the storm. Understood? If I have to take the flak I will. Better that than making a mess of things.'

'Yes, sir.'

'And I want to be kept informed.'

'Yes, sir. I'll keep you up to date on any developments.'

'Good. Now that we understand each other I won't detain you any longer.'

'Yes, sir.'

'Wait for me outside, will you,' Riley said, just as Vallance turned to leave.

Vallance stepped out of the office and back into the cool domain of Miss Julie Perkins. She regarded him suspiciously, as though he were about to pilfer something from the office. Vallance wondered whether she was as haughty with every Detective Chief Inspector or whether she reserved the cold looks and bad attitude just for him.

Superintendent Riley came out a few seconds later.

'This way,' he said, marching through the office and out into the corridor.

'Is there anything wrong, sir?' Vallance asked, falling into step.

'My office,' Riley said, speaking out of the side of his mouth and keeping his face straight ahead.

The Superintendent's office was a less grand affair than the Chief's, and Riley had to make do with the services of Doris, who flashed Vallance a welcoming smile when she saw him.

'I'll make this brief,' Riley snapped, taking his seat behind his compact but neatly arranged desk.

'Sir?'

'I don't know what strokes you've pulled, Vallance,' Riley said, his voice a low, cold whisper, 'but you don't impress me. That case is too important to fuck up, and if it were down to me you're the last man I'd put at the head of it. I'm letting you have Brian Reed, Alex Chiltern and Anne Quinn. They're good officers under the right leadership and I don't want you screwing them up. Is that understood?'

Vallance breathed in slowly before speaking. 'Can I speak frankly, sir?'

'No. You've been warned. Don't mess up my officers and don't mess up this case. Now, out!'

Vallance shrugged and turned on his heel. There was plenty to be said but no chance to say it. For the moment at least.

Cooper and Detective Constable Dave Manning were going through a whole batch of papers when Vallance returned to Ryder Hall. There was hardly room to move in the tiny interview room but the two officers were diligently sorting through the statements and collating the information they had gleaned from Tom Ryder's organisation.

'How was the Chief?' Cooper asked, looking up as soon as Vallance walked through the door.

'We're still on the case,' Vallance said, answering the real question. 'So what have you got for me?'

Cooper spoke first. 'We've got the list of people on the course and where they've come from and what they do. It's not been easy. Either the people running the course don't know what they're doing or they just don't want to help. Dave and I have had to beg for every little piece of information.'

'Tom Ryder's had to give the all clear every time we've asked for something new,' Manning added.

That figured. Nothing seemed to happen without Ryder's prior approval. His management technique was so inspirational it left his staff without initiative or the confidence to make decisions for themselves. Vallance wondered whether Sarah Fairfax had noticed it as well; it was something worth pointing out to her anyway.

'I'll talk to Ryder again myself,' he said. 'So who've you got so far?'

'Looking at the job titles and the organisations these people come from we've narrowed it down to three people who might have medical knowledge of some sort of other.' Cooper looked down at his notes. 'There's a Dr Bharat Patel from a

National Health Service Trust in London. We haven't interviewed him yet but there's nothing obvious to link him to Platt. We've also got an Amanda Edwardes who's listed as working for one of the big teaching hospitals, her job title is "Group Support Officer" but we don't know what that means yet,' he paused to smile sheepishly. 'Finally there's Sue Beamish, Platt's colleague. We've interviewed her already of course and her story tallies with everyone else's.'

It wasn't much of a list. The only one worth talking to was Sue Beamish. The first time round she had been in a state of shock. It was definitely time to go through her statement again. 'We'll talk to Beamish later on today.'

'Beamish has gone home,' Cooper said, 'we've got the address. According to Ryder's people she's planning on coming back for the final day tomorrow.'

'I can't wait that long,' Vallance decided. 'Talking to her at home's probably not a bad idea anyway. I want to pass that list of people on the course, and I mean the complete list, through to Area. If there's anyone on there with previous I want to know, especially anyone who's been in trouble for smoking funny substances or sniffing stuff they shouldn't.'

'Yes, sir, I'll get on to it now,' Manning volunteered.

'I also want a plan of the rooms along from Platt's. I want to know who else was there and we need to talk to people in the rooms above and below it in case they heard anything.'

'People are going to be leaving soon,' Cooper said.

Vallance smiled. 'In that case you'll have to work fast because I want to talk to the people in the rooms adjoining Platt's before they leave.'

'Yes, sir.'

'One last thing,' Vallance added. 'We need to talk to this Peter Shalcott bloke about Platt's bit on the side. I need to speak to Philippa Brady again, so you'll have to deal with Shalcott. Right, get moving.'

Manning grabbed his list of names and headed out to radio them in to Area. Vallance didn't hold much hope of trapping a murderer through a simple name check but stranger things had been known to happen.

There was only one way to get back at Superintendent

Riley and that was to nail Platt's killer to the mast. The sailing analogy was apt and he could easily imagine the Chief Super using it himself.

SEVEN

The news was all over Ryder Hall by the time that classes had ended. The police had started interviewing people who had not been witnesses to the discovery of Alan Platt's body. Rumours were suggesting that more police had arrived, and that these, according to Kate at least, were detectives rather than uniformed PCs. The inference was clear: the investigation had been upgraded. Kate had even suggested, *sotto voce*, that it was being treated as murder.

Sarah had laughed that idea off while privately accepting that it was probably true. Vallance hadn't spoken to her since their interview, even though she felt that he'd promised her more. Had that been a ploy to keep her quiet and out of the way? The course was coming to a dismal end and there was little interesting for her to say about it. There was nothing to Tom Ryder's techniques, and even the promises of time with the great man himself had largely been broken.

The fact that the course was carrying on even with the presence of the police was further proof of Ryder's mercenary attitude. Postponing the rest of the course would have been the decent thing to do, but that would have cost Ryder money. She was surprised that no one else had brought it up; it seemed strange that the things were proceeding in the midst of an active police enquiry. Considering the cost of the course, and the vast chunk of her TV programme's research budget that it had taken out, she had expected much more.

The refectory was half empty when Sarah walked in. A number of people were skipping the evening meals at Ryder Hall and disappearing to local pubs of which there were rumoured to be several where the food was good and the drink even better. Sarah had been asked to join a group of them but somehow the idea of getting drunk in the company of half a dozen middle managers did not appeal to her. Besides which she had work to do. There were notes to write up, ideas to investigate and conclusions to be drawn.

She walked over to the salad bar to pick disconsolately at the uninspired offerings: stodgy potato salad, soggy coleslaw, cold rice clumped together in starchy bundles. Each time she was faced with Ryder Hall cuisine her heart sank. Was DCI Vallance the sort of man to turn his nose up at such boring fare? The answer was a definite no. He was the sort of man who'd throw food down his throat so fast the taste wouldn't even register. Or was he more likely to make a joke of it all before sitting down to a plate piled high?

Why was she thinking of him again? It annoyed her that her mind kept wandering back to his dark, intense eyes, to his good humour and to the surprisingly sharp mind. And why had he not been back to talk to her? She still felt cheated, as though he too, like Tom Ryder, had promised her more and then failed to live up to it. And if he thought that he had gotten her out of the way by promising a deal he was not going to honour then he had no idea who he was dealing with.

She turned from the salad bar and looked around for a place to sit. She couldn't face another minute with Kate Thurston and her collection of new friends. The constant chatter and the insane preoccupation with Tom Ryder were driving Sarah to distraction. It was impossible to think with them around, even though Kate seemed to know more about what was going on than anyone else in Ryder Hall. The latest news had been that the police were interviewing doctors for some reason. A Dr Patel was one of the people on the course and he had been the first to be called in. He hadn't been a witness to the discovery of Platt's body and that fact alone had triggered a new round of rumour and speculation.

The only empty table was at the far corner of the refectory. Keeping one eye out for Kate she walked towards it, hoping to have the time and space to work things out in her head. As she passed one of the tables on the way she glanced at the lone occupant, a young woman, and noticed the name badge. Anita Walsh. There was no sign of the handbag, and this time she was more smartly dressed than when Sarah had glimpsed her before but the badge was clear enough. Had Peter Shalcott given the name of the wrong person? Or was she wrong in linking him to the same woman she had seen with Alan Platt?

There was only one way to find out. And it was time to show Anthony Vallance the error of his ways.

Anita was looking at her plate, keeping her face down as though deliberately warning off prospective company. A quick glance around the room showed no sign of Peter Shalcott.

'Hello, Anita, mind if I sit down?' Sarah asked jovially, sitting down before the other woman had a chance to object.

Anita looked at her warily. Her slim, attractive face was kept expressionless but her bluish-green eyes were filled with suspicion.

'So, how are you enjoying the course?' Sarah asked, picking gingerly at her salad.

'Sorry, but have we met?' Anita replied. She spoke quietly, her voice cool and precise.

Sarah smiled. 'No, but I've seen you around. What do you think of it all?'

'The course is pretty good,' she said, without apparent enthusiasm.

'Really? To be honest I think it's been fairly disappointing. Is it what you were expecting?'

'I think so,' she said without elaborating further.

She didn't want conversation. Sarah could tell that Anita was going to get up and go at any second. 'It's a shame about your friend, Alan,' she remarked casually.

'Who?'

Sarah couldn't help looking surprised. 'Alan Platt. The man who died yesterday morning.'

'Is that his name? Yes, it's a real shame.'

111

The voice was deliberately emotionless, and Sarah could detect nothing in Anita's icy expression. 'He was a friend of yours, wasn't he?' she asked.

'No, I never met him.'

Sarah smiled. Was she wrong? She hadn't seen enough of the woman with Platt to know if Anita was her or not, but something about her made Sarah certain that she was. 'But you did, I saw you together,' she insisted.

Anita looked surprised. 'You did? I can't remember meeting him. When did you see us?'

'It was after Tom Ryder's big speech. During lunch. Remember?'

Anita thought about it for a moment. 'No, I can't remember it,' she said. 'What did he look like?'

Sarah could clearly remember the way Platt had been looking at the woman. It was not the sort of look shared by strangers. 'He was speaking to me and then when he saw you he went over to you. A tall man; he wore glasses. You must remember.'

'Is that the man who died?' she exclaimed. 'I didn't realise. My God, you just never think, do you?'

Anita's eyes were averted; Sarah couldn't see what the other woman was thinking at all. 'I thought you two knew each other,' she told her. 'At least that's what Peter told me.'

Anita looked up sharply. 'I'm sorry,' she said, 'what did you say your name is?'

'Sarah Fairfax. I was speaking to Peter earlier –'

'Peter? You mean Peter Shalcott?'

'Yes. You two work together, don't you?'

She looked away again. 'Did he tell you that?'

'Yes,' Sarah lied.

'Is he the old chap, always sounds in a muddle?'

'You mean you don't work together?'

Anita began to get up. 'No, I only met him on the course. If he said we've worked together he probably meant we shared a class or something. I'll see you later, Sarah.'

'Yes, see you,' Sarah said quietly.

She watched Anita take her tray to the collection point and then walk out of the refectory without a backward glance.

Had she spoken a single word of truth? Sarah could not believe that Anita didn't know Alan Platt, nor that she did not know he was dead, nor that she did not already know Peter Shalcott.

Damn! She'd been so taken aback by the lies that she had forgotten to find out what Anita did for a living. There was a medical connection there, just as there was with Peter Shalcott. What would that information be worth to Anthony Vallance, she wondered?

Cooper looked up from his notes just as Dave Manning arrived with Peter Shalcott in tow. Shalcott came into the interview with a vague smile on his face. He looked relaxed rather than nervous. Who was it had called him the nutty professor? It had been either Kate Thurston or Sarah Fairfax. Cooper could see that the description was apt in either case.

'Please sit down, Mr Shalcott,' Cooper said, pointing to the stiff-backed chair in front of the table. 'We're just looking at the events surrounding the death of Alan Platt,' he continued once Shalcott was seated, 'and we believe you may be able to help us.'

'A terrible business,' Shalcott said, shaking his head sadly.

'Yes, it is. Now, as we understand it Mr Platt was seen in the company of a young lady whom you might know.'

Shalcott raised his eyebrows. 'A young lady? I don't think so.'

'Our witnesses tell us that you've been seen in the company of this same young lady. A friend of yours perhaps?'

'A friend of mine? No, I'm here alone.'

He wasn't lying. Cooper had been through the records and there was no one else present from InfoCorp, Shalcott's company. 'Think back, are you sure that there's no one you've met? By all accounts she's quite a good looking woman.'

Shalcott smiled. 'I think I'd remember a pretty young lady.'

Manning, sitting to one side of Shalcott, referred to his notes. 'Can you think back to Tuesday lunch time? Straight after Mr Ryder addressed you all.'

'Oh, yes, I remember that. An excellent speaker, have you heard him?'

113

Cooper looked at Manning and then back at Shalcott. 'We're not asking you to remember the speech. Can you remember what happened at the lunch afterwards?'

Shalcott looked blank. 'I remember the lunch of course. Tom Ryder joined us for a while, though I regret to say I didn't have a chance to speak with him. Other than that –'

Cooper couldn't hide his irritation. 'You don't remember speaking with anyone?'

'I may have spoken to people in passing, but nothing comes to mind.'

'Did you know Alan Platt?'

'No. Though obviously many people have spoken of him since his death. It's caused quite a stir.'

'Please, Mr Shalcott, try and think back. Afterwards, in the afternoon session, did you meet anyone there?'

A long pause produced nothing but an apologetic shake of the head.

Cooper turned to Dave. 'Manning? What have we got?'

'The afternoon session was in room 5. According to our statements it involved some sort of game playing.'

A smile of recognition dawned on Shalcott's lined and curiously transparent face. 'I remember that now. Bridges. Yes, I did meet a rather fetching young lady there. An extremely pretty young thing in fact.'

At last! 'Her name?'

'I'm not always very good with names.'

Cooper resisted the urge to drag Shalcott across the table. 'Please try and remember,' he pleaded.

'Very pretty. Clever too. The name though – I have it!'

'Yes?'

'Sarah. She was definitely a Sarah. Clever girl, very pretty as you say. Is she a friend of Alan's as well?'

Cooper froze. 'What do you mean as well?'

Shalcott caught the inflection instantly. 'I mean, was she a friend of Mr Platt's?'

'You said "as well" and you meant she was a friend of Platt's as well as you.'

Shalcott smiled uneasily. 'I think you've misconstrued. I meant was she a friend of his as well as a friend of mine.'

'You're a friend of Sarah Fairfax?'

'Yes, we've spoken a number of times since we met on the course.'

Cooper inhaled sharply. 'May I remind you, Mr Shalcott, that I am a police officer.'

Shalcott grinned amiably. 'I do understand that, officer. And I repeat, the only pretty lady I've met on the course is Sarah Fairfax. Do you wish me to make some sort of official statement to that effect?'

'What game are you playing, Mr Shalcott?'

'Game? Oh yes, there are lots of games we play here. It's to help us learn to manage things.'

Cooper closed his eyes wearily. Either Shalcott was a superb actor or he really was an eccentric old buffer; in either case he obviously knew more than he was letting on. 'Detective Constable Manning will draw up a statement for you to sign,' he said finally.

It had been a hard day and Diane's feet ached and her head buzzed with the beginnings of a headache. There were so many things happening and most of them were not good. The police were suspicious of her and the pressure was making it difficult to concentrate on anything. Trying to keep up the enthusiastic smile and positive outlook in front of class had been near impossible. The only thing that had kept her going was the knowledge that Tom had things under control.

'Is Tom in?' she asked Laura, who was just getting ready to leave for the day.

'Hi, Diane. He's in but he's got Philippa Brady in with him. He kind of asked that they not be disturbed.'

Laura sounded slightly nervous. Diane smiled serenely. 'How long have they been in conference?'

'Most of the afternoon. I think they're working on some kind of press statement.'

'Hey,' Diane said, 'it's getting late. It's OK, I'll look after things here until they finish up. You get going.'

Laura seemed uncertain. 'I can stay a bit longer, I'm sure they're going to be finishing up soon.'

'It's OK. I need to talk to Tom so I'm going to be waiting around anyways. You get off now, there ain't no use in all of us hanging around.'

'Sure thing, Diane. I'll see you tomorrow then.'

Laura put her jacket on and grabbed her handbag. As always she was immaculately dressed and her long slim legs were displayed to best effect by a short grey skirt. Diane knew that Laura was the prettiest woman working for Tom but it didn't bother her. There was a world of difference between pretty and beautiful and that was another world away from desirability. Besides, she trusted Laura; there was never any hint of something between her and Tom.

'I'll see you tomorrow,' Diane called as Laura walked to the door.

She slumped down in the comfortable chair behind Laura's desk, glad to get the weight off her feet. High heels were fine but they hurt like hell by the end of the day. Not that she minded, if it was how Tom wanted her to dress then that was all that mattered.

She tried not to think too much about Detective Vallance. He made her feel nervous and edgy and she was sure that he could read her like an open book. He had dark, intense eyes that seemed to see and understand everything. Did things look that bad? It was hard enough to believe that Alan Platt had been killed, let alone to imagine that she was a suspect. For Christ's sake, that was just plain dumb. Except that Vallance obviously didn't think so.

Was she scared? She and Tom had bent the rules so many times now that it was hard to remember what was true and what wasn't. And if Vallance decided to dig deeper – the thought made her feel even more nervous.

And what about Tom? What if Vallance switched attention to him?

The sound of laughter invaded the room. Diane turned and saw Tom and Philippa Brady at the door to his office. He was holding the door open for her, his eyes looking into hers as they laughed together. She had long blonde hair and a smile that was open and inviting.

Diane froze. What the hell was going on? She could see

the way Tom was looking at her, and the way the bitch was looking back.

'Diane,' he said, noticing her suddenly, 'I hadn't realised you were waiting.'

'Good meeting?' she asked, trying to keep the anger from her voice.

'Yes, thank you,' the Brady woman replied. 'I think we're close to formulating a workable plan of action.'

'That's good,' was the only thing Diane could think to say. The exhaustion washed through with her anger but her face was frozen into a rigid smile.

'I'll see you tonight then, Tom,' the blonde said, beaming him another smile.

'Sure, I'll see you later,' he agreed quietly. He glanced at Diane and then back at Philippa. 'I'll meet you at the restaurant.'

'OK. I'll probably be seeing you tomorrow, Diane,' the blonde said as she walked past the desk. She was looking mighty pleased with herself.

'You'd better come in,' Tom said, retreating back into his office.

'Tom,' Diane said, following him in, 'what the hell's going on there?'

He took his place behind his desk. He looked at her calmly, his deep blue eyes fixing her in place. 'What does that mean, Diane?'

'It means I want to know if there's anything going on between you and her.'

He laughed softly. 'You know what's going on,' he said. 'I'm doing my best to keep this mess out of the newspapers. I don't have to tell you that. Hell, you know it Diane. And before you say any more, I'm taking her out to dinner tonight. I need for this to be right, and if that means working this evening then that's OK.'

Diane wanted to scream. 'Working? You call taking her out to dinner working?'

'Diane, don't go getting jealous on me,' he warned softly. He was leaning back in his seat, his attention focused entirely on her. There was no anger in his voice, only the soothing, calming tones that said he was in complete control of the situation.

'Can you blame me?' she asked. 'Tom, I know we can both be in trouble here –'

'No we can't,' he stated boldly.

'But the police are looking for a medical link to Alan's death.'

The news seemed to take him by surprise. She saw the momentary hesitation in his eyes. 'We've still got nothing to worry about,' he said. 'Just keep a calm head and we'll get through this. Damn it, Diane, at a time like this I've got to keep a clear head more than anyone. Do you really think I'm going to jeopardise things by doing anything stupid with Philippa Brady? Do you?'

He was mad and the power in his voice was strangely reassuring. 'No, I'm not saying that,' she said.

'Then what, Diane? We can't afford to slip up here. Don't screw up on me, please.'

He stood up and walked around towards her. She looked up at him, into his clear blue eyes that could see everything. 'I'm sorry, Tom,' she whispered, 'but I'm feeling kind of vulnerable. I feel like fingers are pointing at me. I feel like the police think I was involved.'

He put his hands on her shoulders and looked into her eyes. 'I don't want you to worry,' he said slowly. 'I want you to know that I've got everything under control. You've got to trust me on this one. Totally and absolutely.'

'I do, I do.'

He leant forward and kissed her on the mouth softly.

'Do you?'

They kissed again, his tongue pushing between her lips.

'You know I do,' she whispered.

He kissed her once more and then moved away.

Sarah knocked gently and waited for a reply. She recognised Detective Sergeant Cooper's curt voice instantly.

'Excuse me, Sergeant,' she said, poking her head round the door of the interview room. 'I was looking for Mr Vallance.'

He looked at her with stark, suspicious eyes. 'He's not here,' he stated. 'Is it something I can help you with?'

She could think of nothing on earth that a man like Cooper

could help her with. 'No, I just wanted a word with Mr Vallance. Will he be back later?'

Cooper was already affecting to look bored but as an actor he had much to learn. 'I'm not sure. If it's about your statement –'

He was obviously dying to know what she wanted his boss for. 'It can wait,' she said. 'If he arrives back in the next hour or so can you tell him that I'll be in the bar.'

'I'll tell him,' he said, morosely.

She closed the door on Cooper and headed back towards the bar. It might have been interesting to watch Cooper's reactions to her information but not as interesting as watching how Anthony Vallance reacted. It wasn't that she had something to prove, exactly, it was more of a case that she wanted to show him that she was not a person to underestimate.

While Vallance and his men were plodding through the list of witnesses and covering the same old ground she had started to make real progress. If it were true that the police were interested in a medical connection to Platt's death then she had taken a few big steps forward. Using her skills as an investigative journalist on the Platt case was certainly more interesting than trying to piece together her non-story about Ryder and his competitors.

The bar was noisier than it had been for days. It was Thursday evening, for many of the people on the course their last evening at Ryder Hall. The course finished late on Friday afternoon, with most people going home directly, and so everyone was making the most of their last evening of freedom. The atmosphere was smoky, boozy and loud and Sarah couldn't help making a face as she stepped through the swing doors. Her first thought was to do an about turn and go back to her room – there were still notes to write up and calls to make – but then there was a chance she would miss Vallance.

Most of the tables were full and there were few empty seats even at the bar. The moody barman was missing, thankfully, and in his place there were a couple of girls who seemed much friendlier. Sarah got herself a gin and slimline and then turned round to get her bearings. The little cliques that had formed after the first couple of days were in command of the situation. The laughter and the noise seemed to emanate mostly from a group in the corner. Instinctively Sarah wanted to avoid them as much as possible.

'Sarah! Over here!'

Kate was waving from the other end of the bar. Her face was slightly flushed and Sarah guessed that the drink she was holding was not the evening's first.

'It's not often we see you down here,' Kate said when Sarah joined her. 'Got bored did you?'

Kate was smiling but it was hard to say what the feeling behind the smile was. She sounded slightly annoyed and there was an aggrieved undertone to her voice. 'I'm not much of a drinker,' Sarah said.

'I thought all you journalists were drinkers.'

Was she deliberately trying to annoy? 'Not this one,' Sarah stated coldly.

'So, if you're not here for a drink,' Kate surmised, 'then you're here looking for someone.'

There was no point denying the truth. 'Yes, I'm actually looking for DCI Vallance. Have you seen him?'

Kate moved closer along the bar. 'Vallance – is he the slob with the black leather jacket?'

'He's not a slob,' Sarah countered instantly.

Kate giggled. 'Isn't he? Dark-haired, stubble, leather jacket and black jeans, isn't that him?'

She had left out the brown eyes, the smile and the humour but otherwise it was an adequate description of Vallance. Why be upset because he'd been called a slob? 'Yes, that's him,' she agreed. 'Has he been in this evening?'

Kate obviously thought she'd picked up on something and showed no signs of wanting to let go. 'Interested in him, are you?'

Sarah felt her face begin to colour. 'Not in the way you mean,' she said.

'What other way is there? Can't say that he's my type, though.'

'No, you go for the clean-cut American look.'

Kate giggled some more. 'Mmm. Tom Ryder's just my type. What I wouldn't give to –'

Sarah decided to cut the conversation short; she wasn't interested in Kate's silly fantasies. 'You're slobbering,' she said, 'and it doesn't suit you.'

'You can't tell me,' Kate responded, 'that you wouldn't say no to a night of passion with Tom?'

'I can and I am. Anyway, Kate, what's the latest on the police investigation? You probably know more about it than they do.'

It might have been taken as a sly dig but Kate seemed to take the comment as flattery. 'They're still tracking down the medicos,' she said, grinning. Her voice had dropped to a low whisper so that Sarah had to draw closer still. 'They've gone through all the registration papers of people on the course to see who's got medical training.'

Sarah marvelled at Kate's ear for gossip. She would have made an excellent journalist, nothing seemed to get past her. 'Do you know if they've interviewed Peter Shalcott?'

Kate nodded. 'This afternoon. I can't imagine that they got any sense out of him, though. I saw him earlier and he was still in his own little world.'

'And what about Anita Walsh?'

'Who?'

Sarah grinned. She knew something that Kate didn't. 'You're not going to tell me that you don't know her, are you?'

'But I don't. I'll tell you what,' she whispered, 'you tell me your secret and I'll tell you mine.'

'It's not much of a secret,' Sarah said, sitting back up on the stool as she saw Diane Bennett approaching.

'Hi, Diane, how are things?' Kate said, suddenly changing gear as the American blonde joined them.

'I'm bushed,' Diane sighed, signalling to one of the bar girls for a drink.

'You look it,' Kate said. 'It must be hard working with Tom like this.'

Sarah scanned the room hopefully in case Vallance had wandered in. The thought of being stuck between two of the most vocal Tom Ryder obsessives in the world was profoundly depressing.

'Working with Tom ain't so bad,' Diane responded. She

had changed into clothes that were neatly casual and the severity of her make-up seemed to have faded. She looked tired though, her voice had lost the overly cheerful tone that jollied everyone along.

'I bet it's not,' Kate agreed wistfully. 'I suppose you and he are pretty close, aren't you?'

'Pretty close.'

'I suppose that means you and he are friends too,' Kate continued, 'not just colleagues.'

Sarah could sense where the conversation was headed and she sought desperately for a way to extricate herself.

'Sure, Tom's a real good friend,' Diane said. 'But he's my boss too, it pays to remember that.'

Kate wasn't smiling even if Diane was. 'Is he always in command?'

Diane looked warily at Kate and then at Sarah. 'What do you mean?'

'Nothing,' Kate said. 'Except that I was wondering – No, it's nothing.'

'I think I'd better be going,' Sarah said. The atmosphere had changed. Kate was half drunk and beginning to let the jealousy show. It was only a matter of time before she demanded to know if Diane and Tom were lovers.

'No, don't go,' Diane said. She looked at Sarah as if to say 'don't leave me with her'.

'What's wrong?' Kate asked Sarah. 'Has your policeman friend stood you up?'

'He's not my policeman friend, I just wanted to talk to him. Look, why don't you take it easy? You're beginning to sound a bit tired.'

Kate grinned. 'I'm not tired. Not as tired as Diane. I bet Tom Ryder makes all sorts of demands on her –'

'Cut that out!' Diane snapped.

Kate carried on regardless. 'I mean, when you were in medicine I bet you were used to –'

Diane stood up angrily. 'You are just plain drunk!' she cried, her voice rising high above the background conversation so that heads turned and the room was plunged into silence.

Kate turned to Sarah. 'Didn't you know?' she said, her eyes

122

blazing. 'Diane used to be in medical research before she was picked up by Tom Ryder. But I suppose you've told the police all about your medical training, haven't you, Diane?'

Diane, close to tears, slammed her drink down on the counter and stormed off.

So that was the secret Kate wanted to trade.

Vallance eased the car to a halt and then switched the engine off. Ryder Hall loomed up ahead in the darkness, the outline of the grand building blurred against the black sky. Some of the rooms were lit up with a dull orange light that filtered through heavy velvet curtains. He felt exhausted by the long drive. The sooner he had a PC to act as a driver the better. It wouldn't have been so bad had his long journey not been a waste of time.

He had driven all the way to Hampstead in the hope of talking to Sue Beamish. She had told the police that she'd be in all day if they needed to contact her. She needed time to recover from the shock of finding her colleague dead. The recovery had obviously been quicker than expected, because there was no sign of her when Vallance got there. He had waited for a while in the car, hoping that she'd suddenly appear, but in the end a uniformed PC arrived and demanded to know what was going on. She lived in an expensive street and her neighbours were jumpy about people hanging around in cars. Vallance had let the PC get really stroppy before showing him his warrant card. Exit one embarrassed PC.

Things had not improved on the way back. He had decided to stop off at home in the vain hope that Mags had decided to move out again. She hadn't. And she wasn't pleased to see him either. What was one more blazing row on top of the thousands they had already enjoyed? So it looked like another night in the Fox and Frog. As he had driven in through the gates of Ryder Hall he'd been on the look-out for Philippa Brady's car but there was no sign of it. So it was a night in the Fox and Frog on his own.

He hoped that Cooper had had a more successful afternoon. Apart from Sue Beamish the only other person that Vallance was interested in was the woman alleged to have been Alan

Platt's bit on the side. She should have been traced immediately. He was aware that they had let things drag on for too long. They needed to know precisely what the relationship was and whether she could shed any light on Platt's activities that final evening. Whether she and Platt had been having sex was of no interest, unless their sexual encounters were partially fuelled by cocaine. The possibility seemed so remote that Vallance discounted it completely.

The air was pleasantly cool when he stepped out of the car. His heels crunched down on the gravel as he walked towards the entrance. Cooper was probably still at it, and Manning should have finished going through the list of names. He didn't expect much more than a list of traffic offences from the PNC check, but doing the computer check was still a precaution worth taking.

He saw Sarah Fairfax waiting by the entrance. She was waiting for him. She was probably still smarting from the off-hand way he'd treated her earlier that morning.

'What can I do for you, Miss Fairfax?' he said, stopping at the first of the granite steps.

She looked at him coolly. 'I was hoping we could talk about the state of your investigation,' she said, the icy tone of voice matching her expression.

'What about it, exactly?'

'Have you made any progress?'

He wished he could answer positively but there was nothing positive to say. 'It's proceeding.'

She smiled. 'Does that mean you've made no progress?'

He shrugged. 'We've got a long way to go,' he admitted.

'And the medical angle? How does that fit it in?'

'What medical angle?' he asked suspiciously.

Her smile broadened. 'It's common knowledge that you're interviewing people who have a medical connection. You've already spoken to Dr Patel, haven't you?'

That was the problem with a place like Ryder Hall, word travelled too fast. 'You're remarkably well informed. And what about your investigation, how's that proceeding?'

The smile wavered. 'I'm still working on my story.'

He paused. Was there more that she wanted to say? She

hadn't been waiting for him to swap banal pleasantries. 'Is there something else?'

'Should there be?'

'Are you telling me,' he asked, smiling, 'that you've been waiting for me purely to say hello?'

The suggestion took her aback. 'Clearly not. I do in fact have some information which might be of interest to you.'

'We're not going to have to trade again, are we?'

She smiled. 'So you do remember that we had a deal?'

'Yes. We've got a deal, I think. So what is it that you think I ought to know?'

'Have you spoken to Anita Walsh?'

The name was on the list of people on the course but other than that it was unfamiliar, but there was only one person it could be. 'Alan Platt's girlfriend? No I haven't spoken to her yet.'

She looked disappointed that he knew the name. 'I have,' she said. 'She flatly denied knowing him. And she denied knowing Peter Shalcott, despite the fact that I've seen her with both of them.'

Vallance hoped that Cooper had spoken to her too – there'd be hell to pay if Fairfax had got to her first. 'It's not your job to interview witnesses,' he told her. 'I know you're only trying to help but please, our deal doesn't mean you can rush in –'

Sarah's eyes widened and she inhaled sharply. 'Rush in?' she demanded. 'Why haven't you spoken to her yet?'

A sharp scream filled the night air.

There was a moment of silence and then, a split second later, there was a dull, bodily thud.

Vallance was moving before he knew it. He raced back along the drive as lights flicked on in room after room above him. His heart was pounding and he knew with a sickening finality what he would find.

The body was sprawled on a paved area to one side of the building, face down. Blood was beginning to pool like black oil. One arm thrown back, the other curled unnaturally under the body.

'My God! It's Diane.'

He turned to an ashen-faced Sarah Fairfax.

He knelt down quickly and brushed the hair back from Diane's face. Blood warmed his fingers. He searched for a pulse, found nothing for a moment and then felt the faint echo of life under her neck.

'Get a ambulance!' he cried, calling up to the people craning out of the windows above them.

Sarah came closer. 'Is she alive?'

'Only just.'

EIGHT

Vallance yawned, stretched and then yawned some more. Sleeping in the car had not been the best idea in the world. He felt exhausted, dishevelled and in no fit state to function. The only consolation was the thought that he would have felt far worse without the two hours flat out on the back seat. Besides, he was sure that the story would make it back to Area. He liked to make life interesting for people. Now, sitting in the interview room with a cup of black coffee that was sorely lacking a drop of scotch, he had more important things to face up to.

Diane Bennett was alive, barely. An air ambulance had carried her off to the nearest spinal injuries unit where she'd been put straight into intensive care. She had yet to regain consciousness and the doctors were making no promises.

The first question was obvious. Did she jump or was she pushed? The SOCO team were going through her room but the first finds did not look good – cocaine, syringes, needles, latex examination gloves. There was little doubting that the bag of coke was going to match the Platt sample. And Vallance had little doubt that the syringes were going to be similar to the one that had been used to inject procaine into Platt's shoulder.

Had Diane killed Platt and then decided to kill herself? Had she jumped?

He yawned again and tried to rub the sleep from his eyes. There were witness statements to take, facts to collect, alibis to check. Luckily the extra troops had arrived and DS Reed was interviewing one lot of people with DC Quinn while Cooper was going through another lot with DC Manning. This time they were going for broke. Every person in the building was going to be interviewed, no matter what noise Ryder made about it.

There was little doubt that Ryder would try to kick up a fuss about disruption or heavy-handed police operations. Vallance knew that Ryder would be more upset about that than about what had occurred. If Diane died he'd probably be mourning the loss of a valuable member of staff rather than the loss of a friend. Or lover. There was much that had still to be investigated, including the relationships between the personnel at Ryder Hall.

In any case Ryder's reaction was something to look forward to. Ryder was not on the scene. He had left early the previous evening and had not yet returned. Neither was Philippa Brady around. Ryder was probably more her type, and it was hard to imagine the two of them slumming it in a box room in the Fox and Frog.

Vallance stifled the last yawn when there was a sharp, authoritative knock at the door. It was the sort of knock designed to instil fear in the hearts of criminals and evil-doers everywhere. DC Alex Chiltern had no doubt been spending hours practising his knock and now had it down to a fine art.

'Miss Fairfax is here, sir,' he said, poking his head around the door.

Chiltern was young and keen, just out of uniform and enjoying every minute of being a detective. Although he had acquired the heavy-handed approach to the door he still hadn't managed to acquire the steely demeanour of DS Cooper but it was clearly something he aspired to.

'Send her in,' Vallance said. 'There's no need for you to sit in on this one,' he added.

'Anything you say, guv,' Chiltern said, before letting Sarah into the newly commandeered second interview room.

She looked bleary-eyed but otherwise there was nothing

about her to show she'd been up most of the night. As always she was dressed impeccably and her deep blue eyes were alert to everything.

'You look a mess,' she said, and for the first time there was no hint of reproach in her voice.

Her eyes were on him and he suddenly felt grateful for the sympathy of her gaze and the concern in her voice. What could he say to her? His first instinct was to make some clever remark but something stopped him. Their eyes met and he looked at her until she turned nervously away.

'I just need to go through what happened last night,' he said.

She nodded and then proceeded to list the sequence of events that lead to Diane Bennett storming out of the bar.

'How did she seem to you?' Vallance asked when she had stopped.

'Not suicidal.'

Vallance nodded. 'If she didn't look suicidal, how did she look?'

'Extremely upset. I think she'd been hoping to keep the medical thing a secret. When Kate blurted it out Diane just looked very shocked.'

Diane's career in medical research had been well hidden. Vallance had not suspected a thing. 'What about Kate? What sort of mood was she in?'

'Not in the mood for murder,' Sarah said with a half smile.

'How can you tell?'

For a second Sarah looked shocked. 'You're not serious,' she said.

'We're looking at everything, and everyone, seriously.'

'Including me?'

Vallance smiled. 'I think you've got a good alibi for this one. Apart from the fact that Kate was drunk, what sort of mood was she in? Depressed, angry, elated?'

There was no doubt in Sarah's voice. 'She was jealous. The only reason she's here is to meet Tom Ryder. She's obsessed by him. She's read all the books, seen the videos, collected the magazine articles. Twenty years ago it would have been a rock star or a film actor, now she's into Tom Ryder in the same obsessive way. She's been getting edgy because we're here and we've hardly set eyes on the man.'

'So why get at Diane Bennett?'

'Because Diane Bennett was –'

'Is,' he said, correcting her, 'she's still alive.'

'Diane is also in love with Tom Ryder. You've only got to hear her talk about him, or to see the way she looks adoringly at him. She also gets to spend time with him, she's one of his closest colleagues. That makes Kate insanely jealous.'

'Insane enough to attempt murder?'

'This is silly. There's no way Kate would do that. I mean she was in a bitchy mood last night but that's not the same as being ready to murder in cold blood.'

'You don't think it was an attempted suicide?'

Sarah smiled. 'I was with you and I noticed the whisky as well. It was there mixed in with the blood and I'm pretty sure it was spilt all down her front. I doubt that anyone would commit suicide with a glass of whisky in her hand.'

Vallance smiled too. Full marks for observation and deduction. He'd thought that in the confusion no one else had noticed the whiskey. 'Ever thought of a job in the police force?'

'I'm right though, aren't I?'

She was waiting for approval. He nodded. 'The glass was thrown wide as she fell, it landed out on the grass behind the drive. The crime scene boys have recovered most of it. That's not conclusive proof that she didn't jump, though.'

'It is,' she said, 'and we both know it. And that means she didn't kill Alan Platt as well.'

She was on the right track, again. Vallance wanted to say more but he couldn't take the risk. Evidence was still being gathered and the less that people knew the better. 'I can't say more,' he apologised, 'at least not for a while.'

'Whoever killed Alan Platt also tried to kill her. Don't you agree? The plan was to make it look as if she were guilty and that she jumped because of it?'

There was no denying that logic; every officer on the case saw it the same way. 'I agree, it was a botched attempt at framing her for Platt's death. Which is why we're interested in Kate

Thurston. How did she know about Diane's history?'

'I don't know. She knows a lot about Ryder and his organisation, perhaps she read it somewhere. I could do a literature search for you if you want.'

It was a good idea. 'Yes please. Do one on Tom Ryder too, if you can.'

Sarah looked pleased. 'Anything else?'

'Yes. You said that Diane Bennett was in love with him. Do you think that the feeling was mutual?'

She paused for a moment. Her eyes looked distant and her hair fell across her face as she tried to find an answer. Vallance could hardly keep his eyes off her.

'No,' she responded finally. 'I never saw him look at her with any real emotion. He's not the sort of man I imagine as being very emotional.'

'But that doesn't seem to stop women falling at his feet,' Vallance said, thinking of Philippa Brady.

'I said he's not very emotional,' she replied, keeping her eyes averted. 'That doesn't mean he's not very sexual.'

Vallance could sense that she was uncomfortable but he valued her honesty. 'So you don't think that he was in love with Diane Bennett?'

'No, though I suspect that that doesn't mean he and Diane didn't sleep together. I think Kate had come to the same conclusion, which was why she was being so bitchy.'

'What happened after Diane left the bar?'

'I told Kate that she was drunk.'

The disapproval was still clear in her voice. 'Then what happened?' he continued.

She sighed expressively. 'She argued for a minute and then confessed that she was disappointed with the course and that she was sorry she'd taken it out on Diane. She suggested going up to Diane's room to apologise but I told her that it wasn't a good idea. Instead I took Kate back to her room and helped her settle down before coming back down to look for you.'

'When you left her how was she?'

'Exhausted, miserable and ready to sleep it all off.'

'You're sure?'

She shrugged. 'I think so, but I can't be sure. I'd done my

best even though I was sick to death of her. She was whinging about Tom Ryder, about her boring husband, about the course, about her life. I didn't want to hear it, to be honest, but there was no way I could just walk away from her.'

He could easily picture the scene. Sarah's reproachful manner and disapproving eyes, Kate's self-pitying whine, the feeling of claustrophobia in the cramped little bedroom. Was Kate really a suspect? The full extent of her obsession with Tom Ryder had not come through clearly in Kate's statement. Sexual jealousy was a potent motive and it could turn even the most innocuous person into a raging psychopath.

It was time to switch from an attempted murder to a successfully accomplished one. 'Did Kate ever talk to you about Alan Platt?' he asked.

'No, not properly. While we were waiting for Diane to open the door to his room she said that he didn't look much like Tom Ryder. That was the extent of her interest; if he didn't look like Ryder she wasn't interested in him.'

Kate's room was at the far end of the corridor to Platt's and she had been there at the discovery to the body. Vallance remembered Sarah's original statement. Kate had woken her to tell her something was going on. 'What about Anita Walsh? Did Kate ever talk about her?'

'No.'

'In your statement you said that Kate came to your door that morning. How did she seem then?'

'Nosy. She's the gossippy type, always curious about what people are doing. It's not a trait I find particularly attractive in people,' she added.

He couldn't resist the obvious comment: 'Isn't that what journalism is about?'

Her eyes narrowed. 'What exactly is that supposed to mean?'

He'd screwed up again. She was offended and he hadn't even meant to try. 'I'm sorry, but it wasn't supposed to be −'

'I am not a gutter journalist,' she stated. 'I do not pry into people's private lives, look for scandal or revel in other people's misery. I leave that sort of behaviour to the tabloids and to the police. It's what you do best, isn't it, Mr Vallance?'

Things had been going so well. There was nothing for it

but to defend. 'What we do best is catch criminals. I have as little time for busy bodies and tabloid journalists as you have. I'm asking you these questions in the hope that we can catch Alan Platt's murderer, and if that offends you then that's just tough.'

Her eyes had lost the earlier look of concern. All he could see in them was cold anger. It transformed her face instantly. She now looked disdainfully at him, as though he had committed some bodily indiscretion.

'Do you have more questions, or perhaps you'd rather cast aspersions about my work?'

'For goodness sake! I wasn't casting anything.'

'There's no need to raise your voice, Detective Chief Inspector, you're not at the police station now.'

He looked at her for a moment and then laughed. She was going for a below the belt shot but she'd missed the mark by a mile. 'Nice try,' he said, enjoying her obvious annoyance at his refusal to play. 'Let's get back to the morning when Platt was found. What were you doing when Kate knocked on your door?'

'Working,' she said, defying him to make a comment about it.

'So you were awake and yet you didn't hear any commotion outside?'

'None.'

'But Kate, whose room is further from Platt's than yours, did hear it and came running out to get you as well.'

'She may have been passing at the time,' she pointed out.

'But why knock on your door?'

'I don't know. Because she wanted someone to gossip with?'

'But if she's the gossippy type then she'd gossip with whoever was already there. I mean, are you two such great friends that she needs to be with you all the time?'

Sarah looked as though none of it had occurred to her before. Vallance could see the way she was trying to fit it all together. 'I don't know,' she said. 'I don't know why she came knocking on my door that morning.'

Interview over, Vallance decided. 'Thank you, Miss Fairfax. You've been most helpful.'

She stood up. 'Is there anything I should know?'

She was waiting for information. What was there to give her that wouldn't compromise the investigation?

'Yes, just one thing. Tom Ryder's trying to pull strings,' he said. 'He's getting jumpy about the bad publicity and all that sort of stuff. There's a woman from the Home Office here, Philippa Brady. You ought to know that they're going to be doing their best to cover things up.'

The smile came back to Sarah's face. 'Thank you. I think it's about time that I asked to see Mr Ryder again.'

That wasn't the response Vallance had been hoping for. 'I don't think you should do that. Do I have to remind you that we're the ones doing the interviews in this investigation?'

She smiled sweetly. 'I have my own story to write,' she pointed. 'I only want to find out how inspirational management works in the face of a real crisis.'

Cooper stared icily at Anita Walsh as she took the seat opposite him. So this was Platt's away game. She had bobbed, strawberry blonde hair, pale skin and distinctive green blue eyes. Whoever had said she was attractive hadn't been lying. It was difficult to see how a man like Alan Platt could attract her. Unless he had been much better looking alive than dead.

She looked uncomfortable, shifting around on the stiff wooden chair for a while before she became aware that he was watching her closely. Their eyes met only for a moment and then she looked away nervously. She wasn't there through choice and they both knew it. Cooper also knew that she should have been interviewed earlier, the boss was right about that.

'As you know,' Cooper began, glancing at DC Manning to make sure the other man was ready to take notes, 'we are interested in the events surrounding the death of Alan Platt, in addition to Diane Bennett's fall last night.'

Her voice was surprisingly calm when she spoke. 'Yes, people have been talking about nothing else now for days.'

'Yet you chose not to come forward of your own accord.'

'Why should I? I don't know anything about either incident, officer.'

Cooper looked at her closely, scrutinising her calm, impassive features. 'You deny knowing Alan Platt?'

She shrugged. 'I've been told that I met Alan Platt,' she said, as though doubting the fact. 'If I did it hasn't stuck in my mind particularly.'

'Are you saying that you don't remember meeting him at all?'

'There's lots of people on this course. I've probably said hello to all of them at one time or another but that doesn't mean I can remember them all.'

She sounded so reasonable yet it rang false. 'I find it hard to believe that you've met so many people here that you can't remember them all,' he stated.

'I'm sorry but I really can't remember very much about meeting him. We may have said hello but I hadn't even realised he was the dead man until it was pointed out to me.'

'Who pointed it out?'

'A woman called Sarah Fairfax.'

Fairfax? What the hell was she playing at? The boss was going to have to have a word with her.

'Our information suggests that you and Mr Platt were on much closer terms than that.'

She looked surprised. 'I think there's been some sort of misunderstanding. Where did you get this information from?'

'Are you denying categorically that you knew Alan Platt?'

She shook her head. 'I've already explained this. I may have met him but I can't be sure one way or the other.'

'Can you tell me what you were doing on the Tuesday evening?'

'I was in my room, probably. Reading.'

'Probably? We're only talking about a few days ago, surely you can remember more precisely than that.'

She shrugged again. 'I've spent most evenings in my room. I definitely went to the bar on the Sunday evening when I arrived, and again on Monday. Since then I've stayed in my room every evening.'

Manning decided it was time for a contribution. 'That's pretty unsociable, isn't it?' he said.

'I'm not paid to be sociable,' she replied coolly. 'I'm here to study, so that's what I do.'

He glanced at his notes. 'What exactly do you do at Domino Systems?'

'We develop computer software.'

She had stopped. She was not going to volunteer any more information than she had to. 'And what exactly do you do, personally?' he asked.

'I manage a team of software developers. Which is why I'm here.'

'Doesn't managing people mean you have to be sociable?' Manning asked.

Cooper glared at him. It was time for Manning to shut up.

'It does,' she agreed. 'But I'm not here for the social life, I'm here to learn how to be a better manager.'

'That's very conscientious, Miss Walsh,' Cooper said. 'You must be one of the few people to take that point of view.'

'No, I don't think so, officer. To return to your question, I was definitely in my room on Tuesday evening.'

'All evening?'

'Yes. I finished my class, had dinner, went for a walk in the grounds and then went to my room to do some reading.'

'What time did you go to your room, roughly?'

Another shrug of the shoulder. 'Around half past eight.'

'You didn't leave your room at all after you went up to read?'

'No.'

'And where exactly is your room, in relation to Alan Platt's?'

There was a glimmer of a smile on her lips as she answered. 'I don't know, you're assuming that I know where his room was.'

Cooper didn't blink. 'Room 23.'

'Which is where? I'm afraid I haven't learnt to navigate my way around this old building.'

'It's on the second floor, on the east side of the building.'

'My room is on the fifth floor, on the west wing. Room 55.'

'Isn't that near Diane Bennett's room?'

She nodded. 'Yes, I understand that all the staff quarters are

136

on that side of the building. There was certainly enough of a commotion last night.'

The next question had to be asked in spite of the fact that the answer was completely predictable. 'You were in your room again?'

'Yes, reading. I can't say what time I went up exactly, but I'd say it was probably before nine again.'

'And you stayed there all night?'

She smiled openly for the first time. 'No, I came out when I heard all the noise and rushing about. I wanted to know what was going on, just like everybody else.'

'Did anyone see you?'

'Yes, lots of people I imagine. I walked up to the sixth floor to see what was going on and there were lots of people there. I'm sure you'll find lots of people to corroborate that.'

'We'll check of course,' he said. She was beginning to get on his nerves. 'What do you know about Peter Shalcott,' he said, remembering that she was seen with him as well as with Platt.

She didn't look in the least bit surprised by the sudden change of focus. 'Is your informant Sarah Fairfax again?' she asked.

'What?'

'It's just that she asked me the same question. I'll give you the same answer I gave her, sergeant: Peter Shalcott is someone I met on the course. I've never met him before and when the course ends I'll never see him again. I'm not close to him and I don't know where his room is. Is that enough?'

DC Manning was looking at her with raised eyebrows. 'Why are you so touchy?' Cooper asked her.

'Because I really have nothing to say that can help you,' she said, her voice cool and calm again. 'I don't even know why I'm being questioned, to be honest.'

'You're being questioned because we need to establish the facts.'

'I've given you all the facts as they relate to me. I'm sorry if I can't be of more help, officer, but there's nothing else that I know.'

Cooper looked at her and then at Manning. 'Constable

Manning will draw up a statement for you to sign, Miss Walsh. That's all. For now.'

'Thank you,' she said. Her face was expressionless again, her eyes averted, giving nothing away.

Her answers had all been delivered with an unhurried certainty that contrasted with their defensive nature and the nervousness with which she had kept her eyes shielded. She was lying. There had to be more witnesses who'd seen her with Platt. Cooper vowed to find them, even if it meant questioning every person in the building.

Ryder's secretary, Laura, looked as cool as ever. Her long brown hair was swept back and her eyes were fringed by long dark lashes. She half smiled at Vallance as he walked towards her, swivelling round in her chair to face him. The hesitant smile was just for show. He could see the worry behind the long lashes and glossy lips.

'Is he back?' he asked. One of the uniforms had reported Ryder's return and Vallance wanted to talk to him immediately.

'Yes, sir,' she replied. 'But he's only just found out –'

'You told him?'

She nodded. 'He had no idea. He's taken it real bad. You know he and Diane were really close, they've been working together since the beginning.'

Had Laura been interviewed yet? Vallance couldn't remember seeing a statement from her. He made a mental note to talk to her later. There was probably a lot of background detail that she could fill in if questioned properly.

'I need to talk to him,' he said. 'Shall I just go in?'

The suggestion was met with a shake of the head. 'No, sir. He's in with Miss Brady, I'll just buzz through to let them know you're here.'

She did it immediately and Ryder came to the door straight away. His face was suitably sombre but it looked like the sort of expression driven by the need for propriety than by any real feeling. Sarah was right to describe him as unemotional.

'You'd better come in,' he said.

Philippa Brady was sitting by Ryder's desk. She looked at Vallance briefly, their eyes meeting and then she looked down at her notes. She clearly knew that Vallance had guessed she'd spent the night with Ryder and now she was probably wondering whether it mattered. It didn't, at least not to Vallance.

'Hello,' she said, looking up once more.

'Hi.'

'Is there any more news?' Ryder asked, closing the door and then walking back towards his desk.

'None at the moment. Diane's condition is stable at the moment, that's all they can tell us. She's on a ventilator and there's no word yet on the extent of the injuries she's suffered.'

'I just can't believe that this is happening,' he said, shaking his head sadly. 'What's going on here, Chief Inspector?'

No more questions about Diane? Not even an expression of sympathy or concern? Vallance felt the anger begin to rise inside him. 'What do you think's happening, Mr Ryder? You tell me what's going on here.'

Ryder looked at Philippa for a moment. 'I wish I knew the answer to that. Hell, I admit I don't know what's what anymore. I mean I saw Diane last night and she looked fine to me. Just fine, and then I get back just now and she's in ITU.'

'ITU?' Philippa asked.

'Intensive Treatment Unit,' Ryder explained. 'At least that's what we call it in the States.'

'How was she when you saw her last night?'

'Tired,' he replied. 'Just dog tired. The course is hard enough, but what with everything else she was exhausted, physically and mentally. Do you think that had anything to do with her accident?'

So, Ryder was going with the accident theory. It was the least plausible of the three possibilities but that didn't stop it being the preferred explanation for the moment. 'You think she was looking out of the window,' Vallance said, 'and was so tired that she lost her grip and fell out?'

Neither Ryder nor Philippa looked convinced by the scenario. 'Didn't she jump?' Philippa asked. 'I mean maybe she was so tired that things got on top of her and in a moment of madness she –'

Ryder stopped her immediately. 'No way! I've known Diane

a long time, there's no way she would have done that.'

'Are you saying that she wasn't the suicidal type?' Vallance asked.

There was a long, hesitant pause before Ryder answered. 'I'm not saying that. I'm just saying that there's no way sheer tiredness would have done it alone. There's got to be more to it than that, if it was an attempted suicide.'

Vallance could guess where things were headed. 'Such as?' he asked.

'I'll be straight with you, Mr Vallance. When I spoke with her last night she was real upset. She'd got it into her head that you were trying to pin Platt's death on her. I told her that it was crazy but there was no arguing with her. She was sure that you had her marked as suspect number one.'

It was hard to believe that Ryder couldn't argue with Diane; anything he said to her was better than gospel. 'Why did she think that?'

'Because of all the questioning you'd put her though. I'm not saying that you weren't justified in doing that, it's just that she interpreted things in a certain way. She told me there was a whole lot of circumstantial evidence which pointed at her and that it was making her real jumpy.'

Philippa got in before Vallance could frame a reply. 'Is it possible that she really did kill Alan Platt?'

'No way,' Ryder replied, but not with the same emphasis as before. He almost sounded doubtful and the look on his face reflected that.

'It's possible,' Vallance agreed. 'But there's no motive. Why should Diane want to kill Platt?'

'I don't know,' Ryder admitted.

'So that brings us back to the idea that she tried to kill herself,' Philippa said. It sounded as though the idea appealed to her less than the idea that Diane had killed Platt. If Diane were Platt's killer than everything would fit into place and her job would suddenly become a lot easier.

'What about the possibility that she was pushed?' Vallance suggested. 'Have either of you considered that possibility?'

Ryder looked suitably shocked. 'Why? Why the hell would anyone want to kill Diane?'

'Why would anyone want to kill Alan Platt?'

'Do you think the two things are linked?' Philippa said. 'Do you have any evidence to show that they're linked?'

Evidence there was – the cocaine and the medical equipment – but it wasn't the time to divulge it yet. 'It's too early to say for sure. But this place has been standing for more than a hundred years without a murder, to have a murder and then another unconnected attempt at murder in the space of one week stretches credibility a bit.'

'But it is possible,' Philippa insisted. She turned to Ryder. 'While Diane's still alive we're still dealing with a single murder. It's time we hit the press properly, Tom. If we delay any longer then we'll be reporting two murders and that's just not an option I care to contemplate.'

Ryder nodded. 'You're right. We've prepared a statement and a strategy,' he explained to Vallance. 'We hammered out the details last night,' he added.

Vallance smiled. 'I'm sure you did,' he said. Philippa glared at him and then looked away. 'You do appreciate I'm going to need a statement from you both?'

'Why?' Philippa demanded.

'Because we need to know exactly where people were last night.'

'You're asking for an alibi,' Ryder said. 'Philippa and I were together last night. All night. We returned to Ryder Hall less than an hour ago.'

'That's the truth,' Philippa added. 'You can check the restaurant and the hotel if you like. Will that be enough?'

She was irked by the demand for an alibi. But it wasn't her that Vallance was interested in, it was Ryder. 'I'll need to interview you alone,' he told him. 'I need to understand exactly what Diane's frame of mind was last night.'

Philippa was angered by the request. 'He's told you already,' she snapped. 'Diane was tired. I saw her here last night as well. Just before I left.'

'She saw the two of you leave together?' Vallance asked. He could easily picture Diane's face when she realised that her beloved Tom Ryder was about to bed Philippa Brady, a younger and more attractive woman than herself.

141

'No,' Ryder said. 'Diane spoke to me after Philippa left.'

'But she knew that you two were going to go out that evening?'

'Yes.'

Vallance couldn't go on with the both of them present. 'I'll need statements from both of you. If I could have some time alone with Mr Ryder,' he said, looking at Philippa.

She stood up. Her eyes were fixed on Vallance. She was angry with him and he knew that any kudos he'd earned with her had been well and truly spent. Was there still time to make it up to her?

'I'll wait outside,' she told Ryder.

Vallance watched her leave. His eyes travelled the length of her long, lithe legs. He'd messed up any chances of spending another night with her. But then Tom Ryder had that under control anyway.

'What is it you want to know?' Ryder asked, once Philippa was gone.

Vallance finally sat down. 'I don't suppose there's any chance of some coffee?'

Ryder buzzed through to Laura and ordered some. 'Now, Mr Vallance, what is it you want to know?' he repeated.

'You told Diane you were going to be working late with Philippa. Diane guessed that you were going to be spending the night together,' he surmised. 'How did she react?'

'Diane and I had a working relationship, Mr Vallance,' he explained calmly. 'I won't deny that we had sex sometimes, but that was purely a physical thing. She knew and accepted the fact that I see other women. There was no problem there at all.'

He spoke calmly and without emotion. There was not even a hint of swagger in the way he spoke. He was talking man to man and there was as little need to be coy as there was to boast.

'Did she accept it last night?'

'She was unhappy,' Ryder said. 'But she was more upset by your questioning than anything else, Mr Vallance. In fact I'd say I'd never seen her look so upset before. Don't you think you could have handled her more gently?'

Vallance met Ryder's cold eyes head on. 'Don't you think

142

you could have handled her better? Walking out on her to go and fuck with Philippa Brady doesn't strike me as especially sympathetic.'

'Hell, I've told you already, she was OK about that. Is that it?'

There was a knock at the door and Laura came in with the coffee. Vallance waited for her to leave before continuing.

'Tell me about Diane's medical experience,' he said.

Ryder's expression showed no flicker of surprise at the question. 'I first met her when I was doing a seminar at one of the smaller drug companies in the States. She was just moving out of research and into management. We hit it off straight away and then when I needed help to expand my operation she was the perfect person.'

'She was medically trained?'

Ryder nodded. 'Yes. This is one of the things she was afraid of, Mr Vallance. Last night she was terrified that you'd find out about it and that you'd jump to the wrong conclusion.'

'And what's the right conclusion?'

'That Diane knew how to handle drugs but that she had nothing to do with Alan Platt's death.'

Vallance nodded. 'How can you be so sure?'

'Because she spent the night with me,' Ryder said. 'There's no way she could have slipped out of my room to go out and kill Platt.'

'That doesn't match Diane's statement at all,' Vallance pointed out. 'She claims to have been in her room after 11.30 that night. Why didn't she tell the truth and take herself out of the frame completely?'

Ryder smiled. 'A misguided sense of loyalty perhaps. She didn't want people to know what was going on. She imagined that it reflected badly on me.'

'Of course,' Vallance said, 'now that she's on life support there's no way she can corroborate that, one way or the other.'

'That's true, Mr Vallance,' Ryder agreed. 'Is there anything else?'

Vallance downed a mouthful of coffee. 'Yes, I want the name of the restaurant and hotel and the times you arrived and left.'

'As you wish. Am I a suspect in Diane's death?'
'Only morally,' Vallance said.

NINE

The sun was high in the sky but its warmth seemed not to filter down to ground level. It was probably better for Kate Thurston that way, Vallance decided. A long walk and a dose of icy fresh air were supposed to be good for a hangover. He wasn't sure that it was necessarily true, but the act of doing something, even if it was just taking a walk, was better than moping around vowing never to touch the hard stuff again. Luckily the grounds around Ryder Hall were fairly extensive and a long walk could take you far enough away from the grand house to escape its claustrophobic atmosphere.

Vallance was glad of the chance to get some air. The atmosphere in the interview rooms tended to become stifling, as though the air was recycled along with the endless variations on the same story. A familiar pattern was beginning to emerge: no one saw anything untoward; motives were vague or non-existent. The truth was there but no one had seen it yet. Someone had been trying to frame Diane Bennett for Alan Platt's murder. Was the attempt on her life explicable only in those terms?

He crossed a stretch of lawn and then turned on to a paved path that paralleled the high perimeter wall that ringed Ryder Hall. There were bushes and shrubs along the wall, not that Vallance recognised any of them. Gardens were not his strong point and he was usually hard pushed to tell one species of tree from the next. The cool air was good though, it cleared the head instantly. He just hoped that it was enough to make Kate Thurston lucid enough to talk without loosening her tongue so much that she went on for hours.

The question came back again: was there another explanation for Diane's attempted murder? There were several, of course, but none of them seemed particularly probable. The cocaine stashed in her room was proof enough that Platt's murder and the attempt on her life were definitely linked. However it could have been that Diane was the intended victim from the start, that Platt had been killed in order to create a false trail. It was unlikely but possible, just.

The path rounded a sharp corner and Vallance saw Kate. She was sitting on a bench opposite a small pond, her hands deep in the pockets of her coat, her eyes fixed on the murky brown waters in front of her. She looked as though she were about to be sick and her eyes were only half open as she stared at the unmoving water. From the look of her Vallance judged that she was suffering a hangover of massive proportions.

She looked up at him as he approached. His hands were thrust deep into the pockets of his leather jacket and he guessed that he probably didn't look in much better shape than she did.

'Kate Thurston? I'm Detective Chief –'

She didn't let him finish. 'I know who you are,' she said weakly. She seemed to sink further down, slouching on the stiff wooden bench as though she had no energy to hold herself up.

'Have you promised to go on the wagon yet?'

'I'm not normally much of a drinker,' she croaked. 'I mean I do like a drink, socially, but – well, never again. Not ever.'

'You realise I need to question you about last night, even if you do feel like death warmed up.'

She moved her head a fraction to nod her assent. 'I'm just so sorry it happened. Really I am.'

'Tell me about it, from the beginning.'

'I was angry,' she said, keeping her eyes on the unmoving muddy water in front of her. 'I came here to see Tom Ryder,

146

that's the main reason. I mean I'm here to learn about management and all that, but I didn't pay all that money to learn it from Diane Bennett and her colleagues.'

She fell into a tired silence for a moment. 'And?' he urged her.

'And I was sort of angry. I know I shouldn't have said anything to her, it wasn't her fault. But I couldn't help myself. I can't blame it all on the drinking, though if I hadn't had so much I would have stopped myself in time.'

Vallance listened to her tired voice as she described the by now familiar encounter with Diane in the bar. It was exactly as described by Sarah Fairfax, though delivered with a double dose of apology and self-pity in equal measure.

'How did you know about Diane's medical background?' he asked after she had finished.

'I can't remember,' she sighed. 'I think I might have read it in one of the brochures or in an article somewhere. It's one of those things that you forget the minute you read but somehow it came back to me yesterday. It was when I realised you were after people with medical experience.'

'Does that mean you think she killed Alan Platt?'

The shock registered instantly. Her eyes opened fully and she inhaled sharply. 'No, she didn't do it.'

'That's pretty categorical. How can you be so sure?'

'Because I was there when she opened the door, remember? I saw the shock on her face, there's no way it was faked. Not unless she was a brilliant actress.' The shock seemed to have cleared her head a bit. She sounded stronger and more certain of herself.

'Are there any other little nuggets of information that you've buried in your head that you think might help us?'

'No, I can't think of any,' she murmured.

'What happened after Sarah Fairfax put you to bed?'

She turned from the water and looked at him. 'Nothing. I conked out. I mean it, I've never blacked out like that before. I just felt so ill.'

'When did you come round?'

'This morning, just after about six. I was sick all over the floor of my room. I couldn't help it, I tried to get to

147

the bathroom but I couldn't. I felt so ashamed.'

Thankfully she lapsed into an embarrassed silence that Vallance used to lob another question. 'Tell me about Tom Ryder,' he asked, changing direction once more.

She looked suitably disoriented by the question. 'He's just perfect,' she replied. 'I don't know of another man like him anywhere. Don't look at me like that!'

'Like what?'

'Like I'm some sort of stupid schoolgirl,' she snapped. 'I know everyone thinks I'm acting like a silly girl with a crush but it's not like that, not at all. You just don't understand what it's like.'

'What is it like?' Vallance asked softly, surprised by the sudden passion in her voice.

She looked at him with tears sparkling in her eyes. 'You just can't imagine . . . It's not that I don't love Paul, I do, but sometimes – we've been married for twelve years now. Twelve years. He's a wonderful man but – but there's nothing there now. Is it too silly to want more than routine? I just want more from life than a comfortable home, a good car and a holiday every year.'

'And Tom Ryder?'

She looked at him fiercely. 'Tom Ryder is a man of passion, DCI Vallance. I don't expect you to understand what that means, but it means the world to me. Tom Ryder is everything I ever dreamed of in life –'

Her voice trailed to a sad, resigned silence once more. 'You don't have children, do you?' he guessed.

The tears trailed from her eyes, falling across her pale, sickly face. 'No. It's Paul. We've tried everything but there's nothing the doctors can do. It's not me, there's nothing wrong with me. I know what you're thinking: poor frustrated cow, she can't have kids, she's stuck in a cold marriage and all she's got are her stupid fantasies about Tom Ryder. That's what you think, isn't it?'

He looked away. She was painfully right; she knew herself too well not to see what other people saw. 'Sometimes it's the only thing that keeps me going. Don't you think I know that it's a fantasy? Do you think I'm so besotted that I can't see that it's a silly dream? I just wanted to meet him, that's all. I just wanted to be close to him, to hear him speak, to look into his eyes. That's all. It's pathetic, I know, but that's all I wanted.'

'And when that didn't happen you turned on the nearest target.'

'I'm sorry,' she whispered, wiping her eyes with her fingertips. 'I said things I shouldn't have, but that doesn't mean I killed her. You do believe me, don't you?'

'That's not a question I can answer,' he told her softly. 'At this stage everyone is suspect.'

'Including Tom?'

Vallance nodded. 'Including Tom Ryder.'

Kate was still gazing disconsolately at the dirty brown water of the pond when Vallance left her to trek back to the house. He felt sorry for her; she knew herself far too well to be fooled by her own fantasies yet she clung to them tenaciously. She felt trapped in a marriage without passion when it was the one thing she craved. The ticking of her biological clock didn't help; a few more years and it would be too late for children. If she didn't have romance then she wanted the pure, unconditional love of a child but that too was out of the question.

She sounded desperate but was the motive enough to attempt to murder Diane? And if so where did Platt fit it in?

The sky started to darken, the crisp blue becoming streaked with wisps of grey. It was going to rain again. Vallance hoped that the scene of crime boys had finished combing the area where Diane had fallen. They'd probably recovered everything useful but there was always a chance that something unexpected would throw new light on the case.

He saw Philippa Brady pacing up and down alongside her car as he drew closer to the entrance of Ryder Hall. As usual she was speaking quickly into her mobile phone. Her long legs were poised on sharp high heels that she crunched into the gravel with a hard, satisfying sound. Was she on the phone trying to get him shifted from the case? It would mean having to retract whatever it was she'd said the first time around,

149

which was something he found difficult to imagine her doing easily.

She turned and saw him approaching. 'I want to talk to you,' she told him, covering up the phone with her hand.

He felt tempted to carry on walking. The look on her face would have been worth the hassle, but things were too serious for games like that. She turned away again to finish her call, giving him a chance to study her from behind. Her body was outlined perfectly by her tight-fitting clothes and her black stockings contrasted well with the dark green of her skirt and jacket.

'What went on between us meant nothing,' she told him, turning sharply on her heels to face him with blue eyes blazing.

'Did I say otherwise?' he demanded, taken by surprise.

'Then why the third degree earlier?'

The third degree? What was she on about? 'You mean treating Ryder like a suspect rather than someone who walks on water?'

'You know he was with me all night, so why the heavy-handed questions? I told you yesterday morning, what happened between us was just one of those things, nothing more nor less.'

Vallance laughed. 'You think that I was having a go at Ryder because you spent the night with him?'

The anger in her eyes grew suddenly more intense. She looked fit to burst. 'Don't laugh at me! Don't you think I can see what's eating you?'

'Listen, we fucked and that was it. Maybe it was a mistake, maybe it wasn't, but there's no way I'm going to let it get in the way of this investigation. Now, you'll make a statement to one of my men or I'll make Ryder's life hell. Do you understand me? He's a bastard as far as I'm concerned, but what you two do is up to you. I don't give a shit. Is that clear?'

She looked at him for a moment, sizing him up with cool deliberation. 'You'll get my statement, don't worry. What you think of him or me means nothing to me. I'm here to do my job just as you're here to do yours. So long as we understand each other then that's fine.'

'And does he understand that as well?'

She shrugged. 'He doesn't like you, Vallance, but then you know that already. And he knows that you and your men don't like him either.'

'That's because my people can smell bullshit at a hundred paces,' he said.

The shiny long blonde hair, blue eyes and tanned skin put Cooper in mind of Diane Bennett. Diane and Josephine, the young receptionist, were made of the same stuff, right down to the Southern drawl and the over-heavy use of red lipstick.

'Everybody's got to register soon as they arrive,' she explained, standing stiffly behind the counter. 'Just like in a regular hotel. People arrive, register and then get shown to their rooms.'

'There's a register of some kind?' Cooper asked hopefully.

She smiled. 'Sort of. Everything's computerised. Reservations, bookings, payments and just about everything else is on the machine these days.'

The monitor was there beside her, on a shelf on the other side of the counter, with the keyboard in front of it. 'Can you call up details?'

'It's kind of confidential,' she explained hesitantly.

He knew the magic words by heart; they all did. 'Mr Ryder knows all about this,' he explained.

She fluttered long eye lashes nervously. 'I haven't been told –'

'You've been told to cooperate,' he stated coldly. 'This information is vital if we're going to catch the man who killed Alan Platt.'

'I can see that,' she said, 'but it's just that everything's got to be signed for. It's some kind of Data Protection thing, that's all.'

Cooper smiled. 'But we're the police, we're exempt from that kind of thing.'

'You are?'

'Of course.'

For a second she looked ready to cave in but then something snapped back into place and she looked nervous again. 'Can I just check up with Tom's office?'

'Please will you just think for yourself!' he said through

151

gritted teeth. 'I'm trying to catch a murderer here, do you really need to check every bloody detail with Tom Ryder? What's wrong with you people?'

Josephine's eyes looked fit to burst.

'What's this?'

Cooper turned to face his boss. 'I'm just trying to get some information from this young lady, sir,' he said.

'What information?'

'A look at the registration times for everybody on the course.'

Vallance turned to Josephine. 'And what's the problem?'

Her voice came out as a whisper of indecision. 'I just think I need to check this out with Tom.'

Vallance smiled at her sweetly. 'If you don't give the sergeant all the information he needs I will personally call our computer people, who will come down and impound all the pieces of computer equipment in the building and take them away for analysis. Now, how do you fancy passing that news on to Tom Ryder?'

The boss was still smiling when Josephine's trembling fingers began tapping away rapidly at the keyboard. A moment later the printer started to churn out line after line of black print.

'Thank you, Josephine,' Vallance told her. 'Cooper, is there anything else you'd like?'

Cooper grinned. Watching Vallance in action was sometimes a joy to behold. 'I just need to go through this, sir.'

'In that case what's Manning doing?'

'Going through the last lot of statements for me,' he said. Josephine was listening so it was best not to say more. Manning was scouring through the statements seeking witnesses to verify that Anita Walsh and Alan Platt had done more than say hello.

Vallance frowned. 'I need a driver,' he explained. 'I've just called Sue Beamish and she's definitely at home this time.'

It was weird the way the boss hated driving. Fast cars were part of the territory for everyone on the force except for Vallance. 'What about DC Quinn? She's in doing interviews but we can get a uniform in to take her place.'

Vallance smiled. 'Quinn? Isn't she one of Riley's favourites?'

Considering Vallance hadn't been around that long his

information was spot on. 'Yes, sir. Superintendent Riley's keeping her under his wing, sir.'

The printer stopped and Josephine carefully tore the perforated paper from the roll. It fell into a concertinaed pile which she handed to Cooper. 'Thanks,' he said, grinning.

'You're welcome,' she responded automatically but there was anything but welcome in her eyes.

'Now that you've got that,' Vallance said, 'you can go and sort out Quinn's replacement. I'll be waiting in the car for her.'

Cooper wanted nothing more than to sit down and sort through the computer listing. It was important. He knew instinctively that its contents contained some hidden truth that would knock holes in Anita Walsh's story. But it had to wait. 'I'll go and tell her now,' he agreed.

Anne Quinn looked decidedly nervous when she got into the car. Superintendent Riley had no doubt warned her to be on her guard when it came to Vallance. And from the nervy look and the quiet way she spoke it looked as though she'd taken the warning to heart. It suited Vallance fine for a while. He needed time to think and the long drive up through London promised time enough for that.

Was it time to forget about motive and look at who was capable of murder? Kate Thurston? She was a desperately unhappy woman who projected all her failed hopes and desires on to the figure of Tom Ryder. Whether that meant she was capable of cold-blooded murder Vallance wasn't sure. In a moment of madness perhaps, but Platt's murder was anything but a crime of passion.

Tom Ryder? He was cold, calculating and ruthless for sure, but a murderer? If he had to kill then perhaps the answer was yes, but in that case Vallance guessed that the act would be executed with premeditated thoroughness. Just like Platt's murder in fact. But then why attempt to kill Diane Bennett? Unless she had guessed that Ryder had killed Platt.

Who else was there? Diane Bennett was still officially a suspect in Platt's death. Was she capable of it? Vallance doubted that she would have the courage or the motive to carry out such a crime on her own. On the other hand there were probably few limits to her devotion to Ryder. If he had ordered her to kill then it would be easy to believe that she'd obey blindly. And then afterwards? She'd be dangerous to have around, especially if there was a jealous streak in her. That put Ryder back in the picture for her attempted murder.

Peter Shalcott? According to both Cooper and Sarah Fairfax he was a bit of a doddering old fool, but perhaps there was something lurking beneath the surface. In any case Vallance decided it was time to talk to him in person. The witness statements alone were useless.

And what about Anita Walsh? Cooper was going through her statement but Vallance guessed that there'd be little of value there.

That left Sue Beamish. She'd been away from Ryder Hall at the time of Diane's fall, which left her out of the picture. Did that also mean she was no longer a suspect in Platt's death? Had she ever really been considered a suspect? Her statement had been watertight and had been in line with what everyone else had said. And few people doubted her genuine distress at the death of her colleague. But distress could be faked and a good story was easy to come by.

And after that? There were over a hundred people at Ryder Hall and every one of them had to be counted as a suspect. And that included Sarah Fairfax. Was she capable of murder? It was hard to figure out what her motive might be, but then Vallance was deliberately discounting that. The question had to be faced: was Sarah Fairfax capable of the cold-blooded murder of another human being? He wanted the answer to be a resounding no; despite her prickly personality, he liked her. Could she kill someone? She had a temper; he'd been on the receiving end, as had Cooper and half a dozen other people. But murder?

'A penny for your thoughts, sir,' Quinn said.

She'd decided on conversation at last. It had only taken her half an hour through heavy traffic to get her to talk. That made her practically a push-over. 'They're not worth that much,' he said. He'd not been able to come to a conclusion about Fairfax and was glad of the interruption.

They were heading towards the Thames, making good progress through the traffic that had thinned out considerably. She drove carefully, keeping her eyes on the road as though he were a driving examiner she was keen to impress.

'Aren't you supposed to keep away from me?' he asked, realising that she'd taken his reply as the end of the conversation.

'No, sir. Why, should I?'

He smiled. 'Your CO seems to think of me as a corrupting influence,' he said.

She glanced round quickly at him and then back at the road. 'And are you, sir?'

She was still straight-faced but there was something playfully coy about her voice. 'Terribly corrupting,' he warned. 'Especially to ambitious young officers of a female nature.'

The profile of her face changed as she smiled. She looked much better smiling than not. 'I'll have to be careful then, sir,' she said.

'On the other hand it's not a bad idea to keep in with your guv'nor,' he pointed out.

She mused on this as she steered the car round a tricky roundabout between a bus belching noxious fumes and a cyclist with a death wish. She managed to edge out in front of the bus and then accelerated away sharply. Not a bad bit of driving and the sort of thing that Vallance could rarely be bothered to try.

'Isn't Superintendent Riley my guv'nor?' she asked, glancing round at him again. She was still smiling and her dark eyes touched his for a second.

'Not on this case he isn't,' he said, a little too defensively perhaps.

'I wasn't having a go or anything, sir,' she said.

'How long have you been CID, Anne?'

'Six months.'

'Then you've got a lot to learn,' he sighed. 'Which is probably why the Super was so happy to have you assigned to my team. There's a danger you might learn how to solve crimes and how to catch criminals, which won't do at all.'

'Do I just listen at this point, sir?'

He smiled. She wasn't the sweet innocent he'd imagined

and he liked that. 'You catch on quick,' he remarked. 'Don't lose that, it's important.'

'Thank you, sir.'

He hadn't been around Area long enough to know who was screwing who. Was Quinn currently attached? 'And don't lose sight of the fact that I'm heading this case,' he said.

'Yes, sir.'

'And that means you keep me happy.'

She laughed and he liked the sound of it.

It was only after Sue Beamish had shown Vallance and DC Quinn into her living room that he had a chance to get a good look at her. She was a heavy-boned woman in her middle or late forties, with a round face, long black hair and intelligent, knowing eyes. Her clothes were neat and unadventurous but expensive and chosen with care. She still showed signs of shock: her eyes were ringed with darkness and despite the clearness of her voice she sounded tired.

'Before we start,' she said, showing Vallance into the large, spacious room at the front of the house, 'we must have some tea. Would Earl Grey be OK?'

'Yes, fine,' Vallance agreed, and he was echoed by Anne Quinn.

'I'll only be a minute,' she said. 'Please take a seat.'

'She's got a nice place,' Quinn remarked, sitting down on the far end of a three-seater sofa.

Vallance took the other end of the sofa, which faced a coffee table with two armchairs positioned one at each corner. 'It's an expensive place,' Vallance said, making himself comfortable. A sturdy Victorian town house so close to Hampstead Heath was out of the price range of most people. And Quinn was right, the house was furnished well and decorated with a style that suggested the hand of an interior designer at some stage.

Quinn looked around the room, surveying it more critically. 'Does that make you suspicious?' she asked.

Did it? He had no idea of what a high ranking civil servant brought in, but it was hard to imagine it funding a mortgage big enough for this house. The few gilt-framed photographs showed Sue Beamish at various ages and what he took to be members of her family. No sign of a wedding photo or any pictures of her with children.

'Everything makes me suspicious,' he said finally.

Quinn smiled. 'Doesn't that mean that nothing makes you suspicious, sir?'

He noted that she appended 'sir' to the end of her remark, dressing it up as a question to her superior officer. 'Is this the sort of question you address to Superintendent Riley?'

Her smile wavered for a second. 'No, sir,' she admitted. 'The Super doesn't like us asking difficult questions.'

'No, I don't suppose he does. And the answer to your question is that I don't allow suspicion to get in the way of what I see and feel. Too much suspicion makes you hostile and that's not good for you and it's not good for everyone else.'

Quinn's follow-up was disturbed by the return of Sue Beamish. She was carrying a silver tray bearing a fine porcelain teapot, three matching cups and saucers, a milk jug and a silver sugar bowl. Carefully she set the tray down on the coffee table and then knelt on the rug beside it to pour the tea. Her attention was focused completely, as though investing ceremonial significance in the act.

'How do you take it?' she asked Quinn first, looking up at her with her large round eyes.

'Just one sugar please.'

Sue passed the cup to Quinn and then offered her the sugar bowl, waiting until Quinn had spooned the sugar before turning to Vallance.

'It's milk and sugar for you, isn't it Mr Vallance?'

Dead right. 'How did you know?' he asked, intrigued that she should feel so confident about his tastes only minutes after meeting him.

She smiled. 'Taking tea is very important,' she said. 'It's one of those trivial, functional activities which reveals so much of our inner selves. Does that sound silly?'

He took the cup which she offered, breathed the distinctive aroma of Earl Grey before adding a single spoonful of sugar and a drop of milk to it. 'It doesn't sound silly, it just doesn't answer my question.'

'Earl Grey is meant to be drunk black,' she explained. 'No milk and no sugar. However you strike me as a man who knows what he wants and is not bound by convention. Therefore I surmised that you'd drink it the way you wanted, not the way you are supposed to drink it.'

She was still smiling but her face bore a slight pink flush and she hardly dared look him in the eyes. Was she naturally the shy type or was she embarrassed by her explanation? 'There is another explanation,' he suggested.

She looked surprised. 'There is?'

'Yes. I might not know how Earl Grey is supposed to be drunk. To me it might be just another brand of tea, and so I drink it the way I'd drink the slop from the police canteen.'

Her face reddened a little more. 'I hadn't considered that possibility,' she said quietly.

'You know why we're here?' he asked.

His question signalled the end of the tea ceremony. She poured her own tea – kept it black – and sat in the armchair directly opposite Vallance. 'To ascertain my whereabouts during the last few days,' she said.

'Let's start with the last two days.'

'As you know, I came home yesterday morning. I thought I was far stronger really, but the shock of finding poor Alan like that – I couldn't carry on with the course.'

Mindful of his wasted journey of the previous afternoon, Vallance wanted more details. 'You came straight home?'

'Yes, I informed Sergeant Cooper that I'd be at home should I be required. In the afternoon I went to visit my mother briefly. She lives not far from here and as she knew Alan I wanted to tell her about it before she heard it from anyone else.'

'We'll have to talk to her to confirm all that,' Vallance said.

'Of course. I was with her from about 3.30 to the middle of the evening,' she added. 'I was home before nine because I remember watching the news on television a little after coming in.'

'And once you were home?'

She sipped her tea before answering. 'I watched the news for a while then I switched it off. I don't watch very much television, I prefer the radio or else I read. There are no witnesses I'm afraid.'

'What about the neighbours?'

'It's possible of course that they saw me arrive home, but that's all. Once I was home I saw no one and spoke to no one until the morning.'

'You do know about Diane Bennett?' Vallance asked. He had deliberately not mentioned it but her answers to his questions covered precisely the period of her fall. She had not detailed her movements at the time of Platt's death.

She inhaled sharply. 'I'm stunned, quite frankly Mr Vallance. I couldn't call Diane a friend but I think we could have become friends given time. We met on a number of occasions before Alan and I signed up for Ryder Hall and I have to say she was the best advertisement for Tom Ryder's course. Do you know if there's any change in her condition?'

Her voice had been edged with concern and with a feeling of exhaustion. 'No, there's no news at the moment,' he said. 'Diane Bennett is still critical but stable, that's all the hospital is willing to say. Can I ask how you know about her fall?'

'I called Ryder Hall this morning,' she said. 'I spoke to Josephine in reception. I had promised to go back to finish the course but I was having second thoughts. I called hoping to speak to Diane.'

Vallance looked at Quinn, who scribbled something in her notebook. They would have to check the time and content of the call with Josephine. Not that it told them anything useful if it were true.

'And are you still planning on returning?'

Sue looked horrified by the suggestion. 'No. I'm sorry but I just cannot cope. I've always considered myself level-headed and able to handle any situation, but I realise that I've never had to deal with anything like this before.'

'Like what, exactly?'

'The death of a close friend and colleague. The serious injury of someone I liked.' She paused before adding: 'I realise that I've led a very safe, and in many ways a very sheltered existence. Some lives are easily touched by tragedy, it shadows them from year to year, but that hasn't happened to me before.'

When she lapsed into silence he felt it was time to switch back to the murder case. 'Tell me about Alan Platt,' he said.

Her eyes were suddenly fixed on him. 'That's an open question, Mr Vallance. What precisely do you wish me to tell you?'

Precise questions were what she wanted. Precise, detailed questions which she could answer succinctly and intelligently. Open, messy, unformed questions which meandered without direction were anathema to her. It was easy to see why she had chosen the career that she had. 'Tell me about the reasons for your attendance at Ryder Hall,' was the first question which came to Vallance's mind.

'We wanted to judge the effectiveness of Tom Ryder's management techniques,' she replied simply.

'But why? Of what interest is it to your department in the Home Office?'

'For the same reason that it's of interest to the Metropolitan Police Service,' she replied, carefully putting her empty cup back on the tray. 'We are living in an increasingly commercial environment, Mr Vallance. We are being judged on the commercial criteria of efficiency, effectiveness and competitiveness, as are police forces in every part of the country. As you are aware, this change creates many pressures within existing organisations, which can hamper the cultural change which has to take place if our respective organisations are to survive. Alan and I were charged with the task of investigating methodologies which promised to facilitate this transition to a commercial environment.'

She sounded as though she were dictating a report, but it was a clear enough answer. 'And were you both happy with what you saw?'

'I believe so,' she said. 'At least until these terrible events took place.'

Diane Bennett had said that Platt was unhappy with the course and so had Sarah Fairfax. 'You were both impressed with what Ryder was teaching you?'

'We were most impressed by him on an individual level,' she replied, speaking with the same calm and clear voice. 'However we were not there to judge the man, we were there to judge the effectiveness of the course itself. Alan was reserving judgement, he felt that it was too early to comment on its effectiveness. Should it prove to match our requirements we will recommend that all senior managers within the Civil Service attend.'

'That sounds like it could cost a lot of money,' Vallance pointed out.

'Obviously it's not our department, but a contract will have to be negotiated between Tom Ryder's organisation and the different departments within the Civil Service. I would estimate that this contract will be measured in the millions rather than the thousands.'

It was the sort of money to kill for. 'What will you be recommending now?'

She looked at Vallance strangely. 'Nothing, of course. There is no other option. Our report will have to wait until I, with or without another colleague or colleagues, return to Ryder Hall to complete the course properly.'

'Do you think that Alan would have recommended the course?'

'I suspect that is the case but that is merely conjecture on my part.'

'When do you think you'll go back?'

She shook her head sadly. 'I need time to recover. Unlike you, Mr Vallance, I am not used to dealing with trauma. It may be that in a few days I'll feel able to return, it may be that I'll not feel ready for months.'

'Do you think that someone else might be sent in your place?'

She looked unconcerned by the possibility. 'That may be the only sensible option.'

Vallance looked at Quinn and then back at Sue Beamish. 'Thank you very much, Miss Beamish. DC Quinn will draw up the statement for you to sign.'

'Of course, Mr Vallance. You'll be wanting mother's address and telephone number,' she added.

'Yes. Do you mind if I use your phone for a moment?'

'You can use the phone in the kitchen if you like,' she said.

Vallance followed her from the living room out into the

hall and into the spacious kitchen at the back of the house. It was neat and tidy but obviously a kitchen that was used rather than one for show. The spice racks were full of half-empty jars, the chopping board on the counter nearest the door was scored with cuts that tracked in all directions.

'Would you like more tea?' she asked.

'No, it's OK, thank you.'

He waited for her to return to the living room before closing the kitchen door. The room was pervaded with the scent of herbs and spices and it reminded him that he was starving. As he tapped in the number on the phone he wondered if Quinn was interested in stopping for dinner somewhere on the way back to Ryder Hall.

It took a while but eventually he was through to Intensive Care and talking to the sister in charge. Luckily she remembered him immediately.

'How does it look?' he asked.

'It doesn't look like anything, Detective Chief Inspector. She died half an hour ago.'

Vallance swallowed hard. 'What was it in the end?'

'Internal bleeding, probably. It was sudden at the end. We tried everything, but there was nothing we could do.'

He believed it. He'd seen it often enough in the past. 'Is anyone from Ryder Hall there?'

'No. We're trying to get through to them to see about the next of kin. I'm sorry the news couldn't be better.'

What could he say? What could anyone say?

At least he wouldn't have to break the news to Diane's grieving family. That was something for Ryder to do, he thought grimly.

TEN

Sue Beamish was signing her witness statement when Vallance returned to the room. He had waited for a long while after hearing of Diane Bennett's death. The murderer had claimed a second victim. He knew for certain that Diane Bennett had not jumped, or at least not any more than Alan Platt had chosen to snort cocaine.

Quinn looked up sharply. 'Is anything wrong, sir?'

Sue looked up at the same time. She had initialled every page of the statement and was preparing to sign the declaration at the end of it. She looked at him expectantly with her eyebrows raised and her lips slightly pursed.

'I've just had news from the hospital,' he said. 'Diane Bennett died about an hour ago.'

Sue put her hand to her mouth, a look of horror filling her eyes. The colour seemed to drain from her face and suddenly she seemed much older, the shock merging with the exhaustion to make her look haggard.

'Are you OK?' Quinn asked, putting her hand on Sue's shoulder. 'Would you like me to make some tea or something?'

'No,' Sue replied softly, 'I'll make it.'

She stood up shakily and moved across the room, walking towards Vallance in a daze. Their eyes met briefly and he saw the tears sparkling brilliantly as they waited to fall. He stepped aside quickly, afraid that she'd walk into his arms and weep on his shoulder.

'Has she signed it?' he asked after she'd gone to the kitchen. There was an edge of anger to his voice that shouldn't have been there, but it was beyond his control.

'No, sir, not yet.'

'Make sure she does,' he said, walking across the room to the large bay windows that looked out on to the small square garden at the front of the house and the steps leading on to the pavement. The rose bushes had been cut back and the paved area under the window had been swept clear of leaves. Neat and orderly, Sue's garden seemed an adequate reflection of her life.

'You're not going for the suicide theory, sir,' Quinn observed.

He turned from the window to face her. 'Officially this is just another suspicious death. That's all we're saying until further notice.'

Sue returned with another pot of tea. 'I'm sorry about this,' she said, setting the second pot down next to the first one which had gone cold. She poured more tea into the three cups and then added milk and sugar for Vallance and sugar for Quinn.

'I know this is a shocking piece of news,' Vallance said, taking the proffered cup, 'but is there anything else you can think of to add to your statement?'

She closed her eyes and shook her head. 'Nothing, Mr Vallance. I didn't know Diane very well but I feel very upset by her death. What is it, Mr Vallance, what is going on here?'

He sympathised with the question; it was one that kept circling in his head without resolution. 'I wish I had an answer. Tell me more about Diane's connection with you and Alan.'

She looked down into her tea as she answered. 'She was the first representative of Ryder's organisation that we made contact with. Alan made the first contact as I recall, though we had both agreed that Tom Ryder's group were high on the list of organisations we were interested in. Alan arranged for Diane to come down to visit and we were both very impressed by her professional presentation and by her as an individual. We set high store on this point. I think that if an individual does not present well then the technique he or she is selling must be of little value. That was our first meeting and it was followed up with two or three more before we registered for the course.'

'When did you first meet Tom Ryder?' Vallance asked.

'Our second meeting. He and Diane presented to a senior group within the Home Office and we sat in on that.'

'Who set that up?'

She looked up from her drink momentarily, as though the question surprised her. 'I did. I had arranged a series of seminars for our more senior people and I felt that it would be interesting to have Tom Ryder there. It wasn't directly connected to our current project but it had a positive spin-off I believe.'

'And did Alan Platt have a say in this?' Vallance continued.

Again the question seemed to surprise her. Perhaps it was the edginess in his voice. 'No. It was a different project altogether, Mr Vallance. However, Alan was present at the seminar, as an observer rather than an active participant. We spoke to Mr Ryder after his presentation and that was when the possibility of our attending the course was first broached.'

'Whose suggestion was that?'

'I can't remember,' she said. 'There is no doubt that all parties were agreed that it would be a useful experience for us to attend. The dates were agreed at our next meeting.'

Vallance turned to Quinn. 'Append that to the statement,' he instructed before facing Sue once more. 'Thank you, Miss Beamish. If you do decide to return to Ryder Hall in the next few days then please inform Sergeant Cooper beforehand, if you don't mind.'

'Of course,' she agreed meekly, staring once more with sad, wide eyes into the tea which was cooling slowly in her cup.

The small lecture room was rapidly filling up when Sarah arrived. People had been called from the different classes and workshops all over the building, though it seemed that she was one of the last to arrive. She did a quick head count. There were about twenty people in the room, about a fifth of the people on the course. Most of them had taken seats at the front of the hall and seemed to be as much in the dark as to what was happening as she was. She stood by the door for a moment, looking for somewhere to sit and also keeping an eye out for Tom Ryder.

'Sarah! Over here!'

Kate, sitting a few rows from the front but facing the lectern directly, was calling her. Sarah smiled to her and walked down the steps and then began to thread her way along towards her.

'I'm glad you're here too,' Kate said, taking her bag off the seat next to her.

Up close the signs of fatigue were still evident on her face and in her eyes, but compared to the wreck that Sarah had seen that morning Kate had recovered well. 'What's going on?' she asked, taking the place Kate had saved her.

'I'm not sure,' Kate whispered, 'but I think that Tom's going to have a word with us.'

'About what?'

'About what's going on, probably,' Kate said. 'Why else would he call us out of our classes like this?'

Kate was probably right, as usual. Her intuition seemed perfect, whether it was to do with the police investigation or the workings of Tom Ryder's mind. 'How did it go with DCI Vallance this morning?'

Kate looked away sharply. 'Not very well,' she murmured. 'I didn't have anything to do with what happened to Diane. You believe me, don't you, Sarah?'

'I know you didn't,' Sarah said, patting Kate's hand reassuringly. Given how much drink she'd had it would probably have been physically impossible for Kate to have done anything had she wanted to anyway.

'I'm so sorry that I was so spiteful,' she added mournfully. 'But you never know what's going to happen. I didn't imagine that she'd –'

Kate was still in need of sympathy. 'It's OK, no one's blaming you,' Sarah said.

'Tell that to that Detective Chief Inspector,' Kate said vehemently.

Did Vallance really have Kate down as a suspect? 'He

doesn't really think you had anything to do with Diane's fall?'

She lowered her voice suddenly. 'He thinks we're all suspects, from me, to you to Tom Ryder.'

Sarah knew that Vallance didn't include her in his list of suspects – or at least she hoped that she hadn't been added back on to it – but what about Tom Ryder? Was he now on the list of suspects too? She was about to ask for more information when she became aware of the sudden silence in the room. Kate had already turned towards the lectern.

Tom Ryder strode confidently out to the front of the stage. He looked cool and calm, moving with measured strides and an ultra-confident manner. He had the audience's attention immediately. His presence was enough to fill the room and to silence every conversation.

'Thank you for being here, ladies and gentleman,' he began, his deep voice imbued with a natural authority. 'I'm sorry for taking time out on your course time once again. I'm all too aware that many of you have been inconvenienced many times already. That's why I'm here in fact. I want to remedy this situation here and now,' he said, pausing to look at the people in front of him.

'Before I start, I just want us all to back up a minute. Let's all detach ourselves from this time and space and let's observe what's being going on these past few days. What do we see? What can we say about this week's events? Well, let's be honest, we all know what the main event has been, don't we?'

He waited for an answer that never came. 'A man died here on Wednesday morning. He had a heart attack in the night and his body was discovered the next morning. It's a distressing occurrence. Death is a truly frightening thing, and there ain't one of us here who doesn't get jumpy in its presence. We don't like to be reminded that time's moving on, or that death can visit anyone of us. Life's a lottery, right? It's a gamble and we're putting our stakes on being here tomorrow – so none of us likes to see it when the gamble doesn't pay off.'

Again he paused for a moment. All eyes were on him, and Sarah knew that like everyone else she was wondering where he was leading.

'Well let me tell you all, life *is* a lottery. There ain't no other way of saying it. It's a gamble and we all know just how random a lottery can get. Well, ladies and gentleman, what better example of chaos do you want? Here it is. It's not just some abstract word that Tom Ryder's pulled out of a hat. It's here, all around us. It's random, it's disruptive, it obeys no law other than its own. This is what we have to deal with every day of our lives. This is what you and your organisations have to deal with all the time.

'So what do we do about it? How do we, as inspired people, handle this prime example of chaos in action? Do you think that Tom Ryder's not aware of how disruptive things have gotten? I know it's a pain in the butt with the police interviewing people, searching Ryder Hall, people coming and going. Hell, I've been on the receiving end myself. This isn't just any heart attack victim, we all know that. This isn't just any bit of chaos, this is chaos squared!

'What do I do? Do I just throw up my hands and say: "Sorry folks, that's just the way things are"? Do I stand back and let you return to your organisations with the idea that Tom Ryder's full of crap? I can hear it now: "He talks a good fight but when it comes down to it he's just like the rest of those management bums". Well, I just hope that you people realise that Tom Ryder's just not made that way. I can't lie to you, this has been a difficult time for all of us but who needs a technique and philosophy that only works in easy times?'

'You've learnt some good skills so far. You've been given an insight into new ways of thinking, organising and working. You've discovered the inner creative core that each and every one of us possesses and I hope you're getting properly acquainted with it. But I know it ain't enough to make up for the disruption and the time you've all missed.

'What are my choices here? I can close my eyes to it and send you back with bad reports about what I do. Sure, there's a lot of people who'd love the chance to rubbish Tom Ryder and his philosophy. Hell, they'd love to see this whole place fall apart. Revolutionaries can't expect any better, and believe me, ladies and gentlemen, that's precisely what you become when you learn the art of inspirational management.

'What other choices? There's money. I can write you all

out a refund. Pay you back all or part of the fee for the course. But what does that say about our teaching? It says that when it came to the crunch inspirational management can't deliver. End result? You go back with some money and a whole set of bad impressions. Do I want that? Hell no. Do other people want that? You betcha!

'Well, that ain't going to happen!'

He slammed his fist down on the lectern. Jewels of perspiration beaded his face and his eyes were blazing with anger. His voice had taken on an increasing passion, and the fury radiated across the room.

'I'm not going to give anyone the satisfaction of ruining this course. We're all sorry a man has died here, our heart goes out to his wife and family, but the corporate world doesn't stop for anyone. What happens when you manage a project and a key worker dies on you? It's a horrible thought but it happens. Do you let the project fall to pieces? No way! You carry on through, right? Well, this project carries on through as well.

'I know it might not suit you all, but this is my offer: stay over the weekend for some extra tuition. I'm willing to spend my free time helping you catch up on what you've missed and maybe a whole lot more. At no extra cost, of course. If that don't suit you then we can arrange for people to come back. If you want a cash refund then that's fine too – only now you'll know that when it comes to a crisis Tom Ryder doesn't pull back.

'I promise those people who stay that it'll be worth the extra investment in time. That's my word, ladies and gentleman. You don't have to make a decision here and now,' he added, silencing the buzz of comment, 'just let Sally or Josephine know by the end of the afternoon. Thank you for your patience.'

A tall, leggy blonde crossed the stage as soon as Ryder stepped back from the lectern, not one of his usual helpers. She was too expensively dressed and the confident manner with which she approached him contrasted with the meek manner of his subordinates. Sarah took a guess: Philippa Brady.

'Are you staying?' Kate asked, her voice filled with excitement.

'I don't know,' Sarah mumbled. Philippa Brady had whispered something to Ryder. He closed his eyes for a moment and then opened them slowly. He looked a little sick, the flush of colour on his face seemed to seep away instantly.

'I think I'm staying,' Kate said, as though there had been any doubt.

'Something's happened,' Sarah said. She pointed to Ryder, who was listening silently to Philippa. He nodded several times but said nothing.

'Something's wrong,' Kate whispered. 'He looks in shock.'

He'd been on a high after talking; now it was gone. 'It's Diane,' Sarah whispered. 'She's dead.'

Ryder turned and walked away, his ashen face turned towards the ground.

Sarah stood up quickly and threaded her way along the row of seats. She got out on to the aisle and ran up the steps just as Ryder and Philippa Brady got to the door.

'Mr Ryder?' she said, tapping him on the shoulder.

He turned to her, his eyes ice cold. 'Yes, Miss Fairfax?'

'What's the news on Diane?'

He shook his head and walked out of the door. Philippa Brady waited a second.

'We need to talk,' Philippa said.

'Diane's dead, isn't she?'

Philippa nodded. 'She died a little while ago. We do need to talk, you and I.'

Sarah felt cold, suddenly. 'Poor Diane,' she said quietly.

'Let me deal with Tom and then we can talk,' Philippa persisted. 'Is that OK?'

'Yes, we can talk,' Sarah agreed. She turned back towards the stage. Kate was still in her seat, holding her head in her hands.

Cooper watched the line of people emerging from the lecture theatre. Whatever Ryder had said to them he obviously hadn't broken the bad news about Diane Bennett; the conversation was too lively for that. Perhaps he'd given them another of his speeches, it was what these people seemed to want to hear.

What was it about managers that made them want to listen to bullshit when they weren't spouting it themselves?

People were moving off in ones and twos, probably returning to the classes they'd just left. He'd been all around the building looking for Anita Walsh and had finally been directed to the smaller of the lecture theatres by one of the all-American Barbie dolls. She hadn't said why Walsh and the others had been called out, all she would say was that it was what Tom had wanted. That's all they ever said.

He saw her at last, on her own and lost deep in thought as she came out of the room.

'Miss Walsh?' he said, walking up to her.

'Yes, Sergeant Cooper?' she asked, wearing a slight look of surprise.

'I'd just like to go over your statement again.'

'Again? But we've been through it once this morning already.'

'I think we need to go over it again,' he insisted.

'Now?' she asked, scowling.

'Yes.'

She glanced at her watch. 'Will it be quick?'

'That depends more on you than on me,' he said.

They walked to the first interview room in silence. He was aware of the way she looked straight ahead, keeping her eyes away from him at all times. She had sounded more put out by the inconvenience than nervous about his request for an interview.

DC Manning had his feet up on the table when Cooper opened the door for her. Manning sat up sharpish and tried to look efficient. The computer print-outs were there on the table, along with her statement and the interview notes for Peter Shalcott.

'Please, take a seat,' Manning said, pointing to the chair in front of the table.

Cooper walked round to the other side and sat facing her. Her eyes seemed to hover between green and blue and she met his gaze for a moment before looking away.

'In your statement to us earlier today,' he began, picking up the signed document and showing it to her, 'you said that you'd only met Peter Shalcott on the course. Is that right?'

She nodded.

He picked up the print-out that DCI Vallance had frightened out of the receptionist. 'This is a listing of the registration details for everyone on the course,' he said. 'You were registered her at 7.07 p.m. on Sunday. Is that correct?'

'It sounds right,' she agreed. Her eyes were fixed on the sheet of paper that he held so that she could not see the details.

'Peter Shalcott was registered at precisely the same time.'

'Is that significant?' she asked calmly. She looked at him, without a flicker of doubt in her eyes.

'He wasn't registered at seven o'clock or at 7.15. He was registered at exactly 7.07. I asked reception how that could happen. It takes more than five minutes to register someone and get all the details sorted.'

'We arrived at around the same time,' she said.

He smiled. 'You arrived at exactly the same time,' he corrected. 'And the reason is that you arrived together. Isn't it?'

There was a long delay before she answered. 'We arrived by train and caught a cab from the station. In that sense we did arrive together.'

'You were on the same train, in the same carriage and no doubt next to each other too.'

'No,' she said. 'We were on the same train but we only met once we got to the taxi rank. There was no one else around, we each guessed where the other was going and it made sense to share a cab.'

It sounded too coincidental to be true. 'Why didn't you mention this before?'

She smiled. 'Because I didn't think it was significant, officer.'

'But you signed a statement saying that you met on the course,' Manning said. He sounded affronted that the statement he'd witnessed was in some way incorrect.

'That's still the case. If it hadn't been for the course we'd have never met. Is it really so significant that we met at a taxi rank on the way here rather than in one of the classes?'

Cooper inhaled sharply. 'It's significant that he denied knowing you and that your story is now changing.'

She looked at him confidently. 'It's not changing in substance, is it? And I can't be held responsible for his statement, can I?'

'How many other details have you left out?' Cooper wondered.

'None.'

He was certain now that she was hiding something. 'You said that you didn't know Alan Platt,' he said. 'Is that now incorrect too?'

'I said that I couldn't remember meeting him,' she said. 'I don't deny that I might have spoken to him.'

Cooper ignored the ingenuous play with words. 'He arrived at Ryder Hall at 7.45 that evening. At that point there were less than ten people registered here. In your statement you said you went to the bar on Sunday and again on Monday evening. Correct?'

'Yes.'

He put her statement down and picked up another sheaf of computer print-out. 'We know that Platt also went to the bar on those evenings. His bar bill details the exact times he bought drinks. They tally very well with the times you were in the bar.'

'I don't deny I was in the bar,' she said.

Her confidence was beginning to waver. 'There were only half a dozen people in the bar at the time. You were one, Peter Shalcott was another and Alan Platt a third. Do you remember him now?'

It took time for her to respond. 'Where exactly is this leading?' she asked finally.

'That's when you met him, isn't it?'

Again there was a pause. 'And if I did?'

'Then why the lies?' he demanded. 'Why did you make this song and dance about meeting him and not remembering?'

She sat in silence while the question hung heavy in the air.

'Come on, Anita,' he demanded once more, 'why did you lie?'

'Because I didn't want to get involved,' she said quietly.

It sounded too simple. 'Not get involved? Why? What was the big deal that you didn't want to tell us you knew him?'

She looked up sharply. 'Because I knew who he was. He told me all about what he did at the Home Office. When I heard that he'd died of a drugs overdose I knew that there was going to be a big scandal and I didn't want to get caught up in it. That's all there is to it. I just didn't want to get caught up in all the mess.'

'You're caught up in it now,' Manning said, looking up briefly from his notes.

'I know,' she said. 'It was what I was doing my best to avoid.'

She was sounding less and less sure of herself. 'Were you two sleeping together?' Cooper asked.

The question hit her like a slap in the face. She nodded slowly. 'Yes,' she whispered, 'we slept together on Sunday night.'

The rumours had been right all along. It was progress at long last. Vallance was bound to be pleased but Cooper knew that there was more to come. 'You had sex on Sunday night only? Did you spend the night in his room or was it yours?'

'Do we have to go through this?'

The answer was a simple and brutal 'Yes'.

'We met in the bar on Sunday night,' she began. 'It took a while before I realised that I was attracted to him, and he was definitely attracted to me. By the end of the evening I knew that we were going to spend the night together. He asked me to go to his room but I wanted to go to my room instead. That's where we went. We had a drink in my room and then we had sex. He stayed with me until I fell asleep and then when I woke up he was gone.'

'Did he take anything other than alcohol?'

She sounded shocked by the question. 'No, nothing else. He didn't sniff anything or take any pills or anything like that.'

'And what happened the next day?'

'We met at breakfast and I think we both realised it had been a mistake. It was a bit tense but at lunch time we got talking again and we decided that we'd be cool about it. He was married,' she added, 'but I didn't know that on Sunday night.'

'What about you? Are you married?'

'Engaged,' she said softly. 'No one else is going to know about this, are they?'

It was probably time to go easy on her, Cooper decided. 'That depends, but we'll do our best. Did you sleep with him on the Monday night as well?'

'No, I told you. By then I was having second thoughts and I decided to steer clear of him if I could. On the Monday night the woman he works with was around and so I think he was playing it safe too.'

Cooper flicked through the registration details and saw that Sue Beamish had arrived at 11.03 p.m. on the Sunday night, which meant that she hadn't gone to the bar for a drink. If Platt was being discreet then it made sense for him to keep away from Anita when Sue was around on the Monday evening.

'What about the Tuesday lunch time? What was that about?'

'When Sarah Fairfax saw us together? That was nothing, I just wanted to say hello and to find out what he thought of the course.'

'Did you ever go to his room?'

'No. And I didn't lie when I said I didn't know where it was.'

The forensics boys could probably confirm or deny her story. 'We may need to take a set of your fingerprints,' he said. 'Did you notice anything odd about him? He didn't keep disappearing to the toilet, his pupils weren't dilated or anything like that?'

'I saw no signs of drug taking on Sunday night,' she said, 'that's all I can say for sure.'

'Did he talk about any enemies? Was anything troubling him?'

Her confidence was returning. 'No, on Sunday he seemed fine. I mean he seemed more interested in me than in anything else.'

Cooper could believe that. So, it looked like Alan Platt was not the perfect husband and father after all. Adultery was no big deal in the grand scheme of things but it did open other possibilities. Why believe that Anita Walsh was the one and only such indiscretion? Could there be a whole slew of jealous husbands lurking in the shadows?

'You'll have to sign a new statement,' he said. 'And I've no doubt, Miss Walsh, that Chief Inspector Vallance will also want to interview you.'

'I understand,' she said. 'I'm going to be here until late on Sunday night,' she added.

'Why's that?'

'It's Tom Ryder's suggestion. All of us who've had classes disrupted by your investigation have been invited to stay the weekend for extra classes.'

So that explained Ryder's announcement. Cooper was tempted to ask if she knew about Diane Bennett's death but decided that he'd have to wait for the boss to return before he did that.

It had been a difficult phone conversation and even as Sarah sat waiting for Philippa Brady she couldn't help going over it again and again in her mind. It sometimes felt as if every telephone conversation with Duncan was difficult, and often not just the telephone conversations. Not for the first time she pondered on their future together and it looked far from appealing.

He hadn't been happy to hear that the course was being extended across the weekend. The sound of his whining complaint rang in her ears. And when she'd been sharp with him he sulked for a while before accusing her of being glad that it had been extended. She'd denied it vehemently of course, far more vehemently than it deserved. She didn't know what was worse, his whinging complaint or his grovelling apology after she denied wanting to be away from him.

It was a mess and it was becoming harder and harder to extricate herself from it. For goodness sake, Duncan was her fiancé, they were going to get married and live happily ever after. The thought made her blood run cold.

The door to Tom Ryder's office opened and Philippa Brady was there.

'Would you like some coffee?' she asked as Sarah stood up. 'Good. The coffee in here's better than that awful stuff they serve everywhere else. Laura, if you'd be so kind please.'

Sarah followed Philippa into Ryder's office. She half

expected to find him enthroned in the big black leather seat behind the desk but he wasn't there.

'You've had him evicted,' Sarah said, walking across the spacious office to sit in front of the desk.

Philippa smiled as she sank into the heavy leather seat. She looked comfortably in control, as though the space was hers already and she felt no need to prove ownership. 'Not yet. He's had to go to the hospital, there are so many formalities and in the absence of her family it's all falling on him.'

'How's he taking it?'

Philippa shrugged. 'Quite badly. You saw him earlier, he's almost in a state of shock. He and Diane were very close.'

Sarah could guess just how close they were but decided to say nothing. 'I understand that you're helping to handle the media,' she said. 'Is that why you wanted to see me?'

'Yes. Tom has told me a little bit about why you're on the course, but I just wanted to see how that fits with recent events.'

Translation: tell me what you're going to say. Sarah smiled sweetly. 'My job is to report on Tom's management techniques. Alan Platt's death, and now Diane's, aren't really part of my brief.'

It obviously wasn't enough of an answer for Philippa. 'And what are your views on that?' she asked.

Sarah lost her smile instantly. 'As far as I'm aware the British taxpayer doesn't fund Tom Ryder's press and publicity de-artment. Or has that changed suddenly?'

Philippa responded with raised eyebrows and a stony glare. 'I'm interested only in so far as this affects the Home Office. I'm not here to help Tom Ryder's commercial activities. I think it's a reasonable question on my part; I just need to know if you'll be commenting on the two deaths.'

'I'm well aware of the law on *sub judice*.'

'I don't dispute that. I merely want to make sure that we understand each other.'

What was the woman on about? 'I don't think there's anything for us to understand,' Sarah stated. 'I'm here to do a specific job and how I do it and what I say are no concern of yours. Or Tom Ryder's come to that.'

Philippa laughed derisively. 'Of course it's his concern. What you say or do will obviously affect public perceptions of his work.'

'That's still nothing to do with you or with the Home Office.'

'Have pity on the man,' Philippa said. 'He's just lost a dear friend, surely he deserves some consideration.'

It was Sarah's turn to laugh. 'Pity? What the hell does Tom Ryder know about pity? You heard him earlier, using Alan Platt's death as a handy prop in one of his impassioned speeches. Where was his pity then? I've no doubt that had he known of Diane's death then that too would have been an example of chaos in action. Pity? It's the victims' families that deserve our pity not sharks like Tom Ryder.'

'I don't think we've anything more to say to each other,' Philippa said coldly.

'No, I don't think we do. And I'm sure you'll report back faithfully to Tom. It'll do wonders for his paranoia quotient.'

There was a gentle knock at the door. Laura came in with the coffee.

'You're right,' Sarah said, walking to the door and breathing the scent of fresh coffee, 'he keeps the best coffee for his office and serves the crap to the rest of us.'

ELEVEN

It was late afternoon when Vallance arrived back at Ryder Hall with DC Quinn. Conversation between them had been muted on the journey back. The combination of bad news and the heavier traffic killed any mood for conversation, even though a part of Vallance was still attracted to the idea of making a move on Quinn. She was intelligent, good looking and much sharper than the frightened little DC she had first appeared to be.

As she steered the car through the gates of Ryder Hall he was at once aware that time was slipping away rapidly. The course was due to end that afternoon, and when the attendees dispersed it was going to make the investigation that much more difficult. The people on the course had come from all over the country, and so interviewing any of them again was going to become a wearying exercise in logistics.

'Will you be needing me any more, sir?' Quinn asked as she slowed the car to a halt near the main entrance to the building. There were few cars parked at the front. The places there were reserved and the people on the course had to make do with a separate car park to the rear of the building.

'I might need you to do a bit more driving later,' he decided. 'Were you going to be getting back to base?'

'That's up to you, sir.'

'In that case stick around. We might only have a couple of

hours to interview some of these people before they leave.'

He noticed Philippa Brady's car as he got out. He hadn't had a chance to review her statement yet, though he was certain that she would bear Ryder out completely. The primary question remained open: why kill Alan Platt?

'Shall I rustle up some coffee?' Quinn asked as they walked back through the reception area.

'Good idea,' he agreed.'I'll be checking over the latest batch of statements,' he added.

Cooper was already going through the pile of statements when Vallance found him. He had been sitting with his feet up on the table, balanced precariously on the rear legs of the chair as he read through the paperwork. As soon as Vallance walked in he sat up straight again.

'You've heard the news?' he asked, his excitement showing through.

'Diane Bennett?'

'Yes, that and the fact that the course has been extended over the weekend for a set number of people.'

Was it possible that Tom Ryder was doing the police a favour, albeit unwittingly? 'Which people? Our lot?'

Cooper grinned.'Yes, sir. It's good of Tom Ryder to make our life easier.'

'What's in it for him?'

'He thinks it shows what an inspired manager he is, or something.'

'I think it shows what an inspired bullshit artist he is,'Vallance countered. The more he learnt of Tom Ryder the less he liked the man, only now his dislike was starting to become more active. 'What else have you got? What's the story on Philippa Brady?'

'I haven't had a chance to go through it in detail, sir. I had a quick glance and it seems to tie up with Ryder's statement. But I've got better news on Anita Walsh.'

Vallance sat down. Cooper was looking pleased with himself. 'It's true then, she and Platt did have something going?'

Cooper looked deflated.'How did you guess?'

'You wouldn't have looked so happy with yourself if it was anything less. So, what did you get out of her?'

Vallance listened to the story as Cooper related it in detail, right down to cross-referencing the bar bills and the registration details.

'And where does that leave us?' Vallance asked at the end of it.

'It means that we've got a possible motive at last,' Cooper suggested. 'An enraged husband or boyfriend from some previous bit on the side.'

It sounded possible but then why choose Ryder Hall to do the deed? 'Why a previous bit on the side? How's this Anita Walsh fixed? Does she have a boyfriend or husband waiting in the wings?'

'She said she was engaged.'

'Then find him and get his story,' Vallance ordered. He could see the doubt in Cooper's face. 'What's the problem?'

'It's just that I sort of promised that we'd be discreet,' he said, sounding apologetic.

'Make up a story. Get the details from her and then get an alibi from him. Pretend you're checking up on a hit and run or something. Do it soon, we can't afford to take any more time on this. With two murders in one week there's going to be some really jumpy top brass breathing down our necks soon.'

'Yes, sir. How did it go with Sue Beamish?'

'Too well. Every answer was spot on except for one. I'd got the impression that Platt and Ryder were on opposite sides, she tried to give me the opposite story and then back-tracked when I tried to follow up. We need to talk to other people at the Home Office to figure out what's going on there.'

'What about Philippa Brady? Could she fix that up for us?'

Vallance smiled. Brady was no longer an ally but she might be useful. 'I'll have to see if she's still talking to me first. Anything else?'

'Yes, sir. Talking to Anita Walsh was harder than it should have been because she was ready for us. Sarah Fairfax had primed her with all the questions first.'

Vallance nodded. 'I'll sort it out.'

'I've been over her statement again,' Cooper said, pulling it out from the bottom of the pile. 'There's enough holes to sink a battleship and she was there when Platt's body was discovered.'

What the hell was Cooper doing checking up on Sarah? The anger came suddenly and Vallance felt the adrenaline fire through his veins. 'She was there beside me when Diane took a dive,' he said. 'Unless you think I'm not a reliable alibi?'

'That's not what I meant, sir. It's just that she's getting in the way.'

'I said I'll handle it. Understood?'

'Yes, sir, I get the message.'

'There is no bloody message,' Vallance snapped. 'I said I'll handle it, that's all there is to it.'

The door opened at that point and DC Quinn stuck her head round. 'Should I come back later, sir?' she asked, looking from Vallance to Cooper and back again.

'Only if you haven't got any coffee,' Vallance said, his anger falling away suddenly. Why get so uptight over Cooper's comments, especially as the man was justified in what he was saying? If Sarah Fairfax was getting in the way of the investigation then it had to be dealt with before she did some permanent damage.

'I'd better see Anita Walsh again, sir,' Cooper said, getting up as Quinn walked in with beaker full of coffee.

Cooper was clearly affronted. 'Not yet, sergeant,' Vallance said. 'We need to talk this case through a bit more. If Walsh is going to be hanging around through the weekend then you've got time to catch up with her later.'

'Yes, sir,' he said, sitting back down. His face was emotionless, as though he'd shut down or locked himself away.

Quinn was waiting for instructions. Vallance knew that she'd picked up on the tense atmosphere in the room. She couldn't wait to get out. 'I want you to go through Tom Ryder's statement and Philippa Brady's,' he instructed. 'If there's any discrepancy, any inconsistency no matter how trivial I want you to find it.'

Cooper handed her the relevant papers and she exited sharpish. She had the nous to keep out of the way of difficult situations. It was another good sign as far as Vallance was concerned.

'Right, sergeant,' he said, once they were alone again, 'who have you got in your list of suspects?'

'I'm not sure there's enough evidence –'

Vallance waived the objection away. 'Forget evidence. Who's top of your list?'

'Tom Ryder,' came the reply instantly.

Vallance smiled. 'Anyone else?'

'Possibly an unknown husband or boyfriend who'd had enough of Alan Platt.'

'Then why kill Diane Bennett?'

'I knew you were going to ask me that,' Cooper said. 'Either because she knew more about Platt than she was letting on, or because she'd been deliberately set up as the murderer.'

Vallance wanted Cooper to follow it through. 'Which means what?'

'Which means that whoever this unknown bloke is he must be here or must be connected with Ryder's lot in some way.'

Vallance spotted the connection immediately. 'What about Peter Shalcott?'

Cooper laughed. 'You haven't met the man. He's much older than her for a start. He's on another planet most of the time. I mean she's a very pretty girl, why would she, you know, with him?'

It was a good question, but Vallance knew that desire knows no rules and recognises no laws. 'Why is anyone attracted to anyone else?' he asked. 'You've said that she admitted that they arrived here together. And they've both denied knowing each other often enough.'

Cooper looked unconvinced. 'I have to admit, it's a hard one to imagine but I'll have it checked out. You haven't had a chance to interview Shalcott yet, have you?'

'Not yet,' Vallance grinned. 'But if he doesn't check out then I've got that pleasure to look forward to. There's another angle on the jealous partner story which you haven't considered yet.'

'Which is?'

'Vanessa Platt. Perhaps she'd had enough of her husband

straying and decided to put an end to it once and for all.'

'You don't really think that, do you?' Cooper said, looking appalled.

Vallance had seen more than one distraught wife crying crocodile tears over a dead husband. Who would suspect a grieving widow? Gut instinct told him that Vanessa Platt was genuine but that wasn't enough to go on. 'Whether I believe it or not she needs to be alibied. She's got motive, assuming she knows what her dearly beloved got up to when he was away from home, and she might even know who Diane Bennett was, assuming he talked about his work. Get someone to check up on her, only make sure it's discreet.'

'What about Diane Bennett having something going with Platt?' Cooper suggested. 'That gives us motive for both murders.'

He was right. 'Good point,' Vallance said, smiling. 'That might point the finger at Vanessa Platt again, or it might point to your friend and mine, Tom Ryder. We know he plays around but we don't know how he'd feel about one of his women doing the same. Did any of the other Ryder women seem as if she was close to Diane?'

'No, sir, not one.'

It made sense in a sick sort of way. Ryder liked to keep control of his organisation. He'd be wary of close friendships among his key staff just in case they turned out to be alliances that threatened him. 'It figures,' he said. 'If we have to come back to this then Ryder might be the only person who'd know if Platt and Diane were closer than she let on. Or else,' he added, 'we could find out if Sue Beamish suspected anything.'

'And you, sir, who do you suspect? Who do you have on your list?'

'Kate Thurston, Tom Ryder and Sue Beamish.'

'In that order?'

'No, in no particular order,' he said. And then added: 'I'd add Anita Walsh and Peter Shalcott to the list as well.'

'What about their motives?' Cooper asked. He sounded less guarded, as though the affront was beginning to recede into the background.

Vallance shrugged. 'I've not got it all worked out yet,' he admitted. 'But for the moment they're the people we focus on. Get Chiltern or Manning on to forensics; we're getting desperate here.'

The bookshop was located in a small room to one side of the lecture theatre. A large square window shed pale light on to the shelves which lined two of the walls and created sufficient glare on the TV screen that was mounted on the other wall as to obscure the picture of Tom Ryder delivering one of his lectures. The full range of Tom Ryder merchandise was on display: books, magazines, videos, tapes and even a range of computer software.

It was, Sarah decided, a haven for the Tom Ryder junkie. His image was plastered everywhere: on the covers of the books and videos, on the packaging of the computer disks and CDs, on a poster advertising the course. The cult of personality reigned supreme, as though he were a dictator in some part of the world that history had bypassed. It sounded good, she decided, making a mental note to write about the Tom Ryder 'personality cult' in her piece.

As soon as Ellen – tall, blonde, bland and American – had announced 'recess' before the final session of the afternoon Sarah had escaped to the bookshop. Partly it was because she needed space to get away from an increasingly manic-depressive Kate Thurston and partly because she wanted to collect some last-minute materials for research. The shop was going to be closed over the weekend and she didn't fancy having to drive out from London just to pick up a book or a magazine once she'd gone back to write her story.

'Is there anything I can help you with?'

Sarah turned to the assistant who'd just returned to the shop. Not an American blonde for a change; her accent was local though her syntax had been imported.

'I was just looking round,' Sarah told the young woman.

'Well, if there's anything in particular you're looking for then let me know.'

Sarah smiled and then turned back to the bookshelves. There were more than a dozen titles by Ryder as well as a couple of books about him by other people. She picked up the first of those and saw that it had been published by Ryder's organisation, though it hadn't been obvious from the cover. It figured of course. Who else could Tom Ryder trust but his own people? She replaced the book and looked at the second one. It too had been published by Ryder but the book consisted of a series of articles by other people. She was about to put the book back when she glanced at the list of contributors. Diane Bennett's name was half way down the list.

She turned to Diane's article and scanned through it quickly. It seemed to be a brief history of how Ryder's organisation was formed and how it grew. This was the authorised history, the version of events that the early apostles were willing to pass on to their unknown followers. It was all useful stuff. Several of the articles described case studies where Ryder's techniques had been used successfully to steer companies through various crises.

'How much is this one?' Sarah asked, unable to find the cover price anywhere on the book.

The girl looked a bit sheepish. 'It's a bit pricy, that one,' she admitted.

Sarah almost winced at the exorbitant figure when she was told. No wonder he was raking in a fortune.

'It's all right,' the assistant assured her helpfully, 'if you charge it to your company account it'll just be added to your bill at the end of the course. I mean it's not the sort of book you'd buy for yourself, is it?'

The amount was hardly negligible and Sarah knew that accounts were going to query it, but the hassle had to be worth it. 'You're right,' she agreed. 'Is this one popular?'

'They're all popular,' the assistant said. 'Would you like anything else? The videos are useful.'

'No. Do you have anything else? Something less expensive, preferably.'

The girl grinned. 'We've got some of the books in older editions,' she offered. 'They might be a bit tatty but they're still worth reading.'

Sarah had a quick look at the dog-eared books but none seemed as interesting as her find. 'What about some of the brochures?' she asked. It might be useful to have some of the glossies for stills or for quoting from.

It was only after she had returned to her room loaded down with a pile of brochures, catalogues and other promotional material that Sarah made the connection. Quickly she dumped the brochures on her bed and then flicked through the over-priced book. There were ten contributors listed in the book, excluding Tom Ryder himself who'd written the introduction, and four of them were connected to the pharmaceuticals industry. The two case studies were both for drug companies. Diane included a brief sketch of her work in medical research and one other contributor was listed as working in an American teaching hospital.

This was where Kate Thurston had picked up on Diane's medical background. She had boasted before of having read everything by and about Ryder. So why had she kept the knowledge secret instead of trumpeting it immediately, like every other piece of gossip? Why had Kate waited for so long before blurting out what she had known from the beginning?

There wasn't time enough to read the book properly. The next session was about to start. None of the contributors to the book were English, that much was obvious, but it made her wonder just how closely Ryder was working with the UK drug companies. She flipped through a couple of the brochures before she found what she was looking for: a list of British corporate clients. It was an impressive list of blue-chip companies, and drugs and pharmaceuticals were very well represented.

She glanced at her watch. The session was probably already starting. She dumped the brochures on her bed and hurried out. There was a connection, somehow, between Tom Ryder and the drug industry and she was certain that it was significant. The only problem was to find the connection and then understand its significance.

What's more, she thought, rushing down to her class, it was a connection that Anthony Vallance hadn't stumbled on.

Vallance was half way through the pile of statements when Anne Quinn came rushing in to see him. She was clutching

187

the statements she had taken with her earlier.

'What have you found?' Vallance asked, quietly pleased to see her again.

'There's a mismatch in the times that Ryder and Brady have given about their movements on the night Diane Bennett was pushed.'

'How much of a mismatch?' he asked, afraid to let himself get too hopeful. Misplaced enthusiasm was acceptable in a young, ambitious DC. In a DCI with a dodgy reputation it was downright obscene.

'Forty-five minutes, give or take ten minutes,' she said. 'She says they met at a restaurant for dinner between nine and half-past. He says it was earlier, at around 8.30. If we split the difference that means there's forty-five minutes that are missing.'

'We don't split the difference,' Vallance warned, trying not to let his excitement show. 'The most we can say is that there's half an hour missing. It might sound a lot but people can be really imprecise about times.'

But not Philippa Brady, he wanted to add. She was not the type to lose half an hour. And neither was Tom Ryder.

Quinn sounded disappointed. 'Half an hour?'

'How far's this restaurant?'

'It's the Les Amoureux, it's about fifteen or twenty miles from here.'

Vallance had never heard of the place, but he knew that it was probably way out of his league price-wise. 'Twenty miles along straight road or along country lanes or what? How long would it take to drive there?'

Quinn shrugged. 'I'm not sure, sir. If it was forty-five minutes then I'm sure he'd have time to make it easily.'

'We'll have to find out later tonight. I told you that you might have to do a bit more driving for me,' he added. 'Well done, by the way. Now, see if you can find anything else in these statements that doesn't add up.'

The smile on her face disappeared when he handed over the half dozen statements he had already been through.

Although Tom Ryder still looked authoritative and composed on stage, Sarah immediately recognised that something had changed in him. The technique which she had so much admired at the beginning of the week failed him miserably. The words were all there: chaos, turbulence, inspiration, control. But now they sounded like stale formulae instead of grand concepts and pointers to a better future.

For most of the audience this was to be the end of the week-long course. They had been through a day of tests and questionnaires followed by four long days of role playing and classes and now, to gather it all together, Tom Ryder was supposed to be weaving his spell again. Rather than a *dénouement* his final talk was turning into a damp squib which failed to do anything except for the small core of purists like Kate Thurston.

Sarah sat back and let the words pour over her. Without the grand oration and the passion, Tom Ryder was just another salesman. It was apt of course, and she scribbled the note down quickly. Just another salesman. And his biggest and best product was himself. He was letting himself down badly, though. It wasn't a performance to be proud of, and certainly not one to act as an advertisement for his theories and his courses.

For a moment he paused, giving himself time and space before launching into the next part of his summing-up speech. It should have been a dramatic pause, a rhetorical trick to build the tension but instead it served to highlight his sudden and unexpected failure of nerve. His eyes darted through the audience, as though in search of someone or something. Tired eyes, Sarah noticed, without the hardness of self-control that touched everything he looked at. Perhaps he was gauging just how badly he was doing. That was one of the techniques that they'd been shown in class. It was time to change gear, 'to push on the gas pedal' as Diane had put it.

Diane was dead. The thought jolted Sarah back to the moment. Was that why he was messing up so badly? Had the realisation finally dawned on him that she was dead, deceased, gone forever?

'There isn't a man alive who can say what tomorrow brings!'

She sighed inwardly. He was indulging his passion for stating the obvious in the most banal terms possible. Had she already made notes on that? She flicked through her notebook quickly, only half listening as he continued in similar vein. He hadn't pushed on the gas pedal. His speech was continuing in the same gear, there had been no change in direction or pace or rhythm. He was looking more and more desperate up on stage, as though he could sense that he was losing his audience but could see no way of winning them back.

Kate Thurston was sitting a few seats from Sarah. Her expression changed from moment to moment, one second delighting in the words of wisdom and the next filled with concern as she saw her hero faltering. It was a measure of how bad things had become that even Kate was beginning to show signs of restlessness. She was still on the edge of her seat, but this time it was because she was worried about Tom and not because she was entranced by him.

Sarah looked to the wings. It was where Diane Bennett used to stand and wait, gazing adoringly at Tom and waiting with quiet anticipation for the moment when he'd finish and she'd rush to his side. Her place had been taken by Sally, a younger and less intelligent version of Diane, and by Philippa Brady. What was Brady doing there? It annoyed Sarah that Brady should be there, lending support in that way. Tom Ryder was a businessman, making a fortune by the look of things, why should he have the support of a civil servant funded by the taxpayer?

'And we've shown them, haven't we, ladies and gentleman? We've shown that in spite of the worst kind of events, in spite of the most chaotic conditions, we've carried on through,' Ryder was saying. 'Let's be honest here,' he continued, 'there's times it would have been easier for Tom Ryder to say: "Hey, this is just too much! Let's just call it quits now." But that's not the way Tom Ryder works. I won't give people that satisfaction.'

He was being paranoid again. It made Sarah wonder who the nefarious 'people' were. Who did he perceive as enemies and what did he imagine that they had done? There was a streak of paranoia that ran through most things he said, and in the beginning she had hardly been aware of it except in the vaguest sense. Now it made her feel uneasy. Paranoia on that scale was dangerous, and at the very least it was evidence of an ego that had outgrown any kind of rational control.

'Together we've worked through things,' he was saying. 'We've shown, together, all of us, that inspiration works. Inspiration is what put men on the moon. Inspiration is what puts music in our hearts. Inspiration reveals the key to the universe. Inspiration can make a difference. You, ladies and gentleman, know how to be inspired and how to become the most effective and efficient people in your organisations. That's it, ladies and gentleman, thank you all for being with us and we thank you for helping us to learn along the way as well. Thank you.'

The applause was perfunctory but he accepted it gratefully. He stood on the edge of the stage and smiled weakly at his audience, the sweat falling freely from his brow. Sally was beside him ready to dab away at the perspiration and to whisper whatever words of encouragement or congratulation his ego desired.

Kate was standing up, applauding furiously, her eyes fixed on Tom Ryder with a look of wonder. It was as if she had not noticed, or had chosen to forget, his dismal performance. She was not alone. Sarah could see the rest of his devoted following doing the same, but this time they were outnumbered by the people who sat in their seats waiting for the moment when they'd be able to escape. For most of them there was the long journey home to look forward to, and for a few there was the promise of two more days cloistered in Ryder Hall to ponder.

Sarah filed out slowly, wondering whether to chance another phone call to Duncan. She knew that she'd hurt him by refusing to go home and that a quick apologetic phone call would clear the air for the rest of the week. On the other hand she knew that he'd be impossibly grateful to her and that his fawning behaviour would drive her to blind rage once more. Did he really imagine that they'd ever get married? Sometimes she hated herself for her moment of weakness in saying yes to his proposal.

'Sarah? A quick drink later?'

She turned to Kate, who'd followed her out of the lecture theatre. 'Yes, sure,' she agreed instantly. A drink in the bar would be a chance to do more research and if it meant no phone call home it couldn't be helped.

Kate smiled. 'Good,' she said.

'What did you think of Tom's performance?'

Kate exhaled heavily. 'The poor man,' she said quietly. 'It can't have been easy for him, really. What with Alan Platt's murder and this with Diane. Any other man would have just given up and handed over to one of his assistants. You've got to admire his dedication, haven't you?'

Sarah smiled politely. A woman like Kate was a hopeless case.

Quinn opened the door to Diane's room and stepped aside. The SOCO team had marked out a safe path through the room, delineating those areas which were still of interest to forensics. Vallance stood on the threshold for a moment. It still felt like Diane's room: her presence was there in the arrangement of the furniture, in the pictures that cluttered up her dressing table, in the scent that hung in the air, in the books that were forced across bookshelves heaving under the strain.

'Shall I start the clock now?' Quinn asked.

He turned back to her. She was eager to get on with the reconstruction and she had her stop-watch ready to begin clocking up the seconds. 'When I give the word,' he said and then turned back to the room.

It was a pitifully small room and he felt a sense of claustrophobia as he tried to picture Diane's life in it. There was so little space, so little room to live and breathe. How did she stand it? How did any of them stand it? Vallance had no doubt that Ryder's quarters were vast in comparison and furnished with an eye to style and comfort with money no object. Diane was his most senior assistant, surely he could have allowed her more space?

He stepped into the room finally. It was time to reconstruct the sequence of events which lead to Diane's fall from the window. In his mind he had worked it out again and again but now that he and Quinn were to act it out he felt less sure of the scenario.

'There were no signs of struggle,' he said, walking carefully between the taped lines to the window. It was closed now but it had been wide open when Diane fell. 'No scuff marks on the floor, nothing turned over in the room, no drink splattered over the carpet except here under the window sill.'

'She obviously knew her killer and trusted him or her completely.'

'Or else the murderer was already in the room and she didn't hear him,' Vallance suggested. 'Perhaps whoever planted the drugs was still here when she returned.'

'Have forensics turned up anything?'

'The usual collection of fibres and dust but nothing that points to a murderer. So, let's assume Diane came in. She was angry after her argument with Kate Thurston. She comes to the window to get some air and to have a drink to calm her nerves. The murderer's already here, hiding. He or she emerges from the shower or the toilet, creeps up on her and then gives her an almighty shove to send her over the edge. Does it sound plausible?'

Quinn nodded. 'Yes, sir. The shower or the toilet, there's nowhere else to hide in here really, is there?'

'The wardrobe could take a person but it's jammed solid with clothes,' he explained. 'It must have been a struggle for her to get anything in or out of it. That really only leaves the shower or the toilet, and before you ask, there's nothing that forensics have found in either.'

'What if she knew the person and had invited him or her into the room for a chat?'

It was an equally valid scenario and one that Vallance had not discounted. It did nothing to narrow the field in terms of suspects; they were all known to Diane Bennett. 'I haven't dismissed that as a theory,' he admitted. 'But then what about the drugs planted in the room? There wouldn't have been time to plant them after Diane had been pushed. And in a room this size it's likely that Diane would have found anything that had been planted for more than a day or two. Which suggests that they were planted on the day she was killed.'

Quinn seemed satisfied with the explanation. 'Shall we begin now?' she asked, not bothering to hide her impatience.

Vallance took one last look at the window, guessing that it wouldn't have taken too much force to push Diane over the low edge. One hard, unexpected push and Diane had plummeted.

'Start the clock now,' he said.

He turned quickly and then jogged the few steps required to get himself out of the room and into the corridor. It was deserted, just as it had been on the night itself. He paused momentarily, glancing quickly just to make sure that the coast was clear and then ran along the corridor to the door marked FIRE. He shoved against it with his shoulder, the door clicked and then gave way. It was dark but not pitch and he glanced down the winding stairs to the bottom.

With Quinn close behind him he ran down into the darkness. Down one flight, turn, down the next, turn and down again and again until he was on the ground floor. The fire door was closed but he pushed hard against the bar and it sprang open without protest. The cool night air was a welcome blast against his face and he sucked it down quickly.

No one had seen him yet, and he in turn had seen no one but Quinn, as close to him as his shadow. He let the fire door slam shut behind him as he set off across the grounds. He jogged easily over the lush moist lawn, glancing back at the big house as it receded from him. There were lights on here and there but already it seemed as though the entire house slept soundly. On the night in question lights were beginning to snap on as people realised what had happened but who would have thought to look out across the dark expanse of the grounds for someone fleeing the scene of the crime?

'How am I doing?' he asked breathlessly as he stopped at the perimeter wall. His lungs felt on fire but that was because he was a lazy slob and not because the run had been especially arduous.

'Just under five minutes,' Quinn replied, flashing a light across the face of her stop-watch.

He edged along the perimeter wall in the darkness until he found the door he was looking for. Recessed into the wall and stiff with age it was an exit that Quinn had found earlier. He pushed hard and it creaked open a fraction for him to slip through. It should have been locked but someone had forced it open and not bothered to repair the mechanism. Forensics had been on to it immediately and had taken pictures and samples so it was safe to use it.

The door opened out on to a wooded section of the road that ran parallel to Ryder Hall. There were few street lights but Vallance saw the unmarked police car waiting for them. Would Ryder have left his car here on the night?

He jogged to the car and then slumped into the passenger seat gratefully. His part of the reconstruction was over at last. There was no point in his driving the car with his sense of direction. Quinn was in the driving seat and starting the car before he'd even slammed his door shut. She accelerated away with a satisfying screech of rubber.

'Remind me to see if we can get witnesses to the car driving away,' he murmured.

Quinn's attention was firmly on the road. She drove at high speed along the narrow lane and then out on to the dual carriageway. Traffic was busy but not so heavy that she couldn't hop from lane to lane, picking up speed – and collecting dirty looks from other drivers. He made a note to see if there were any relevant traffic reports from the evening of the murder. If the murderer had driven the way Quinn was driving then perhaps he or she had annoyed someone enough to complain to the police.

He kept glancing at his watch as she drove. He had no idea where they were going but the minutes were ticking away. 'How far have we got left?' he asked as they jumped a light turning from amber to red.

'Nearly there,' Quinn told him, steering the car off the main road and on to another narrow lane.

They drove in silence, passing few cars coming in the other direction and easily overtaking anyone going their way. At the first junction they were back in the land of the living. They turned on to a main road, sped along it and then stopped suddenly.

'This is it,' Quinn announced.

The restaurant was there in front of them.

'How long?' he asked.

'Thirty-eight minutes, give or take a few seconds.'

'Time enough for Tom Ryder to kill and still make his date,' Vallance said.

TWELVE

There was no news from Ryder Hall. Cooper was still trying to track down more on Anita Walsh and Peter Shalcott. Tom Ryder had given his closing speech to end the course officially, though a small group were going to be staying on over the weekend. There had been nothing new from forensics. Vallance finished making the call to Ryder Hall, switched off the mobile phone and turned to DC Quinn.

'Where next, sir?' she asked.

She had dark brown almond-shaped eyes that sparkled with excitement. Speeding along breaking every traffic law in the book was precisely the sort of police work that appealed to young and ambitious officers and she was no exception. It easily beat slogging through witness statements, doing house-to-house enquiries or handling bits of dead bodies.

'I think we call it a day,' he said. It had been a long, hard day at that and the accumulated tiredness was beginning to kick in. The adrenaline rush of speeding through the streets in reconstructing Ryder's movements – or possible movements – was starting to wear off.

'Yes, sir,' Quinn said, not bothering to hide the note of disappointment in her voice.

'Of course we could race back to Ryder Hall in an effort to break a new speed record,' he suggested. 'If we're lucky we can get chased by some of the lads from traffic; there's nothing they like better than nicking one of their own.'

She grinned. 'It's all right, sir,' she said, 'if we get caught I can always blame it on my superior officer.'

'You catch on quick,' he said, leaning back in his seat to gaze at the expensive French restaurant in front of the car. He was starving again but he knew that a meal for two in Les Amoureux was out of the question. 'Are you hungry?' he asked.

'Yes, sir.'

'Do you know anywhere round here that's any good?'

She shrugged. 'It depends on what you want. Indian, Chinese, Italian, burgers –'

'What do you fancy?'

She looked at him and smiled. 'Are lowly Detective Constables allowed to eat with Chief Inspectors, sir?'

'Only on direct orders, Constable Quinn.'

'Yes, sir,' she said, her smile wavering. Her dark eyes were locked on his and he could see that she was suddenly nervous.

'Where shall we eat?'

'There's a nice little Italian place near my sister's flat,' she said. 'It's about fifteen minutes from here.'

'You don't have to eat with me if you don't want to,' he said, losing his smile. 'If you want to drop me off there that's fine, I'll get a cab home.'

'I do want to eat with you, sir,' she replied quietly.

'Is there a boyfriend or a husband I should know about?'

She started the car as she answered. 'There's a boyfriend,' she admitted. 'But you don't need to know about him, sir.'

Vallance kept the smile from his face. 'Good,' he said. 'We'd better get going then.'

Detective Sergeant Cooper was standing just inside the bar when Sarah arrived. He heard the doors swing open and turned to look at her. His cold eyes fixed on her and she could feel his intense dislike of her radiating across the room. As always he wore an expression that mixed dark suspicion with angry belligerence. She looked at him disdainfully and then walked right past him, knowing that her haughty attitude would anger him still further.

The atmosphere in the room was far brighter than it had been for days. It looked as if a number of people had decided to stay for a last drink or two before heading home. She had imagined that only those people staying over for the rest of the weekend would bother coming up for a drink but there were too many people for that. There seemed to be a palpable sense of relief in the air. It had been a long week and some people at least were making sure it ended on a high.

Kate was sitting in the far corner of the room with a group of people that she had shared classes with. A pall of cigarette smoke hung over them and the table was already stacked high with empty glasses. Was Kate going to get drunk again? The idea of it made Sarah's heart sink. The idea of having to look after her again was distinctly unappealing. With everything that had happened, she knew that Kate would get maudlin and start bemoaning her fate or else she'd launch into some unprovoked attack on a hapless victim.

With relief Sarah saw Peter Shalcott walk towards her.

'Are you staying for extra tuition too?' he asked.

She turned and saw that Sergeant Cooper was glaring at them. The man was making no attempt to hide his dislike and it annoyed her intensely. Did DCI Vallance know how his subordinate was acting?

'Yes I am, Peter,' she said, taking him by the arm. 'Shall we sit down?'

'Of course, of course,' he said, looking around the room for a convenient place.

She waited for a second and then realised that he was gazing across the room without actually seeing anything. It was as though he'd already forgotten what he was doing.

'Over there,' she suggested, nodding towards a small table near the door to the toilets.

Cooper was still watching them when they sat down. He had obviously been looking for someone too but had drawn a blank. Sarah met his eyes for a second and then looked away dismissively. A second later she looked and Cooper was on his way out.

'So you're staying for extra tuition,' she said, facing Peter properly.

'Oh yes,' he agreed readily. 'I'm not sure what the topics are going to be mind you.'

'No, neither do I,' she agreed. 'Medical research perhaps?'

The old boy's face brightened at the prospect. 'Not sure that this Ryder chap's the man to do it,' he said.

'Who would you suggest?'

He furrowed his brow thinking through his list of candidates. 'I understand that Bertie Atkins still does a course on quantitative analysis, I'd say he's the man for the job. Not so hot on computer simulation; it's all the rage these days you know.'

He was speaking clearly and rationally again, a different person to the absent-minded old boy who seemed to lose track mid sentence. The change from one to the other was always instant, as though he switched from one side of his personality to another. The trick, Sarah decided, was to keep him talking on a subject he was interested in.

'What about Ryder?' she asked. 'You don't think he'd be any good lecturing on medical research?'

'Ryder? Not at all. He was hopeless in the field. Got nowhere of course, which is why he switched to teaching.'

Sarah resisted the temptation to rush forward with the endless questions the revelation triggered inside her. 'Was Diane any better?' she asked.

'Diane Bennett? Not first-class material,' he judged, 'but then again she dropped out of it fairly quickly.'

'You knew them both?'

Peter looked at her strangely. 'Who?'

She sensed that his defences were starting to rise. 'I understand that Ryder's still closely linked in to research,' she said hastily.

'Ryder linked to research?' he repeated, as though the idea were preposterous.

'Isn't that the case?'

'I'm sorry,' he said, 'but as far as I know he only teaches about management theory now. Not that it's a real discipline you understand.'

'Did Ryder ever work with Alan Platt?'

Peter smiled. 'The dead chap? Yes, of course.'

At last! Progress! 'When? On what?'

'Here of course. Ryder was teaching Mr Platt about the management of things. It's quite interesting you know, this chaos theory. Interesting maths but I'm not sure that Ryder's up to it.'

Sarah looked at him sharply. 'Peter,' she said, looking him directly in the eye, 'I want you to be honest with me. Tell me what you know about Alan Platt and Tom Ryder.'

He held her gaze for a while and she saw the expression change and mutate, growing clearer for a second and then becoming more distant. 'Tell me!' she said, grabbing him by the shoulder forcefully. 'I've had enough of this stupid game! What's going on?'

'Games? Not more of these games? When are we going to get some hard science?'

It was hopeless. He knew more than he was letting on, much more. It was infuriating because she knew that he wasn't putting it on. There were two Peter Shalcott's and the one with the answers always retreated behind the doddery old fool when things got interesting.

It was towards the end of the meal that Anne Quinn let slip the fact that her sister was away for the weekend. She didn't need to say that her sister's flat would be empty and available. Vallance made no comment, there was no need to. It had been a good meal; the food was good, the wine better and Detective Constable Quinn had become Anne Quinn. He in turn had stopped being DCI Vallance and had allowed her to call him Tony. It was a gamble that she'd be able to revert back to him being DCI Vallance later on, but not much of a gamble as she was too bright not to know the difference.

The conversation had skirted the difficult issues: the case, his failed marriage and her boyfriend that he didn't need to know about. It helped that she combined a flirtatious attitude with a sense of humour that coincided with his. The fact that she was London born and bred probably helped, he decided.

The air was cool and bracing when they emerged from the restaurant late in the evening. He stood on the edge of the pavement breathing the cold air deep into his lungs.

'Is your sister's flat far from here?' he asked, turning to face Anne.

'A two-minute drive,' she said.

The flat was in a small purpose-built block at the end of a narrow cul-de-sac. Vallance sat in silence as Anne manoeuvred the car into a tight space along the kerb. He kept glancing at her, wondering whether he was doing the right thing or not. If he had any sense he'd kiss her goodnight and then get a cab back to the Fox. Messing around with junior officers was not a good career move. He knew that. He knew it just as he knew that he'd not be able to stop at just a kiss.

'We're here,' she said, turning to face him after switching the engine off. The car was shrouded in darkness, with even the brightness of the moon obscured by a row of trees that lined one side of the narrow street.

He looked at her in the darkness, trying to work out was going on in her eyes that were hidden by shadow. 'I can piss off home if you want me to,' he said, finally.

'Did I say I wanted that?' she asked.

She moved forward, closer to him so that he could look into her dark brown eyes. He reached out and touched her, his fingers travelling down her cheek to her throat. When he pulled her closer she came to him, her lips open to his. They kissed just once, long and slow, and then he released her.

'Let's go up,' he said softly.

He followed her from the car and up the single flight of stairs to her sister's first-floor flat. She fumbled with the key for a second and then the door was open to a narrow hall that was littered with children's toys.

'My niece,' Anne explained, kicking away the bright plastic shapes strewn across their path.

He followed her into the living room and flicked on the light. The room had a comfortable, lived-in feel to it, with the walls dotted with framed family pictures, more toys stacked untidily in a corner and a glass-topped coffee table around which the sofa and armchairs were arranged.

Anne surveyed the room quickly, slipped off her jacket and threw it over the arm of a chair and then turned to him. 'Do you want some coffee?' she asked.

Coffee? Why was she playing that game? He looked at her coolly, fixing her with his eyes, holding her in place. 'No. I want you.'

She smiled nervously and looked away.

'I mean it,' he said, his voice lower. He stepped towards her and took her by the hand. She looked up into his eyes and he saw the excitement clearly in hers. He put his hands on her shoulders and held her for a moment, gazing at her intently.

When they kissed she gave herself to it, parting her lips as his tongue pushed forcefully into her mouth. He held her close, pushing their bodies together, breathing her scent as he pulled his face away from hers. Her face was flushed and she was breathing hard, her moist lips still parted.

'Where's the bedroom?'

'Across the hall, sir,' she whispered.

Sir? Why had he stopped being Tony? 'Don't call me that,' he said, looking from her to the door. He guessed that the blue door on the other side of the hall led to the bedroom.

'I want to,' she whispered, her face flushing red suddenly. 'Let me call you sir. Please?'

He smiled. She was embarrassed. If that's what she wanted – 'Show me where the other room is,' he ordered.

She looked at him with wide, brown eyes and then turned. He followed her, aware of her excitement and finding that it triggered something in him too. The bedroom was cramped but tidy, the big double bed filling the room so that there was hardly space to move. She walked over to the dressing table quickly and turned down a framed picture of her sister's family.

'Come here,' he said, keeping the hard edge to his voice.

'Yes, sir,' she said quietly.

He held her by the waist and kissed her forcefully, pushing open her lips with his tongue, sucking hard at her breath. His hands were tight around her waist and he could feel her body against his. He squeezed tighter and felt her respond immediately. When he pulled back she moved towards him, as though afraid to lose him.

'Do you still want coffee?' he asked, smiling.

'No. You know what I want.'

'Tell me,' he said. She was evasive, looking away from him,

unable to answer. He held her under the chin and forced her to look at him, waiting until her eyes met his before speaking again. 'Tell me,' he demanded coldly.

'I want you, sir,' she said, the colour still in her cheeks and the excitement in her eyes.

'What does that mean?'

'Please – do I have to do this, sir?'

He smiled. 'Yes, you have to. I want to know, I want you to tell me.'

'I want you to make love to me, sir.'

'You want me to fuck you, don't you?' he said, brutally.

She tried to nod but her face was fixed into position. 'Yes, sir,' she whispered. 'I want you to fuck me. Please. Sir.'

He let go of her and she bowed her head once more. Very slowly he began to unbutton her blouse, taking care not to fumble or to appear too excited. Her dark blue top contrasted with the creamy whiteness of her skin and the white lace of her bra. When the last button was undone he gently slipped the blouse from her shoulders and let it fall to the floor. At last she looked at him, sneaking a nervous glance before bowing her head again.

What next? She looked so vulnerable, so innocent and yet so sexual that it made his cock bulge painfully. He touched her softly, running his fingers across her shoulder so that he could hold the back of her neck. She was trembling slightly, as though afraid of what was to follow.

'Will you do as you're told?' he asked.

She nodded but as he tightened his hand on her neck she whispered 'Yes' in a voice so quiet he could have imagined it.

He lifted her face towards him and kissed her soft, warm mouth. She responded with a half-whispered sigh and then he pushed his tongue between her lips. She put her arms around him tentatively, holding on to him as he kissed her passionately.

'Hands down,' he ordered harshly, pulling away from the kiss while she was still open to it.

Her hands fell to her sides instantly and she looked away. Her nipples were dark, hard discs that pushed against the white lace of her bra. He smiled as he stroked each one in turn, brushing his fingers over the protrusions in the lace so that she moaned softly with pleasure. It seemed as if the harsher he became the more she responded.

He slipped her bra straps over her shoulders, sliding each one down towards her elbows but without undoing it. A black bra would have been better, he thought, the straps would have been perfect against her pale skin. As it was the straps were tight over her arms, restraining her field of movement so that she could not easily lift her arms. It turned him on to think of her held in place by her own garments; the idea had never occurred to him before but now it excited him immensely.

She was wearing a long skirt that reached down to her ankles. It was sensible of course, and it stopped anyone leering at her long legs but all day he'd been wondering what she wore underneath it. He began to pull it up gently, gathering the material in his hands as it rose higher and higher. Her legs were smooth and well shaped, tanned slightly and toned by regular exercise. He lifted the skirt higher, inching it slowly above the knee to enjoy the sight of her thighs emerging from under the dark shroud.

Her panties were snow white and pushed tightly into the bulge of her sex. He held the skirt high for a minute, enjoying both the look of her exposed body and the red blush on her face. She was embarrassed but not enough to get in the way of her excitement. Somewhere in the back of his head he was wondering why he felt so in control and asking how he could be so sure of what she felt, but for the moment he just knew what to do and that was all that mattered.

'Hold this,' he said, indicating that she should hold her skirt up for him.

She obeyed at once, taking the bunched-up hem of her skirt in her hands. He stepped back to get a better look and then walked around her slowly, admiring her long legs and the pert roundness of her backside. Her skin was smooth and unblemished and it was a pleasure to stroke her with the tips of his fingers. He slid his hand between her legs and stroked softly, enjoying the feel of her inner thigh and pushing gently against the moist warmth of her panties.

'Are you wet?' he asked, walking round to face her again, his hand on her inner thigh.

'Yes, sir,' she whispered, closing her eyes rather than look at him.

He allowed himself a smile at last. She was enjoying every minute of the game.

'Why are you wet?' he demanded, sliding a single finger under her panties.

She gasped for breath as he touched her pussy lips, teasing gently between the puffy labia and towards the liquid evidence of her desire. 'Because I – because I want to be fucked, sir.'

He pushed his finger into the moist heat of her sex, felt the wetness and then withdrew as she moved towards him. She wanted him to touch her, to push his fingers into her sex, to give her pleasure there and then. Too greedy, he decided, she would have to wait. He stepped back and she looked at him with wide, disappointed eyes.

'What?' he demanded angrily.

She started to say something and then changed her mind.

'Undress for me,' he ordered.

Again she obeyed without question. He watched her dispassionately as she undid her skirt and then let it fall to the floor around her ankles. She stepped out of it and then reached up to undo her bra. She hesitated for a moment, mock coyness in her eyes as she held the white lace to her chest. One look from him was enough to make her change her mind. She dropped her bra to the floor and then pulled her panties off so that she stood before him naked.

Her breasts were peaked with dark nipples that were fully erect and aching to be touched and teased. The dark tangle of hair between her thighs was neatly trimmed and covered a pussy that he knew was wet with pleasure and excitement. She was waiting for him, waiting for his order, waiting to obey. To obey. That was what she found most exciting. Command and obey, it seemed to be an aphrodisiac more potent than any he'd ever found before.

He moved to the bed and began to undress himself. Should he get her to undress him? It would only take one order, one command delivered with a hard edge to his voice and she'd be down on all fours begging to please him. Maybe that was going too far? He didn't know and rather than risk destroying the moment he stripped off slowly. It felt as if the whole experience were balanced on a knife edge. There was something intense and brittle between them and the wrong word or action might ruin the whole thing.

When he was naked he turned to her. His cock was hard, jutting from between his thighs, the glans already slick with silvery fluid.

He swallowed hard before issuing the next order. 'Get down on your hands and knees,' he whispered hoarsely.

She did as she was told and then crawled towards him, her lithe body moving with a feline elegance as she crossed the room on all fours. She stopped in front of him and waited, looking up at him expectantly, a look of fire in her eyes.

He grabbed a handful of her hair and pulled her face towards his hard cock. 'I want you to suck me,' he said threateningly. 'Understand?'

'Yes, sir,' she responded weakly, 'I'll suck you.'

Her lips on his cock felt like heaven as she kissed him gently before licking away the jewels of fluid that leaked from the slit. She licked slowly and then moved her mouth lower, rubbing her lips softly from the glans down to the base of his hardness. There was no hurry in her movements, she was going to make sure he enjoyed every second of it. She licked and kissed her way back up towards the glans and then stopped to look at him, her mouth slightly parted and her eyes full of questions.

'That's it,' he said, 'suck it properly now.'

She closed her lips around his glans, taking it into the warmth of her mouth and tracing the underside with her tongue. He inhaled sharply, the pleasure passing through him in a wave of pure sensation. She moved up on to her hands and knees and then plunged her head over his cock, taking it deep into her mouth. She moved up and down slowly and then faster as she gained confidence, making him moan softly with pleasure.

She seemed to think nothing of her own pleasure, it was as though she were completely focused on the act of pleasuring him. She withdrew completely and then let him push his hardness back into her mouth, fucking her between the lips in a wild, passionate motion. He grabbed her by the hair and steered her into place, holding her in position as he fucked her rhythmically, forcing his hardness against her tongue and deep into her mouth.

The pleasure grew more intense and he knew that he was moments from orgasm. He gasped and then pulled her away quickly, tugging sharply at her hair so that she cried out in pain. For a moment he felt lost and out of control but then the second passed and he looked down at her, there in front of him on her hands and knees. Her face was red and her breasts and upper chest were flushed pink with pleasure.

'Why?' she asked softly, the disappointment clear in her voice.

'I didn't want to come in your mouth,' he said, still breathing hard.

'But I wanted you to do that,' she said, 'I wanted you to fuck me in the mouth, sir. I wanted you to make me swallow your come.'

She wasn't joking. She really did get off on being told what to do.

'Get on the bed,' he ordered.

He watched her get up off the floor. She looked vulnerable and nervous again. She lay down on the bed, face down, her backside lifted slightly. He passed his hand down her back, marvelling in the smoothness of her skin and the contours of her body. When he reached under and touched her pussy she moaned softly. Her pussy was running with her juices and she moved towards him, lifting her backside higher, opening her sex to his fingers.

'Do you know what I'm going to do now?' he asked.

'No, sir,' she said, closing her eyes as his fingers pushed deeper into her pussy.

'I'm going to fuck you hard,' he whispered hoarsely.

She moaned softly as he continued to fuck her sex with his fingers. Her voice was a soft, quiescent murmur of pleasure that echoed the movement of his fingers between her pussy lips. He moved round and slipped his other hand under her belly, reaching round to find the apex of her sex. He began to tease her clit in long, slow strokes that matched the motion of his fingers penetrating her wet slit. She clutched at the bed wildly, turning her head from side to side as the pleasure grew more intense. He began to kiss her on the back of the neck, and then moved round to bite her neck and shoulder as her cries of bliss became more insistent. She screamed her climax as his fingers pushed into her sex and her clit throbbed under the fingers of his other hand.

He pushed her over on to her back and waited for her to open her eyes. She looked dazed, sleepy almost and her chest rose and fell as she breathed deeply. He leant over and kissed her softly.

'That was so good,' she whispered, putting her arms around him to draw him closer.

'We're not finished yet,' he told her, pushing her hands over her head.

'But –'

He got up on hands and knees and pulled her towards his hard cock. Her eyes were fixed on the thick, veined flesh of his erection.

'Now I'm going to fuck you in the mouth properly,' he said.

She touched her lips to his hardness. 'Yes, sir,' she sighed, opening her mouth obediently.

Sarah breathed a sigh of relief as she managed to get out of the bar without attracting Kate's attention. It had been touch and go for a while but luckily Kate had been side-tracked by extended farewells from some of the people leaving the course. She was busy swapping addresses and phone numbers when Sarah had last seen her. No doubt she was the sort of person who swapped phone numbers and life stories with the strangers she met on holiday too.

There were more important things to think about than Kate Thurston. Much more important. Like who killed Alan Platt and Diane Bennett.

Her room was a haven of peace after the noise of the bar. She locked the door quickly, poured herself a juice from the mini-bar and then fished out her notes. The answers were all there, written down but locked away somehow, the clues noted down at random so that a pattern had yet to emerge. But now, perhaps, the time was right to tease out the story that she should have been looking for from the beginning.

She found her original list of keywords for Tom Ryder: mesmerising, evangelical, sexy. After his closing speech she had listed a new set of words: formulaic, unconvincing, paranoid. The difference was startling. It was as though she were writing about two entirely different people. Was that significant? On its own the answer was probably not, but when pieced together with the other facts?

A new piece of paper was needed to list the salient points. Firstly there were the links to all the drug companies. Secondly the fact that Diane Bennett had been in medical research. And if Sarah understood Peter Shalcott correctly then Tom Ryder had been in research too.

Why had that last point been kept secret? Surely a man with an ego the size of Ryder's would let the world know of his achievements? Ryder had something to hide. Diane knew about it. She had to know him inside out. Did Platt know about it too? It was possible.

She returned to the list of points. Ryder was paranoid, he had been all along. It had only become more apparent because of the two deaths, which he seemed to be ascribing to some conspiracy aimed at destroying him. Or else that was an elaborate bluff to hide his own involvement in the murders.

What else was there? She put her pen down for a moment to flick through her notes. Why had she written so much about Anthony Vallance? His name appeared again and again in her notes. She had not been impressed by him at first, but her initial reaction had softened. He was scruffy, disorganised, flippant and not always the easiest man to get on with and yet –

She got up and walked to the window. It was no time to be thinking about Anthony Vallance, she decided. Tom Ryder was the key to the entire case. He was intelligent, ruthless and paranoid, a combination which sounded explosive. Add to that his undoubted charisma, his government contacts and his high profile and you had a very dangerous individual.

She turned back from the window without really looking out into the darkness. The question had to be asked: was Tom Ryder a murderer? There were no other real candidates; he was the only one with motive, opportunity and the skills to carry out the murders. As a former researcher he'd know how to handle drugs, both the stuff used to knock Platt out and the cocaine which finished him off. And Diane would have let him into her room without question.

Why hadn't Vallance arrived at the same conclusion? She smiled to herself. Because he hadn't spoken to Peter Shalcott and so didn't know that Ryder had been in medical research as well. The case was balanced on that pivotal fact. Once Vallance discovered it then the conclusion would be inevitable. Should she tell him herself? It was her duty to inform the police of any information pertinent to the case, of course, but –

But what if it were not true? What if she had read more into Peter Shalcott's meanderings than was there? The old boy seemed to move in and out of focus all the time, skipping from point to point without obvious rhyme or reason. It was possible that she'd misinterpreted what he'd said. Possible? Probable more like. The police would have no problem confirming the facts given their resources, but then they would be able to claim all the credit and all she'd be left with was an uninteresting feature on management theory.

The idea came to her suddenly. Ryder's offices were there on the ground floor. Surely the information she needed to prove his past would be there? He had to have archive material, or perhaps copies of medical papers he'd worked on.

She glanced at her watch. It was late. There would never be a better time.

As she walked through the silent corridors she tried not to think of all the risks she was taking. She might be caught by the police and she was sure that Sergeant Cooper would want to charge her with an offence – any offence would do, in fact. Or else Tom Ryder might catch her. The thought made her flesh crawl. In his paranoid state there was no knowing what he might do to her. For a second she was ready to stop and turn back, but then that would be admitting defeat.

Besides, she needed the evidence if she was going to solve the case before Anthony Vallance.

The lobby was quiet, thankfully. Someone was on duty at reception, but with no one around the receptionist had probably retreated into the back office. It was now or never.

By the time Sarah had crossed the lobby and walked through the STAFF door her heart was pounding so loudly she was certain it echoed throughout the entire building. No one had seen her, she hoped. The lights were dimmed low but the open-plan office was unoccupied.

The secretary's desk faced a glass-topped coffee table and a row of seats along the wall. It was all carefully arranged, modern and spacious compared to the cramped lecture rooms and tiny bedrooms that the people on the course had to put up with. There was a faint aroma of good coffee in the air, the coffee that she had almost had a chance to sample before her argument with Philippa Brady. There was a filing cabinet to one side of the secretary's desk but Sarah was willing to bet that anything worth looking at would be kept away from Laura's eyes too. Ryder didn't trust anyone.

The sudden murmur of voices made Sarah freeze. Where the hell had that come from? She stood stock still for a second, waiting for her heartbeat to drop below danger level so that she could listen to something else. She turned back towards the door before she heard it again, and this time she realised that it was coming from Ryder's office. She recognised his voice from the low and indistinct murmur but the female voice that followed she couldn't quite place. Was it Philippa Brady?

There was only one thing to do. She walked carefully over to the door to Ryder's office, hoping above all that it wouldn't suddenly fly open in her face. The voices were there again, much clearer though not enough for her to recognise the female voice that she knew she had heard before. Was there an argument going on?

She pressed her ear to the door. 'It just doesn't work that way,' she heard Tom Ryder saying.

'Please, can't you make an exception in my case?' came the plaintive reply.

'I'm sorry, but there's just too much going on for me to even think about –'

'But this is a chance to be different,' the woman insisted, 'to be inspired.'

This time Ryder's tone was harsher. 'Look, I've explained the way things are already. There's people out there who want to destroy me, don't you think I need to get a handle on that first?'

'I know that Tom –'

Sarah recognised the voice suddenly. Kate Thurston. What the hell was going on?

'Then if you know that you'll back off,' he said. 'You'll give me the space to organise things. I mean I'm giving you my word on this one.'

'But how long do I have to wait? How much longer?'

'I can't promise you a time and date, Kate, you know that. You know that I'd like you with me.'

Kate sounded sharp. 'Is that true? Or are you just playing for time? You know what the police will think if I tell them everything?'

'Don't try to push me, Kate,' he warned in a voice so low that Sarah could hardly make out the words.

'I'm not pushing, Tom,' Kate replied. 'It's just that you need me. Now that Diane's gone you need someone who understands you and who'll care for you the same way she did.'

'You're right,' he said. 'But I still need time to make arrangements. Will you do that for me, Kate, will you give me the time I need to sort things out?'

'You know I will,' she replied.

'It's getting late,' he said. 'Maybe you ought to get back before anyone sees that you've been here.'

Sarah missed Kate's reply. It was time to make a clean getaway before the door opened and Kate emerged. Poor Kate. Poor sad blackmailing Kate.

THIRTEEN

Vallance decided that Philippa Brady was to be the first victim of the day. She hadn't gone back to London as he had feared, and much to his surprise she had arrived at Ryder Hall early that morning. He wanted to make a crack about her dedication to her job but decided against. There was no point in antagonising her any further, especially if it meant that she felt even more protective towards Tom Ryder.

'Yes?' she demanded, marching into the interview room on imperious high heels.

She looked immaculately dressed, with not a hair out of place or a smudge on her glossy red lips. He smiled sweetly. 'I'm sorry about this,' he began, 'but I just need to go over your statement once more before I beg a favour from you.'

'If that's an attempt to be disarming then you've failed miserably,' she said, sitting opposite him. The cramped confines of the interview room at Ryder Hall did nothing to diminish her presence.

He shrugged. 'I was hoping that the boyish charm would work,' he admitted. 'But I still need to beg a favour and there's still this statement I need to check.'

'Why do you need to check it? Don't you trust your own officers to do things correctly?'

That was below the belt but he smiled any way. 'You're

right, they might have made it all up for all I know. Tell me about your meal with Tom Ryder.'

She looked exasperated. 'How many times must I do this? I've been through it already. We ate at Les Amoureux. The food was excellent and Tom chose a superb bottle of wine to accompany it. Do you want a run-down on what we ate and the name of the wine?'

'No. What time did you eat?'

'About nine, I think.'

'Is that when Tom arrived?'

'Obviously not,' she said, raising her eye brows. 'This wasn't a burger bar, you don't just wander in and pick something from a list on the wall. We took our time with the menu and with the wine list.'

It was hard ignoring her sarcasm but he had no choice. 'How long did that take? Ten minutes, twenty, half an hour?'

She shrugged. 'Something like that.'

'Like what? Be precise, was it ten minutes or half an hour?'

'What is the point here? What are you trying to prove?'

'Will you answer the bloody question! How long, ten minutes or half an hour?'

She looked slightly shocked by the raised voice. 'It was more like quarter of an hour, I think.'

He inhaled sharply. 'So you're saying that Tom Ryder arrived at the restaurant at 8.45?'

She hesitated for a moment before answering. 'About that, I think.'

'And what mood was he in?'

'Normal.'

'Describe that.'

The new question seemed to unsettle her once more. 'Why? You're not seriously suggesting that Tom's a suspect, are you?'

The answer was a definite yes, but that wasn't something to admit. 'I'm not suggesting anything. I'm only interested in establishing the facts. Tell me what you mean when you say he was acting normally.'

'He looked relaxed, he was smiling when he came in. He chatted normally about the closing session of the course and then we both talked through the menu and the wine list before ordering our food. Over dinner he was still very relaxed and he seemed to enjoy the meal almost as much as I did. Do I need to go on?'

'How did he feel about the end of the course?'

'Not very good. He felt that he'd done badly and that it wouldn't reflect well on the course as a whole.'

'Did he appear agitated by that?'

Philippa laughed. 'Of course he did, but then he shrugged and put it down to experience. He's got a very good positive mental attitude,' she added, looking at him meaningfully.

'You mean as opposed to my negative mental attitude?'

'Yes,' she said simply.

'Did he appear angry or upset about anything else?'

'No.'

'Did he appear elated?'

'No.'

'Emotionless? Passive?'

'No and no again. Why don't you just ask directly? Did he look like a man who's just murdered a close colleague?'

Vallance grinned. 'And how would he look if he'd done that?'

'I don't know,' she admitted quietly.

'From what you know of him,' he said, 'how would you imagine he'd be in that situation?'

It took a while for her to arrive at the answer. 'Normal,' she said finally.

'Are you still saying that was the mood he was in?'

'Yes, I'm telling the truth here,' she insisted. 'I'm not lying to protect him if that's what you think. I still don't think that he's done anything wrong.'

'Thank you for that. Now, about this favour.'

She smiled but there was no warmth in her eyes. 'Do you deserve any help?'

'No, but if you want to help prove that Tom Ryder's as pure as driven snow then you'd better help me.'

'What is it that you need?' she asked in a voice that suggested agreement depended on what he was asking.

'Get me Alan Platt's boss. I need to speak to him or her today. I don't care who they are, where they are or what they're doing, I need to talk today.'

The request seemed to elicit no excitement. 'I'll see to it,' was her reply.

It had been a long night and Sarah felt exhausted by the time she came down for breakfast. There had been too many urgent and unanswered questions to allow for sleep but by the time the light had filtered into her room she was no nearer a solution. She'd gone through all the evidence building up scenarios which she then demolished as easily as the bridge she and Kate had built at the beginning of the week.

The dining room was almost empty in comparison with the relative bustle earlier in the week. Kate was already there, sitting in a corner alone and contemplating her half-eaten breakfast of cereal, toast and coffee. She looked every inch the frustrated middle-aged professional woman that she was. Her hair was neatly fashioned and any hint of grey had been ruthlessly dyed out, her clothes were comfortable, sensible and purchased on any High Street. She was probably good at her job but she had enough self-awareness to know that she had reached the pinnacle of her career.

On the surface there was nothing remotely extraordinary about Kate and her position in life. Was it at all likely, then, that she was a blackmailer? Even more unlikely was the possibility that she knew that Tom Ryder was a murderer and that she was willing to cover it up so that she could be with him? The whole idea was preposterous and yet Sarah could not get it out of her head. How else could she interpret the conversation she had overheard?

She spooned some muesli into a bowl, added milk and poured herself a glass of awful synthetic-tasting orange juice and then walked over to Kate's table.

'Mind if I join you?'

Kate looked up suddenly; she had been miles away. 'Of course,' she said, making space on the table. Her voice was cheery and welcoming but it was a message at odds with the look on her face.

Sarah set her tray down carefully. Kate was already acting differently, or was Sarah merely looking out for signs that

218

had been there all along? 'Looking forward to it?' she asked, attempting to emulate the cheerfulness.

'It should be good. At last we'll get a chance to work with Tom directly.'

'Yes, that should be good. Do you know,' she added, looking down at her bowl as she spoke, 'the more I find out about him the more I appreciate just how talented and original he is.'

Kate sounded genuinely surprised. 'Really?' she asked, putting down her coffee.

'Don't sound so shocked,' Sarah laughed. 'In spite of how things might have seemed I've never been out to nail him. I thought we'd been through all that.'

'I know, I know,' Kate said. 'It's just that there are so many people out to get him. He's got so many enemies in the media, they'd just love to destroy him.'

Ryder's paranoia was obviously catching. 'Well,' Sarah insisted, 'I'm not one of them. I mean if I was then I would have had plenty of chance this week to write about the goings on here, wouldn't I?'

There was no faulting that logic and Kate didn't even attempt to try. 'So what have you been finding out about Tom then?' she asked.

'All sorts of things,' Sarah said airily. 'I've been reading through a lot of the old books and articles on him. I mean did you know about the work he's done in medicine?'

Kate hesitated momentarily, her pupils dilating suddenly before she spoke again. 'Did he really?' she asked, as though it were not obvious that she already knew.

Sarah laughed. 'I thought you knew everything about him,' she said, making a big joke of it all. There was no point in making a big deal of the fact that she knew Kate was lying.

'It shows how wrong you were then,' Kate said, forcing a smile. 'Still, it's good that we can get some time with him today, isn't it?'

'I'm looking forward to it,' Sarah said. 'By the way, what happened to you last night?'

'What do you mean?' Kate demanded.

Another raw nerve had been touched. 'Nothing really. It's

just that I was looking for you to have a drink and you'd disappeared.'

'I hadn't. I saw you with dotty old Peter and then you went off on your own.'

Kate deserved full marks for observation, Sarah decided. 'I went up to my room for a while and then came down again. You'd disappeared by then.'

Kate's laugh was unconvincing. 'I couldn't risk another hang-over. I wouldn't want people thinking I'm an old lush. I think I've made a fool of myself once too often already.'

'You haven't made a fool of yourself,' Sarah said. 'We all have a bit too much to drink sometimes.'

'Do we?' Kate asked. 'When was the last time you did that?'

It was a blow well aimed. 'Far too long ago to mention,' she admitted.

'Well, I suppose people are different,' Kate said. 'It's good to let your hair down occasionally, just to let people know that you're human after all. Don't you agree?'

Sarah forced a smile. 'Yes, I suppose so.'

'Well, last night I just decided on an early night, that's all.'

It wasn't that early, Sarah thought. She had left Ryder's office and gone straight back to her room and then, minutes later, she had heard Kate returning. There was nothing more to be said. Kate was definitely blackmailing Tom Ryder.

The boss was busy with Philippa Brady when Sergeant Cooper arrived. He'd stopped off at the Fox in the hope that Vallance was still there but according to the landlord he hadn't showed the night before. Did that mean he had moved back home or that he had found another bed for the night? Was the fact that he was with the Brady woman so early really significant?

He waited impatiently, knowing that the news he had was probably worth more than any information his boss could get out of Brady. Most likely the only reason for talking to her was political. Why did they have to bother with all that stuff at all? It just got in the way of solving the crime in the best way possible. Pussy-footing around because of political considerations was the best way of letting the murderer off the hook.

'Morning, Sarge.'

DC Quinn had arrived as well. She looked far too chipper so early in the morning and it annoyed him because he knew that Vallance was also likely to be disgustingly cheerful.

'What have you got to look so happy about?' he asked, glancing at his watch quickly.

Quinn shrugged. 'Nothing I suppose, Sarge. Do you know if the guv'nor is going to be long?'

'Why?'

'I've just been on to Area that's all.'

'And?'

'And nothing much really. There's nothing on the traffic reports that he asked for. There's nothing new from forensics. And we've not been able to contact Mrs Beamish.'

Was that it? It was a pitifully small haul of information to report back to the boss. 'I'll pass all that on,' Cooper said. 'In the mean time I want you to check up on a couple of companies for me.'

Quinn looked surprised by the request. 'Companies, Sarge? Why?'

'Because I'm telling you, that's why. First off I want the works on InfoCorp. Then I want the same on Domino Systems.'

'Domino Systems? Isn't that who Anita Walsh works for?' Quinn asked thoughtfully.

All that time going over witness statements had done her some good. 'That's right,' Cooper agreed. 'And InfoCorp is Shalcott's company in case you're wondering.'

'What am I looking for, exactly?'

It was question Cooper didn't have an answer for. There was something weird about Walsh and Shalcott and he couldn't quite pin it down. 'It's important background,' he told her instead.

'Yes, Sarge.'

Why was she still waiting? 'Get to it then,' he snapped impatiently.

She looked towards the closed door of the interview room and then turned to go back to Area. He could understand how she felt. Sitting in front of a computer screen getting information on the two companies didn't rate high on his list of things to do either. But it might yield some clue to the relationship between his two prime suspects and so it had to be done.

The door opened suddenly and Philippa Brady emerged. She looked at him coldly, as though he were some kind of lower life form and then she stormed off on her big high heels. He glanced appreciatively at her legs and then walked into the room.

'How did it go?' he asked Vallance, who had already planted his feet on the edge of the table and was leaning back in his chair thoughtfully.

'That woman is not an easy person to ask a favour from,' Vallance said.

Cooper slumped into the seat that she had just vacated. 'Rather you than me, sir,' he admitted.

'It's one of the joys of command. Now, where are we?'

An early morning chat was the nearest they got to having a proper case conference. The boss was not one for doing things formally, no matter how much training was put into man management at Bramshill. 'I've just been talking to DC Quinn, sir. There's nothing new to report. She said there's nothing from the traffic reports you requested. Nothing from forensics and nothing from Sue Beamish.'

Vallance sighed. 'Another successful mine of information. Where are we with Walsh?'

Cooper smiled. 'She disappeared last night. I checked the bar and then her room but she was definitely away from the premises. She returned in the early hours of this morning, just after four. I had a PC on the entrance sir, he tracked who came and went all night.'

'Have you spoken to her yet?'

'Yes, sir. She said she'd gone home to talk to her fiancé.'

'Has he been checked out yet?'

'I'm having someone check him out now, sir. I only got his name this morning. He's her boss apparently.'

'Where's this leading us?' Vallance wondered.

It was time to hazard a guess. 'Towards Peter Shalcott, I think.'

Vallance didn't need to ask the question, his face said it all.

'I spoke to him this morning too. He's definitely not all there, sir. But there's enough there for him to know when to lie and when to tell the truth. His room is next to hers and from the way he denies knowing her I suspect that he's either involved in some imaginary relationship with her or else he harbours ambitions in that direction.'

Vallance raised his eyebrows. He looked unconvinced. 'Evidence?'

'The way he looks at Walsh. The way he looks at any of the younger women on the course, including Sarah Fairfax. The way he denies knowing Walsh when it's obvious he does know her. Add this to his obvious mental instability and you've got yourself a potential killer. I've also checked his background and there's a Peter Shalcott listed as a pharmacological researcher but he denied it this morning. I'm pretty sure it's the same Peter Shalcott, the ages fit even if I wouldn't trust this one with a bottle of aspirins.'

'Are you really suggesting that out of some kind of tangled sexual desire Peter Shalcott killed Alan Platt and then Diane Bennett?'

The boss sounded even more unconvinced. 'Platt because he really was having it off with Anita Walsh,' Cooper said. 'Bennett because she might have made the connection with medical research. Who knows, perhaps he fancied her as well and then when she told him where to go he killed her.'

'Where's the evidence for all this? All you've got are suspicions.'

There was no point denying the lack of hard evidence. 'It's all circumstantial. I mean his room is close enough to Bennett's to give him time to push her and get back before anyone really knew what was going on. His medical training would give him the skills to kill Platt easily enough. The fact that he's lied consistently must make him a suspect.'

'What are you doing next?'

'I've got Quinn checking out the company he works for. I also want to know if there's some other connection between him and Walsh. I'm sure there's something going on between them. It's a gut feeling, sir, I can't say why but I know there's something there.'

Vallance nodded. 'I can understand what that's like, but it's never enough. Do you really think this doddery old guy carried out two ruthless and well executed murders?'

Cooper inhaled deeply. 'Hand on heart I can't say I believe it completely,' he conceded. 'But he's still a prime suspect as far as I'm concerned.'

'Do we collar him for another interview?'

Vallance had only seen the interview notes and the signed statement. He had yet to meet Shalcott face to face. 'It can't do any harm, can it, sir?' Cooper said.

'Where are they now?'

'Getting down to the first session this morning, I imagine.'

'OK, but before we talk to him we need to pull Ryder in once more. DC Quinn picked up on the fact that his statement doesn't tally with Philippa Brady's; he's out by time enough to have pushed Diane Bennett out of the window and still make the drive to his date with Brady. She's sticking to her statement, which means we have to see what he's got to say for himself.'

A discrepancy? And it had been picked up by Quinn. No wonder she was looking so pleased with herself. It also meant that his theory about Shalcott looked like a load of crap. Why hadn't Vallance said so? Why the hell was a bloody Detective Constable deeper into the case than he was?

'Is there anything else I should know?' he asked, keeping a lid on the fury building up inside him.

'What is it?' Vallance asked.

'I just want to know if there are any other developments I should know about.'

'We only picked up on the discrepancy late yesterday, and then we had to retrace Ryder's route to the restaurant to see if the gap gave him the time he'd need. By the time we finished it was late and there was no way I was coming back here to look for you. Do you have a problem with that?'

'No, sir,' Cooper said, unable to shake off the impression that he'd fouled up in some way. He was the one who should have picked up the discrepancy in the statements; he'd had the chance and yet he'd let it go.

'In that case we still need to follow up on Shalcott. Just

because this has cropped up with Ryder it doesn't mean we close down any other lines of investigation. Understood?'

'Yes, sir.'

'In that case it's time that nice Mr Ryder had the pleasure of our company.'

Ryder was giving the first class of the morning, aided and abetted no doubt by one of his blonde assistants. It would have been interesting to sit in for a while in order to listen to the man in action but Vallance knew it was out of the question. His presence would probably distract Ryder completely. It would have been worth doing on that account alone but then it would probably elicit howls of outrage from Philippa Brady. And Ryder wouldn't have been too happy either, though his opinion counted for a lot less than Philippa's as far as Vallance was concerned.

Cooper was silent as they walked along a deserted corridor towards the class room. He was probably still nursing his pet theory about Peter Shalcott. It was possible that the man considered least capable of the evil deeds had actually committed them; possible but not probable. Nothing that Vallance had heard about Shalcott marked him as a potential murderer. Vallance's own instincts said that Cooper was way off the mark, but then he had yet to meet Shalcott and perhaps Cooper had picked up on something genuine.

As they neared the reception area they heard voices, chief among them the authoritative tones of Philippa Brady.

'Yes, I'm here,' Vallance said, coming down the stairs just as Philippa was about to go looking for him.

'You're in luck,' she said, fixing him with a cold, unfriendly stare. 'This is Dr Wingard, the man Alan Platt reports to.'

'Reported to,' Dr Wingard corrected. He was a slim, bearded man in late middle age with hair and beard both more grey than black. Dressed in dark blue trousers, white shirt and a comfortably shabby jacket he stepped towards Vallance and offered him his hand.

'Dr Wingard lives a few minutes' drive from here,' Philippa explained as Vallance shook the man's hand. 'He's generously agreed to give us some of his time this morning.'

'If it will help,' Dr Wingard added.

The timing was out but it was a stroke of luck anyway. Ryder was going to have to wait, Vallance decided. 'Thank you, Dr Wingard, I'm grateful that you could spare some time for us.'

'If you need me I'll be in Tom's office,' Philippa said.

She'd done well again. 'Thanks, I'm grateful,' Vallance told her. Whatever it was they paid her at the Home Office it was worth it. She knew how to get results even if her taste in men did run to the likes of Tom Ryder. 'If you'll just give me a second, Dr Wingard,' he said and then walked out of earshot accompanied by Cooper.

'Shall I get Ryder now?' Cooper asked, lowering his voice.

'No, let him finish his classes first. I want people on the entrances and exits to this place. I'd hate for Mr Ryder to do a sudden runner.'

Cooper nodded. 'If you're not finished with Dr Wingard by the time Ryder's finished I'll keep him in the interview room until you're ready.'

'Do that, and if he suddenly feels the need for a solicitor then you come and get me immediately.'

'Will do,' Cooper agreed.

Vallance turned back to Dr Wingard, who was gazing around the interior of the building intently. 'Dr Wingard, would you prefer to talk inside or out?'

'Outside; it's quite a pleasant morning actually.'

Vallance led the way out of the building and then across the gravel drive. The green expanse of the lawns and gardens were dappled with dew and the air felt cool and fresh. The sky was thick with heavy cloud that hinted at the rain that was sure to come later that day.

'It's a fine old building,' Dr Wingard remarked, looking over his shoulder at Ryder Hall as he fell into step with Vallance.

'I suppose it is,' he agreed absently. 'Not that I know much about old buildings. Nor do I know much about this management theory business.'

Wingard grinned. 'Neither do I,' he admitted casually. 'It's all the rage at the moment though, and I'm afraid I've little choice but to go with the fashion.'

'What about Alan Platt, what did he think of it all?'

Wingard thought for a moment before answering. 'The man was an excellent scientist, Chief Inspector, he regarded this fad for management theories in much the same was as I do. It's a spurious collection of ill-considered ideas and buzz words from a dozen different disciplines, none of which are ever explored fully or even understood properly. That's why I wanted him to come here.'

'To show that Tom Ryder was talking rubbish?'

Wingard's grin widened further so that his uneven white teeth showed through his straggly beard. 'I needed Alan to balance the views of Sue Beamish. I trust I'm speaking in confidence here.'

'Of course.'

'Sue was very much taken with Mr Ryder's ideas. She was keen that our whole department undertake this training programme. Can you imagine the expense? My budget's tight enough as it is, and if I can afford to spend on training I'd rather do it on something more useful than playing children's games.'

Vallance grinned too. Wingard sounded like a man who recognised a con artist when he saw one. 'And had you spoken to Alan Platt while he was here?'

'Very briefly. He sounded none too impressed, though he did say that he was reserving judgement. He's a scientist you see; he wanted to test the validity of the claims being made by Ryder and his people. To be honest, I think he was anxious for the whole thing to finish so that he could get back to the lab.'

It had finished early of course, though not in the way that Platt had intended. Vallance resisted the temptation to be flippant, however. 'What was he working on in the lab?' he asked.

'You'll appreciate the highly controversial nature of the work,' Wingard said, stopping for a moment.

Vallance stopped too. They were far from Ryder Hall and away from prying eyes and ears. 'Don't worry,' he said, 'I can keep a secret as well as you Ministry people.'

'Alan Platt was working on drug fingerprinting. Put simply

227

he was looking at ways of marking drug samples so that you people and Customs and Excise could trace their movement across the world and into the country.'

The next question was obvious. 'What drug samples?'

'All kinds. Cannabis, heroin, cocaine, ecstasy, the lot.'

'And presumably he had access to real samples to work on?'

Wingard nodded. 'He'd moved from the theoretical stage some months ago. And to pre-empt your next question, Chief Inspector, I know for a fact that Alan Platt was not a drug abuser.'

'How?'

'All the samples were carefully accounted for and he had undergone a number of random tests in the course of his work. In fact he was a member of the team that first proposed randomised testing a few years ago.'

'Was he involved in administering the tests?'

Wingard's face carried a pained expression. 'I must assume that you ask that question because you have to,' he said. 'It would be insane for us to allow people to administer their own tests. The tests were carried out by your own force, Chief Inspector.'

The fact that Platt had access to samples of cocaine meant that every question had to be asked, no matter how offensive those questions might appear to Wingard. 'Tell me about these accounting procedures,' he said.

'Samples come to us from police and C&E seizures and in addition we occasionally refine and manufacture our own samples of controlled substances. In every case these samples are carefully labelled and stored under high security. Similarly samples are disposed of in accordance with Home Office provision. Every last milligram is signed for and the records are audited at regular intervals.'

'Is it possible that Alan Platt broke the rules? Could he have stolen the cocaine that killed him?'

Wingard remained stony-faced. 'As I understood it, Chief Inspector, there is evidence that Alan was sedated before the cocaine entered his bloodstream. Are you suggesting that he did this himself?'

'No, I just need to know if the cocaine that killed him was one of the samples he was working on.'

'Impossible. I had the records checked as soon as I heard the tragic news. If you'd like to view them yourself I'll make them available to you on Monday morning.'

Damn! Wingard was serious. He had complete confidence. 'I hope you won't be offended if I take you up on that,' Vallance said. 'I have to eliminate that route of supply from this enquiry.'

'As you wish,' Wingard said, turning back towards Ryder Hall.

Wingard started walking back and Vallance joined him. 'Do you know what drugs he was working on recently?'

'Cocaine and opium. It occurs to me, Chief Inspector, that there's a more empirical route to ascertaining whether the cocaine that killed Alan was one of a batch he'd worked on.'

Wingard was talking like Sue Beamish, as though dictating a report or describing an experiment. Platt probably spoke the same way, Vallance realised. 'And how's that?' he asked.

'Test the sample found near his body for one of the radioactive markers that Alan was using.'

The sample had been tested in the lab already, but that would have been to establish the type of drug and the level and nature of the impurities it contained. There was no way that the Met would check a sample of coke for radioactive markers. 'Can you carry out the test for me?'

Wingard smiled. 'I'm sure that it can be arranged. I'm sure that you're barking up the wrong tree here, Chief Inspector, but I'm more than happy to prove you wrong.'

Vallance smiled. 'It won't be the first time,' he said.

FOURTEEN

There was no point in taking chances, Cooper decided. He'd posted uniformed constables on the entrances and exits to Ryder Hall as instructed, and then for good measure he'd assigned DC Manning to keep an eye on the lecture theatre too. With everything covered there was still time to follow up on the other leads. It looked like Ryder was suspect number one but perhaps that was down to the fact that the boss didn't like him. Cooper didn't like him either. If it turned out to be true that Ryder was the murderer then there was going to be added satisfaction in watching him go down. A pompous, jumped-up little dictator like Ryder wouldn't last five minutes into a life stretch.

In the mean time there was still the Anita Walsh/Peter Shalcott connection to uncover. Vallance was right, of course, and there was no doubt that Peter Shalcott made an unlikely double murderer, but then that was the thing about murderers. There was no typical murderer any more than there was a typical victim. And what if Shalcott's mental instability made him prone to sudden rages or psychotic fits? Who was to say that a kindly old boy couldn't turn into a ruthless and calculating killer?

From the window of the interview room Cooper could see the boss and Dr Wingard walking across the grounds at a leisurely pace. It would have been better to make Dr Wingard wait until after Ryder had been interviewed again. The boss was being political again, probably; appeasing Philippa Brady would have had a lower priority if Cooper had been in charge of the case.

Cooper's musings were interrupted by the buzz of the phone.

'DS Cooper,' he announced, taking the call instantly.

'Hello sarge,' DC Quinn said. 'I've dug up a few things you might be interested in.'

'Well?' Cooper demanded irritably. She couldn't have had much time to look at things considering the drive back to Area. If she was really that good then it was only a mater of time before she made the grade to Detective Sergeant.

'InfoCorp is just a one-man band,' she reported. 'It's Peter Shalcott's trading name. It makes him sound like a multinational, doesn't it?'

'What else?' he demanded.

Quinn's manner changed abruptly. 'His line of business is medical diagnostic software, sir.'

There was no point in pretending he knew what it meant. 'Which means what?' he asked.

'It means he writes computer programs that are used in medicine. He's got a whole alphabet of qualifications after his name, nearly all of them in some medical field or other. There's not much else I can get on him. He's not exactly good at filing his accounts, sir.'

Why hadn't he revealed his medical knowledge before? It put Shalcott firmly back in the frame. 'Anything else?'

'Anita Walsh is also back on the list of suspects,' Quinn said. 'Domino Systems is also involved in medical software. It's a newish company with about half a dozen employees. The client list includes most of the big drug companies as well as the Home Office. That puts a possible link between her and Platt that pre-dates their meeting at Ryder Hall.'

Cooper bit his tongue. He didn't want the picture muddied any more than it already was. It would have suited him more if Shalcott had been the only one with the secrets to hide. 'Is there any link between Shalcott and Domino Systems?'

'None that I could find,' Quinn said.

'Then keep digging,' Cooper instructed. He needed a link between Shalcott and Walsh and if it meant that finding that link kept Quinn away from Ryder Hall for a while then so much the better.

'But it's the weekend, how am I —'

'Keep digging,' Cooper repeated firmly. 'If you're half as good as you think you are then you'll get something.'

'There is one other thing,' Quinn said, her voice sounding strained as though she were doing her best to suppress her anger. 'Mrs Beamish has been contacted and her story doesn't tally with —'

'I'll pass that on to the boss,' Cooper said, cutting her off short. Sue Beamish was not an issue, especially with her manager being interviewed by Vallance at that precise moment. 'Call me as soon as you get anything more.'

The line went dead instantly. Cooper smiled to himself. The last thing he needed was an ambitious young DC snapping at his heels; he'd been a sergeant long enough and he was sure that bagging Platt's murderer was the surest way of making the next step up the ladder.

The tension in the class was palpable and no matter what he did or said there was no way that Tom Ryder seemed able to inspire his students. Sarah Fairfax watched him dispassionately; his words barely registered on her consciousness. What he was saying was far less interesting than his body language. He kept glancing towards the door of the lecture theatre, as though the presence of the police officer made him feel even more nervous than usual. His paranoia level had to be sky high if past experience was any measure of things.

In addition Sarah noticed that he kept looking at Kate Thurston, seated down in the front row of seats. She in turn was gazing up at him adoringly. It would have been comical had Sarah not been aware of what was going on between them. What the hell was going on in Kate's head? No matter how Sarah tried she could not understand Kate's weird mentality. How could she sit and stare with such child-like devotion at the man she was blackmailing? At a man who had probably killed twice?

Ryder glanced at the door again, and this time Sarah followed him. The policeman, one of Vallance's team of detectives, was still there, but this time he was joined by another figure, barely glimpsed through the circular pane of glass at the top of the door. Whoever it was caused Ryder to lose track for a moment, his speech faltering in mid-sentence. Sarah looked again but whoever it had been had disappeared.

'I'm sorry ladies and gentleman,' Ryder said, beaming them all an apologetic smile, 'but something serious had just come up. Hey, you're probably all in need of a break right now, so let's just take five for coffee, air and head space. OK?'

He was probably right. His monologue had gone on long enough. To Sarah it felt like he'd been speaking for a couple of hours though the clock on the wall said it had only been an hour. But the fact that it was an unscripted break did not go unnoticed. Kate shot Ryder a concerned glance which he ignored completely.

People started to file out of the lecture hall in ones and twos, most of them looking completely brain dead. Not all of them were suffering the after-effects of too much drink the previous night. Far from rescuing his reputation the extra lessons were positively dragging it down further.

Sarah started to rise from her seat when she saw Tom Ryder make a sudden exit. Kate had been walking towards him when he'd dived into the line of people heading towards the door. He was in a hurry and the look of panic on his face was obvious.

Kate stared open-mouthed for a second and then she joined the line heading out for coffee. Sarah waited a second and then headed out too, hoping to talk to Kate about Tom's performance. People were milling about by the doorway. It was an impromptu break and coffee had not been laid on in the usual way. So much for slick organisation. When it came to the crunch Ryder's organisation was as inept as everyone else's. It was a telling point as far as Sarah was concerned and if she'd had the time she would have noted it down.

But there were more important things to think about and Kate Thurston was top of the list. Sarah caught sight of her just as she disappeared up one of the flight of stairs leading to the bedrooms. She was looking intent, her features were set and she was walking at a speed that said she was in more than a hurry. There was no time to hang back, Sarah realised.

She reached the stairs in time to see Sergeant Cooper and the officer who'd been on the door of the lecture theatre approach Peter Shalcott. She resisted the temptation to get involved. Cooper seemed to have it in for the old boy and she was beginning to get annoyed by it. The old man was harmless and that only seemed to goad Cooper. He seemed to like her even less, which was one good reason to stop and give him a piece of her mind.

Peter glanced up at her and she smiled, shrugged and indicated that she had to go upstairs. Much as it pained her Detective Sergeant Cooper was going to have to wait. Kate Thurston and Tom Ryder were an altogether more interesting prospect. She headed up the stairs quickly.

Vallance watched Dr Wingard drive off in a battered old Ford before turning back to Ryder Hall. The man's faith in the infallibility of the system of checks and balances at his laboratory was everything that could be expected. But systems like that depended on people following the rules and that was where they failed. It was going to be a tantalising wait until Monday morning when the cocaine that had killed Platt could be tested. The possibility that Platt had brought in the drugs that had killed him put a new slant on the case. What it meant with regard to Ryder wasn't clear. Nothing about the case was clear.

It was time to talk to Ryder, he decided, walking back to the main entrance of Ryder Hall. The constable posted at the entrance straightened up instantly.

'Any departures?' Vallance asked him.

'No, sir. No one's left or tried to leave. And there was only one new arrival, sir.'

'Who?'

The constable looked blank. 'I didn't ask her name, sir. I was only told to stop people leaving,' he added in an obvious attempt at mitigation.

'What did she look like?'

'White, middle-aged and well dressed, sir.'

It was a description that fitted a sizeable chunk of the population. In other words it was useless. 'Keep up the good work,' Vallance said, shaking his head sadly.

As soon as he walked into the lobby he knew that something was wrong. There were too many people about. What had happened to the class that Ryder was giving?

'Has your class finished?' he asked one of the people hanging around.

'It broke off suddenly,' the man explained. 'I don't know what the hell Tom Ryder's playing at,' he complained. 'I've a good mind to demand my money back and ask for compensation. This is my own bloody time I'm wasting.'

There was probably more but Vallance didn't want to hear it. 'Where's Tom Ryder now?'

'Buggered if I know,' the man replied. 'He disappeared ten minutes ago.'

He was obviously still in the building. There'd be hell to pay if he wasn't. Vallance jogged across the lobby and along the corridor towards the interview rooms. Something was wrong. Seriously wrong.

The first interview room was empty. He pushed the door of the second room open and three faces looked up sharply. DS Cooper and DC Manning were busy with a man in late middle age. It had to be Peter Shalcott, Vallance realised. There was no time for niceties.

'Where the hell's Tom Ryder?' Vallance demanded, addressing himself to Cooper.

Cooper's face was suddenly drained of colour. 'Still in the building, sir,' he said.

'Where?'

Cooper looked at Manning and then back at Vallance. 'I'm not sure. The class had stopped for a coffee break, I assume he'd gone off for a drink or a piss or something. If he's attempted to leave then –'

'We've got to find him. Now.'

Peter Shalcott shifted uneasily in his seat. 'I might be able to help,' he said.

'Where is he?' Vallance asked. Shalcott wasn't a murderer,

236

he decided. Gut instinct said he was anything but a killer.

'I saw him going up the stairs towards the first floor,' Shalcott said. 'He looked to be in quite a hurry, actually. It's odd, but so many people seemed to be in a hurry today. Even Sarah Fairfax.'

Vallance froze. 'Sarah Fairfax?'

'Yes, a lovely girl. Do you know her?'

'Where is she?' Vallance demanded.

'I think she was going to her room,' Shalcott said.

'Manning, you stay with Mr Shalcott,' Vallance instructed. 'Cooper, you follow me.'

Cooper shot Shalcott a look of pure belligerence and then joined Vallance. 'Don't let him pull the wool over your eyes,' he said as they walked hurriedly back towards the lobby. 'Shalcott's a clever bastard, sir. He might look the picture of innocence but he's been lying to us all down the line.'

'At the moment all I care about is finding Tom Ryder,' Vallance muttered. 'Where's Quinn?'

'She's still at Area, sir. She rang in to say that Mrs Beamish's story doesn't tally.'

Vallance stopped dead in his tracks. 'What exactly did she say?'

'Exactly what I told you, sir.'

It suddenly made sense. The whole thing was clear. There was no more time to lose. 'Follow me,' he said, breaking into a run.

Cooper looked mystified for a second before following suit.

Sarah listened at the door but could hear nothing but the clamour of angry voices. How many people? Three or four? She could make out the low rumble of Tom Ryder's voice and then the plaintive tones of Kate Thurston. Who were the other women? Or was it just one woman?

She leant closer, putting her head right against the door. Tom Ryder was speaking but his voice was a low monotone and she couldn't follow what he was saying. Two voices, both female, replied. She leant closer and then the door creaked. The silence lasted only a heartbeat before the door swung open and Sarah fell into the room.

'Well, well, well, Miss Fairfax, how nice of you to join us.'

Sarah looked up at Sue Beamish, leaning back against the door which she had just closed and locked.

'Hell,' Ryder complained, 'this is turning into a damned convention. How many other people —'

'Be quiet, Tom!' Sue snapped irritably.

'There's no need to take that tone,' Kate said, walking over to Ryder protectively.

Sue looked from Sarah to Kate. 'You stupid woman,' she told Kate. 'Don't you realise what you've got involved in? Do you really imagine that Tom Ryder's the superman he says he is? How easily led we all are; what fools for believing his self-mythologising. Tell her, Tom, tell her what it is that drives you to such fits of eloquence and brilliance.'

'That's enough now,' Tom said, but his voice carried no conviction. He was going through the motions again.

'Look,' Sarah said, 'I'm not part of this. I don't know what you three are doing and frankly I don't care.'

Sue smiled to her. 'Do you really believe that I'm stupid enough to believe that? Surely you of all people must know what's going on here.'

Denying it was pointless even if it was true. 'What do you intend to do with me,' she asked. There was a murderer in the room and as she didn't know who it was she had to assume that it could have been any or all of them.

'If it were not for Tom's weakness this would never have happened,' Sue explained. She walked across the room to pick up her handbag.

'What weakness?' Sarah asked.

Sue reached into her bag and produced a small pink make-up purse. She laughed. 'My dear I really imagined that you were more worldly-wise. His weakness for cocaine, of course.'

So that's why he had appeared so fired-up the first few times Sarah had seen him speak. And presumably his lack-lustre performances were down to a lack of coke. 'And what about his weakness for women?' she asked, hoping to buy some time.

Kate answered first. 'He's a man with natural appetites,' she answered. 'You can't expect him to follow the rules.'

Sue's laugh was short and derisive. 'Don't be so pathetic,' she said. 'Do you imagine that he's really attracted to fat middle-aged women like us? Young, big-breasted blondes are his particular fancy. Unless of course he thinks he can get something other than sex out of you. You're quite a mercenary, aren't you, Tom, darling?'

'This has gone far enough, Sue,' he replied. There was a note of warning in his voice but it wasn't matched by anything in his eyes or his body language.

'Has it?' Sue demanded. She reached into her bag and produced a pair of surgical rubber gloves. 'He had sex with me as long as I supplied him with sufficient quantities of cocaine,' she announced, her voice on the edge of hysteria. 'If he had enough white powder to snort from me he'd be as brilliant in bed as he was on the stage. And fool that I was I supplied him again and again.'

'That's not true,' Kate said. 'Tom, she's lying, isn't she?'

Sue pulled the rubber gloves on while Kate waited for the denial that didn't come from Tom. Sarah swallowed hard. 'You stole the cocaine from work,' she said softly.

Sue turned back to her. 'How very astute, my dear,' she said. 'Unfortunately my colleague came to the same conclusion. Poor Alan, I offered him a deal but the stupid man decided that he had principles. I was fully prepared to turn a blind eye to his adultery if he was willing to turn a blind eye to my little game. I respected him a great deal, but really I had no option but to kill him.'

Kate's face drained of colour instantly. 'You killed him? But I thought that −'

'You thought what? That Tom killed Alan? Do you believe that Tom really has the intelligence and the skill to have committed such a crime? Tom Ryder, the man who was sacked by the only lab ever to have employed him as a researcher?'

Ryder seemed stung more by the accusation of incompetence than anything else that had been said. 'That ain't true and you know that. My methods were unorthodox and if some people can't take the way Tom Ryder works then −'

'Shut up!' Sue snapped angrily. 'Diane Bennett knew enough of what was going on to work out the truth. She realised that

Tom was implicated in Alan's murder and we simply couldn't risk her telling the truth. I had to clear that little mess up too, didn't I, Tom, darling? He wasn't man enough to do it himself, so he had her wait for him and then I gave her that little push to send her on her way.'

Sarah jumped up suddenly and made for the door. She yanked it hard but it was locked tight. Her heart was pounding as she whirled round to face a calm, smiling Sue Beamish.

'It's all right, my dear,' Sue told her. 'This won't hurt a bit. In a few moments you'll be fast asleep and then —'

'What about me?' Kate asked, realising at long last that she too was trapped.

Sue turned to face her. 'You make a poor blackmailer,' she said. 'But I suspect that you'll keep quiet in return for a few favours from Tom.'

'Don't believe her!' Sarah cried. 'She's lying, Kate. She'll kill me and then make sure she gets you too!'

'That's not true,' Tom said. 'I made you a promise, Kate, and I intend keeping to that. You can trust me.'

Kate turned and looked at him. She gazed into his eyes for a long moment and then turned back to look at Sue and Sarah. 'How will you cover this up? Surely it's only a matter of time before the police work it all out.'

Sarah closed her eyes. Her heart was thudding loudly and she felt her knees giving way. 'Kate's right,' she said quietly, 'you'll never get away with all this.'

Sue nodded. 'I know you're right, my dear. But then what choice do we have but to carry on?'

Time was running out fast. 'And what about you?' Sarah demanded, looking directly into Tom Ryder's deep blue eyes. 'Don't you see what she's doing?'

Sue took a step closer and stopped. 'Don't make this difficult for yourself,' she said softly.

'She's setting you up, Tom!' Sarah said, realising at once how Sue intended to get away with it. 'She's going to plant the evidence to pin it all on you and then she'll make sure you go the way Diane did.'

Ryder hesitated for a moment, as though he recognised the truth of what Sarah was saying.

'That's an interesting thought, my dear,' Sue said, her voice still calm, 'but I'm afraid that you forget just how much I need Tom.'

'I trust Sue –' Tom started to say but he had no time to finish.

Sarah jumped out of the way of the door just as it came in. She huddled down in a corner as the wood splintered and gave way. The black leather jacket and boots were followed by a dozen other officers. When she looked again DCI Vallance had Sue Beamish up against the wall, smashing her wrist against it until she released the hypodermic full of clear fluid.

Kate was weeping hysterically on Tom Ryder's shoulder until Sergeant Cooper peeled her away and led her out of the room.

With her heart still pounding and her stomach doing butterflies Sarah managed to stand up. Two of the officers were leading Sue Beamish away. She looked calm, unruffled and supremely at ease with the situation. In contrast Tom Ryder was on the verge of tears.

'Are you okay?' Vallance asked, finally walking over to her.

'Of course I'm OK,' she said. She had never been so happy to see a man in her life. Ever. 'Now, do you want the full story or not?'

Vallance smiled. 'I know that Sue Beamish killed them both. I know that she was stealing drugs and I suspect that Ryder was on the receiving end. Is there more that I should know?'

He knew more than she had hoped but there were still big gaps for her to fill in. Thank God. 'If you get me some coffee,' she said, 'I'll make a full statement.'

EPILOGUE

Cooper had been right all along. He had also been wrong, almost fatally so. Vallance put down the thick report that Cooper had pieced together and leant back in his chair. A few more minutes and Sue Beamish would have been guilty of three murders and not the two that she had been charged with. Of course Cooper had tried to shift the blame but there was no doubt in Vallance's mind that Ryder should never have been allowed to make his way up to Sue's room.

The paperwork was piled precariously on Vallance's desk and he added Cooper's report to it. He'd been going through the lot before making his own report. He needed to know how everything pieced together before starting the arduous task of writing it all out. Writing statements was a pain in the neck. Almost as much a pain as having to deal with subordinates too busy competing with each other to pay attention what was going on.

Cooper had been right about their being a relationship between Peter Shalcott and Anita Walsh. He was wrong on what it meant. The poor old guy had not fully recovered from a nervous breakdown of some sort. He was still good at his job but he had trouble focusing on things. He wasn't being cagey, he was genuinely not all there. Attending Ryder's course was an attempt at some kind of therapy. His daughter, Anita Walsh, was there to look after him and to see that he coped

OK. Her boss, her boyfriend in fact, had no idea that her father was also on the course. He'd forked out the cash to pay for the course because Anita had convinced him it would be beneficial in her work.

Anita Walsh had lied to her boyfriend about other things too. She had been having an affair with Alan Platt for some time. They'd met through work and one thing had led to another. That Anita was on the course at the same time as Platt was one of those coincidences that can mess up an investigation. Cooper had fallen into that trap all too easily.

If Cooper had been on the ball he would have heard Quinn talking about Mrs Beamish. Not Sue Beamish but her mother. The alibi that Sue had given was as full of holes as Ryder's had been. If Cooper had understood then he should have realised, as Vallance had done, that Sue was the murderer.

And if Sarah Fairfax had been less interested in outdoing the police – Vallance smiled to himself. Sarah had been so intent on showing him how to do his job that she had almost got herself killed. She had been grateful for the rescue, of course. For about five minutes. And then she had turned her anger on DS Cooper, DC Manning and any other member of the team who had failed her in some way. Vallance had escaped that particular outburst, though it had been a joy to watch her in full flow. It had made Cooper livid, but there was nothing he could say to her.

Now it was all over and the accumulated tiredness washed over him. He felt exhausted and in no mood to do anything but sleep.

He stood up and yawned. Outside it was cold, dark and uninviting. In a few hours the sun was going to warm the sky as it climbed over the horizon. The day ahead was going to be busy once again as he worked on his report. The only consolation lay in the fact that Sue Beamish had confessed all. Ryder too had confessed his sins, though in his case he laid the blame entirely on Sue Beamish's shoulders. As a performance it was distinctly uninspiring.

As he walked away from his office Vallance paused just

once. Aside from the confessions, the end of the case brought one other consolation: the chance to see Sarah Fairfax again when the case came up in court. He was looking forward to it already.

INTIMATE ENEMIES

by
Juliet Hastings

ISBN: 0 7535 0155 4
Publication date: 15 May 1997

Francesca Lyons is found dead in her art gallery. The cause of death isn't obvious but her bound hands suggest foul play. The previous evening she had an argument with her husband, she had sex with someone, and two men left messages on the gallery's answering machine. Detective Chief Inspector Anderson has plenty of suspects but can't find anyone with a motive.

When Stephanie Pinkney, an art researcher, is found dead in similar circumstances, Anderson's colleagues are sure the culprit is a serial killer. But Anderson is convinced that the murders are connected with something else entirely. Unravelling the threads leads him to Andrea Maguire, a vulnerable, sensuous art dealer with a quick-tempered husband and unsatisfied desires. Anderson can prove Andrea isn't the killer and finds himself strongly attracted to her. Is he making an untypical and dangerous mistake?

**_Intimate Enemies_ is the second in the series
of John Anderson mysteries.**

CRIME & PASSION

A TANGLED WEB
by
Pan Pantziarka
ISBN: 0 7535 0156 2
Publication date: 19 June 1997

Michael Cunliffe was ordinary. He was an accountant for a small charity. He had a pretty wife and an executive home in a leafy estate. Now he's been found dead: shot in the back of the head at close range. The murder bears the hallmark of a gangland execution.

DCI Vallance soon discovers Cunliffe wasn't ordinary at all. The police investigation lifts the veneer of suburban respectability to reveal blackmail, extortion, embezzlement, and a network of sexual intrigue. One of Cunliffe's businesses has been the subject to an investigation by the television programme, *Insight*, which means that Vallance has an excuse to get in touch again with Sarah Fairfax. Soon they're getting on each other's nerves and in each other's way, but they cannot help working well together.

A Tangled Web **is the second in the series
of Fairfax and Vallance mysteries.**

DEADLY AFFAIRS
by
Juliet Hastings

ISBN: 0 7535 0029 9
Publication date: 17 April 1997

Eddie Drax is a playboy businessman with a short fuse and taste for blondes. A lot of people don't like him: ex-girlfriends, business rivals, even his colleagues. He's not an easy man to like. When Eddie is found asphyxiated at the wheel of his car, DCI John Anderson delves beneath the golf-clubbing, tree-lined respectability of suburban Surrey and uncovers the secret – and often complex – sex-lives of Drax's colleagues and associates.

He soon finds that Drax was murdered – and there are more killings to come. In the course of his investigations, Anderson becomes personally involved in Drax's circle of passionate women, jealous husbands and people who can't be trusted. He also has plenty of opportunities to find out more about his own sexual nature.

This is the first in the series of John Anderson mysteries.

HOW TO ORDER BOOKS

Please send orders to: **Cash Sales Department, Virgin Publishing Ltd, 332 Ladbroke Grove, London W10 5AH.**

Be sure to include with your order the title, ISBN number, author and price of the book(s) of your choice. With the order, please enclose payment (remembering to include postage and packing) in the form of a cheque or postal order, made payable to **Virgin Publishing Ltd**.

POSTAGE AND PACKING CHARGES

UK and BFPO: £4.99 paperbacks: £1.00 for the first book, 50p for each additional book.
Overseas (including Republic of Ireland): £2.00 for the first book, £1.00 each subsequent book.

You can pay by VISA or ACCESS/MASTERCARD: please write your card number and the expiry date of your card on your order.

*Please don't forget to include your **name, address and daytime telephone number**, so that we can contact you if there is a query with the order. And don't forget to enclose your payment or your credit card details.*

Please allow up to 28 days for delivery.

A Blakes Cottage for Only £5* per person, per night when you buy any two Crime & Passion books

Offer is open to UK residents aged 18 and over. Offer closes 12th December 1997.

Booking your Blakes Cottage is easy. Just follow the step-by-step instructions listed below:

1. To book your Blakes Cottage for only £5* per person, per night, simply call 01282 445056, quote the Crime & Passion £5 per person, per night offer and reference MPJ702.

2. The Blakes Holiday Adviser will ask you for the following:
   - the number of adults and children in the party
   - your preferred holiday dates (the duration must be a minimum of one week)
   - you preferred holiday area

3. You will then be offered a choice of selected properties and provided with details of price, location, facilities and accommodation.

4. To confirm the booking you will be asked for full payment by credit card or cheque.

5. Send the completed application form show below, together with two Blakes Cottages/Crime & Passion tokens and a till receipt highlighting your purchase to: Blakes Cottages, The Crime & Passion Offer, Stoney Bank, Earby, Colne, Lancs BB8 6PR.

Application Form

Title   Mr/Mrs/Ms ....

First Name(s) ....

Surname ....

Address ....

....

....

Postcode ....

Telephone Number ....

> C & P
>
> *One Token*
>
> A Moment of Madness

If you do not wish to receive further information and special offers from Virgin Publishing or Blakes Cottages you should write to Blakes Cottages, Dept. DPA, Stoney Bank Road, Earby, Colne, Lancs, BB8 6PR